# THE RAKE AND THE FAKE

Husband Material Series
Book One

Goldie Thomas

ISBN 979-8-9878380-0-6



www.goldiethomas.com

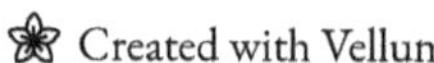 Created with Vellum

*For Pepper*

# PROLOGUE

*London*
*1824*

From her private vantage point behind the curtains on the landing outside her dying mother's bedchamber, young Charlotte Price guessed that their modest townhome had never been so full of people. The housekeeper and cook were there as usual, but the addition of two doctors, combined with the steady stream of her mother's many friends from her career as an opera singer left Charlotte feeling as though they should simply prop the front door open to allow everyone to go in and out as they pleased.

She knew that her mother wasn't going to get better. Celeste Beaumont, her mother's dearest friend, had explained this to her just the other day.

"Darling, the doctors believe that your poor *maman* will pass soon. She will not recover. Try to be strong, pet."

Charlotte didn't know how to be strong, and didn't

understand why the doctors were still here if they had given up on her mother, the most beautiful and elegant woman in all of London (in her estimation, at least).

Charlotte had watched from the wings of theaters all over town as her mother performed flawless arias to houses packed full with the cream of London society, always draped in Mademoiselle Celeste's elaborate costumes. Before the onset of her illness, her mother commanded the stage with her poise and grace, stunning audiences with a singular beauty rarely seen in cold, gray London. When she began to sing, she stunned them further, for even her physical appearance paled in comparison to that of her coloratura soprano voice.

The assembled lords and ladies would cheer her name at the end of each engagement, which Charlotte always found puzzling. If they were so happy to hear her sing for them, why would they refuse to acknowledge her mother as she shopped on Bond Street, or when she and Charlotte took a turn in Hyde Park? If she were to believe the barely whispered insults, it was because Charlotte did not have a father. Either that, or it was simple jealousy—Charlotte knew that her mother was unmatched in both beauty and talent, two of the few things that the monied ladies of London could not buy.

Charlotte peaked her head out from behind the curtain once more as she heard yet another knock upon the door. The housekeeper, her face ashen, rushed to answer. It was the vicar.

The doctors exited the bedchamber and exchanged hushed words with the vicar as they passed him on the dim, narrow staircase. Charlotte assumed the worst.

After a quarter of an hour, the vicar exited the bedchamber, followed by Mademoiselle Celeste, who had been at her mother's side for days. The Frenchwoman approached Charlotte, her cheeks stained with tears.

"Darling, your mother wishes to see you. Come," she said quietly, reaching for Charlotte's hand.

The room was dark, with only a few candles burning. Charlotte was afraid.

"Charlotte, come here so I can see you," whispered her mother. Her voice, once so strong and clear, had been reduced to dust.

Charlotte approached the bedside and took her mother's withered hand. The familiar, firm grip soothed her, even as hot tears stung at the corners of her eyes.

"Charlotte, my darling. I think that its time I tell you about your father."

# CHAPTER 1

*London*
*1842*

Nicholas Felton, Viscount Dorset, was in agony.

*Head throbbing, stomach churning agony.*

Every bump and lurch of his carriage served as a violent reminder that he, at the urging of his compatriots, had poisoned his own body with enough of their club's finest whisky to fell both of the horses currently pulling him toward his parents' London townhouse. The previous night at White's had been more of the same for him and his usual band of companions: card games, whisky, bawdy tales of escapades with their mistresses, yet more whisky, dozens of cheroots, and not a single thought given to the bodily consequences.

After a seemingly endless trundle from his Mayfair townhouse, his carriage lurched to a stop in front of the grand front entrance to Stapleton House, his parents' home while they were in town. Dorset knew that his father would identify his physical ailment and its cause instantly, but he hoped his mother, the Countess of Harrington, wouldn't recognize his pallid skin, sweaty brow, and general ill-humor for what they were: a *blistering* hangover.

Mr. Carter, the family's longtime butler, met him at the large oak door with a practiced bow. "Good morning, my lord. Allow me to show you to your father's study."

"Thank you, Carter," he replied, his voice hoarse. Dorset followed the straight-backed and perfectly composed man through the cavernous marble entryway and down various exquisitely papered hallways to his father's study. His vision swam; he felt bile creep up the back of his dry throat as Carter announced his arrival to his father, who sat at his large desk opposite a roaring fireplace. The Earl of Harrington did not glance up from his papers before addressing his son.

"Nicholas, I'm glad to see you survived the night. Would you care for a strong cup of tea, or perhaps you would prefer an empty basin and some privacy?" How the man knew of Dorset's carousing was a mystery, but the viscount was less concerned about how exactly the news of his debauched evening had reached his father, and more so with staying upright in that moment.

"Good morning, Father. Its nice to see you as well," Dorset replied, his eyes squinting against the light in the room. He felt as though his very bones were rejecting their place inside his body, and he silently cursed his parents for sending for him that morning when he could have been waiting for death in his own bed, without interruption. Rather than respond to Dorset, the earl turned to the waiting butler.

"Carter, it appears that my son requires a hair of the dog that bit him. Please tell the cook that he shall take one of her special remedies this morning. This is likely a two-egg problem." Dorset shivered and stifled a retch at the sound of the word "egg." It seemed that food was not yet an option for the unwell gentleman.

"Very good, my lord," Carter replied. He gave a slight bow and slipped out of the room, closing the door behind him.

"Have a seat, my son. We've something important to discuss, and I'd like to get it over with before your mother returns," said the earl, straightening in his high-backed desk chair. Dorset sat down across from his father, and instantly felt no older than sixteen. His father had been larger than life to him then, and Dorset felt the full weight of the older man's authority now, even as the years had dusted his thick hair and beard with gray.

"Dare I ask where my mother has gone?" asked Dorset, his hands shaking. He assumed it was a medical impossibility, but it seemed that his tongue had turned from flesh into wool.

"I will tell you, Nicholas. But first, you must know that what I'm about to say to you is for your own good, and for the good of our family," his father replied, his gaze serious. This was not the first time they had had this conversation, and Dorset knew what was coming next.

"Let me guess, Father. You and Mother have decided that I am to take a wife, and that I shall have the duration of the season to select her. She shall be of noble birth, accomplished but not ambitious, unblemished in reputation, and prepared to produce an heir and a spare for the Harrington lineage. Have I missed anything?" Dorset uttered all of this with his eyes screwed shut and while rubbing his temples in an attempt to still the ceaseless pounding in his head. When he opened his eyes, he recoiled from the withering stare his father sent from the other side of the oak desk.

*If looks could kill...*

"Nicholas, you are not a child. Because you are a grown man of thirty-three, and the heir to my title and assets which I have worked tirelessly to protect and grow for your future prosperity, I will no longer wait for you to select your wife. Your mother has been in contact with a woman we both feel is a suitable match. Luckily for you, this woman, as well as her parents, consent to the suit. You should be thankful for this news, as you are an aging rake, and have been a disappointment on the marriage mart thus far, despite your fortune. Your mother has gone to meet her this morning, and will be bringing her here for tea so that you may meet her and begin courting her this very day. It is our intention, as well as that of her parents, that you will marry before the end of the year."

At this pronouncement, Dorset was unsure if he could keep from gagging, and for the first time so far that morning, his hangover was not to blame. His skin turned from a pallid, sickly beige to an unpleasant shade of green as the news washed over him.

"How can I be a disappointment on the marriage mart if I have so far avoided it completely and without incident?" asked Dorset.

"Don't quibble with me, Nicholas. It isn't gentlemanly. I doubt that a man earns your reputation without an incident or two to get the gossips talking," Earl Harrington replied.

There had been rather more than two "incidents," but Dorset thought it best to keep that to himself before he got into more trouble.

Had his future wife had been selected for him? He knew that English marriages were arranged by the intended's respective parents for practical reasons relating to business or politics, but he had always assumed that his parents, who were a rare love match themselves, would allow him to take his time and find the same. The search for a respectable wife simply hadn't felt urgent to Dorset, and while he had sat through this lecture many times before, he was feeling for the first time that his father's patience had run out.

Dorset tried to ignore the sting he felt at his father's words, but he knew they were true: He had aged well past the years that his playboy behavior would be excused as a rite of gentlemanly passage. He was growing tired of the late nights, the empty conversations, *the hangovers.* That he might marry and have a son who would grow to repeat this generational cycle filled him with nothing but disgust.

"I'm sure it will surprise you to hear, Father, that you needn't convince me. You see, I am an aging rake, and I would rather die from this hangover than produce another of my kind, lineage be damned," he said, feeling the room spin around him as he began sweating, his forehead resting in one large hand.

"Nonsense, Nicholas. Between your future wife, nurses, tutors, and teachers at school, you will have little to do with the day-to-day upbringing of your children. Do not flatter yourself and assume otherwise," said the earl, his tone light even as his words cut Dorset to the bone. He was about to protest when Carter reentered the study with a tray.

"Ah, I see Mrs. Moore has prepared you her very best remedy, Nicholas," said Earl Harrington. "The recipe is quite simple actually, and one I have taken a time or two after a late night. Carter, will you do the honors?"

"Certainly, my lord," replied the butler. Dorset looked upon the contents of the tray with horror. Next to a large crystal tumbler was a bottle of ale, two cloves of garlic, and two cracked, raw eggs in a small china dish. With a fine cloth over his shoulder, Carter muddled the garlic in the tumbler, added the eggs, and then proceeded to combine the curious mixture together with a long silver spoon. After wiping the spoon clean and returning it to the tray, Carter uncorked the bottle of ale and poured in a measure of the amber, fizzing liquid. He offered the glass to Dorset.

"If I may make a suggestion, my lord, I find that it is best to take this tonic 'down in one,' as the saying goes," said Carter as Dorset took the glass.

"Quite right, Carter. The beauty of this remedy is two-fold: either you will gradually feel better and clearer of mind thanks to the ale and the nutrients in the eggs, or, you will purge your body of the entire contents of your stomach in short order. Either option is better than your current suffering, is it not?" asked the earl, who seemed rather pleased with himself as he sat back in his chair.

"Quite right," said Dorset, echoing his father's words and quietly considering the cloudy, swirling liquid. He brought the tumbler to his lips, and after mastering a spasm, he opened his throat and downed its contents, swallowing once and wincing at the acrid taste and sickly slide the mixture made as it reached the back of his throat.

Finding inner strength that he did not previously possess, Dorset centered himself, knowing that swallowing this putrid beverage would be nothing compared with the trial of meeting the woman his parents had selected as his bride over tea and finger sandwiches.

"Pray tell, Father, what is my future wife's name? She does have one, I hope," said Dorset, after Carter had once again left the two men alone in the study.

"Miss Tabitha Crampton, only child and daughter of Baron and Lady Balfour."

"Balfour...why do they sound familiar?" he asked in response.

"Lady Balfour has long been a friend of your mother's. They were neighbors as girls. The Balfours visited the country house when you were still in short pants, although you may have been too young to remember. Lady Balfour was with child at the time, and they were taking one last trip away from home before she was to deliver the babe. That babe grew to be Miss Tabitha Crampton, to whom I believe you will have no sound objection. Especially due to the fact that I shall happily cut off your allowance and disinherit you should you reject her."

"Father, I have half a mind to send the lady on her way with my regrets and accept the consequences. I have no desire to do my duty for England, you know that I have no need of your money, and I'm not sure that I will survive that cursed glass of ale," Dorset said on a sigh, with his elbows on his knees and his head in his hands. His fogged mind was clearing, but he feared the tonic had permanently sickened his stomach.

"Just meet with the girl, Nicholas. Your mother has assured me that she is pretty, and I'm told she is rather well-read, so you should have plenty to talk about during your courtship," said the earl, his tone softening.

"I shall meet her, but only because I don't think I would survive a carriage ride back to Mayfair. When is Mother returning with her?" he asked, stretching his muscular legs in front of him and crossing one foot over the other as he leaned back in his chair and raised his eyes to the ceiling, silently praying for relief.

"One hour, I should think," replied Earl Harrington. "Your mother got it in her head to commission a gown for the girl, as a kind of pre-betrothal present meant for her to wear to a ball that we shall host, and you shall attend, to be held when Lord and Lady Balfour arrive in London. Miss Crampton has traveled in advance of them and has arranged to meet your mother this morning at the modiste for a fitting, after which they will come here for tea, where you will be ready to begin charming the young woman."

"First, allow me to renew my objection to this arrangement entirely, as I am not a suitable husband for anyone, nor am I interested in acting the part," said Dorset, rising from his chair. "Miss Crampton would do well to run as fast as she can from the modiste's shop without a look back—but if it will make you and Mother happy, I will meet her. I only ask you to prepare yourself for the certain eventuality that she will reject me, if she has even half a brain in her head.

Now, please excuse me, Father. I shall take a walk in the fresh air before this harebrained tea you and Mother have planned. If I'm lucky, I shall be sick somewhere in the garden before the lady arrives."

# CHAPTER 2

To aristocratic ladies during the London season, *nothing* was more important than a fashionable wardrobe of the latest designs. If they were to successfully attract a husband for themselves or their daughters, they would need the finest, from silk stockings trimmed with colorful ribbons to the extravagantly feathered hats pinned atop their monied heads. Luckily for these ladies, Madame Celeste Beaumont, famed French modiste, was happy to oblige them.

Madame Beaumont owned and ran the most exclusive and luxurious women's clothing shop in London. The store, located in a prime three-story storefront on Bond Street, was a living monument to the French design and fine craftsmanship that Madame was known for. To the ladies of London, Beaumont's was a gilded sanctuary, and the closest thing they had to the storied men's clubs their fathers, husbands, and brothers disappeared to so often. To seamstress Charlotte Price, it was the center of the known universe.

Occasionally, Charlotte thought back to the first time she had entered the shop, in her worn brown cloak and walking dress, and with her only worldly possessions tucked away in a small case. The fashionable clientele, the colorful gowns on display, the droves of assistants rushing around from task to task: All of it thrilled and delighted Charlotte then as it did now.

Madame Beaumont had nearly fainted at the sight of Charlotte that day, believing for a moment that she had seen the ghost of her dearly departed friend. Charlotte's resemblance to her late mother, a storied beauty with alabaster skin, naturally peach-colored cheeks, and sable-colored hair, was reportedly so strong that an assistant was sent immediately for cognac to revive the modiste. Only then did Madame Beaumont calm herself and welcome Charlotte with open arms. Madame offered Charlotte a position, and the security of a living wage, on the spot.

That day found Charlotte and Sarah—her closest friend, roommate, and surrogate sister—working together on a rather curious project. In the usual course of purchasing a Beaumont gown, the lady in question would meet with Madame Beaumont to discuss her needs and preferences before being measured by the assistants, at which point the gown would be created to her exact measurements. The lady would return for a fitting, but alterations aside from hem-length were rarely required due to the custom nature of their work.

In this case, the Countess of Harrington, a longtime customer, had requested that they create a gown as a surprise for a young lady she had hoped to impress. She produced a letter featuring the young woman's bust, waist, and hip sizes, although relying on just three measurements self-reported by the young woman without a trained seamstress to measure her would normally be insufficient to produce a gown of such intricate construction. Unwilling to hear the modiste's protestations, Lady Dorset had assured Madame Beaumont that they would worry about further particulars once the young lady had accepted the gift, and had insisted that they create a formal gown fit for a "belle of the ball." As was always the case with the countess's purchases, price was no object.

The staff of Madame Beaumont's shop always rose to the often-exacting challenges presented by their wealthy clientele, and this was no exception. Luckily, the measurements Lady Harrington had provided matched near enough with Charlotte's, so the seamstresses decided to fit the gown to her, leaving generous seam allowances for any possible alterations the gown recipient might require upon receipt.

The day had come for Lady Harrington to arrive with the young woman to try on the gown, and so, final preparations were underway. With only a few minutes to check that all was in order before the ladies arrived, Sarah hurried Charlotte into a fitting room to slip into the gown one last time.

"Come, Lottie, we have to hurry. Lady Harrington should be here in half an hour," said Sarah, helping her friend undo the buttons along the back of her dove-gray work dress, the uniform every assistant in the shop wore so as not to distract from the fine clothes worn by the ladies, who always arrived ready to see and be seen.

"Thank the Lord this is the last day of this torture," Charlotte sighed as she stepped out of the plain frock.

"I'd have guessed that you'd love being fit to a couture gown, and for a wage, no less!" replied Sarah, in her usual lively tone.

"That's the problem. Wearing this gown feels like heaven, and I fear that I'm growing more and more attached with each fitting." With Sarah's help, Charlotte pulled the lavender silk gown up over her underskirts and began fastening the endless row of tiny, silk-covered buttons that perfectly matched the color of the garment. The neckline dipped low across Charlotte's décolletage, while the delicate cap sleeves draped over Charlotte's bare shoulders and created the perfect frame for jewelry. Charlotte thought wistfully of how a pair of her mother's beloved amethyst earrings, her entire inheritance, would match the gown. She felt a pang of sadness deep in her heart knowing that she would never have a reason to wear such an extravagant piece of art.

"All finished with these blasted tiny buttons. Come out to the platform, we've got to show Madame before the ladies arrive," said Sarah, holding aside the heavy brocade privacy curtain.

"The sooner I can get out of this gown and start forgetting about how good it feels to wear, the better," Charlotte whispered in response. They were in a semi-public part of the store now, visible to other customers who there for fittings. Like the other assistants, Charlotte and Sarah had to be careful of what they said in front of the ladies.

Charlotte stepped up onto the platform and turned toward the large mirrors, the full skirts swirling around her as she did so. She had never seen herself like this before; it was like looking at a photograph of another person, someone born into another life. Charlotte had seen firsthand how Madame Beaumont's designs affected the ladies who wore them, and she was feeling that same power herself with each new fitting. She knew she had no right to feel so confident, so *beautiful*— after all, this gown was intended for another, even if it felt like it had been designed and sewn just for her. While Charlotte was lost in thought, Madame Beaumont approached her with an army of assistants at her side, each ready with pins in hand for adjustments.

"*Mon dieu*, Charlotte. You look just like your gorgeous mother, may she rest," said Madame Beaumont, with a hand to her heart. Her eyes grew liquid as she took in the sight before her.

"Madame, it is only because of your beautiful design. We both know that I'm nowhere near as beautiful as my mother was," replied Charlotte, looking away from Madame Beaumont in the mirror lest she grow emotional herself. Charlotte did not want to admit that even though she was ten years old when her mother died, she sometimes found it difficult to recall her face.

"*Non, mon chérie.* I know that you are just as beautiful, if not more," said Madame Beaumont, stepping closer and taking Charlotte's hands in hers and leaning closer to whisper. "You are a vision, and you should know this: Lady Dorset gave me complete control over the design, including the color. Once I knew that you'd be modeling the gown, I chose lavender because it was your mother's favorite."

Charlotte held her breath and closed her eyes as Madame Beaumont spoke. It would not do to present a tear-stained gown to Lady Harrington and her mystery companion.

"Thank you, Madame," she replied on a shaky breath, unable to say more without losing her composure. Where had this emotion come from? It had been years since Charlotte had made peace with her mother's early death; one didn't have the luxury of time for grief when one had to find a way to survive in a society that didn't accept children brought up without fathers.

Madame Beaumont released her hands and addressed the assembled staff members, who were awaiting further instructions. "This gown is as perfect as we can make it without the lady here to don it herself; change nothing. Sarah, you can help Charlotte change. The rest of you, follow me to assist with the Willingham sisters. They have each ordered gowns enough to clothe an army of *débutantes*, and if they are unhappy and decide not to pay, we shall be bankrupt!"

The team of assistants followed Madame Beaumont through a doorway at the side of the room and down the employee's private flight of stairs like a row of ducklings, leaving Charlotte and Sarah alone once again. Charlotte moved to step down off of the platform and out from under the warm candlelight; Sarah held out a hand to help her. Just before Charlotte's slippered foot met carpeted floor, they were interrupted by a familiar voice emanating from the grand, public-facing staircase that led from the ground-floor salon to the fitting area on the first.

"Oh, my WORD, Miss Crampton! You look absolutely STUNNING!"

Charlotte turned slowly. The Countess of Harrington had arrived, and with her trademark combination of bluster and easy confidence, had mistaken Charlotte for one "Miss Crampton," apparently the recipient of the gown Madame Beaumont had designed with Charlotte in mind.

"Oh no, my lady—" Charlotte began to correct the countess, but Sarah stopped her with a gentle touch on the arm.

"Lady Harrington, it is *so* lovely to see you today. Please, take a seat here on the settee. *Miss Crampton* and I were just discussing that perhaps a different underpinning is necessary for this gown. Would you excuse us while I help her change?" Charlotte turned to her friend, her eyes wide, a false smile plastered across her face. Knowing she couldn't speak aloud lest she draw the attention of other guests, she tried her hardest to send a private message straight into Sarah's brain.

*Sarah, what on Earth is the meaning of this?*

"Of course, my dear! Take your time, I shall make myself comfortable right here," replied the countess, settling herself on the low furniture. That day, she wore a large hat decorated with feathers dyed in various shades of deep blue. It matched her ornate gown (trimmed with frills of fine lace and endless rows of pearls) and suede gloves; Charlotte would never say so aloud lest she offend a customer, but she couldn't help the thought that the petite, round-faced woman resembled a very wealthy blueberry.

Sarah took Charlotte by the arm and ushered her into the

dressing room with a firm but subtle shove, before Charlotte could protest. Even behind the heavy curtain, Lady Harrington would be able to hear their conversation. With a mix of frantic whispering and pantomime, Charlotte addressed her closest friend.

"What are you doing? The real 'Miss Crampton' is going to walk in here any moment and you and I will be tossed out on the street for playing a trick on a COUNTESS," Charlotte rasped, furious. She held Sarah firmly by her shoulders, feeling for the first time like she should shake some sense into the woman who was the closest thing she had to a sister. Sarah swatted away Charlotte's hands and grabbed for her wrists.

"No, Lottie, listen to me—"

"Hush! She will hear you," Charlotte mouthed while gesturing in the general direction of where Lady Harrington sat on the other side of the curtain.

"Lottie! While you were getting teary eyed with Madame, Daisy handed me a letter that arrived by post this morning," said Sarah, reaching into the pocket of her apron and holding out a letter that was addressed to Lady Dorset, in care of the shop, and that had been opened. Charlotte didn't have to guess that it had also been read.

"Why does that matter? I am not Miss Crampton. Don't you think the countess, who has been shopping here for *years*, will recognize that I'm a seamstress? *A seamstress who has measured and fit gowns to her and her daughter?*" breathed Charlotte, color rising in her cheeks.

"Charlotte, hush for one moment—"

"Is everything all right in there? I'm sure it doesn't take this long to change your stays and stockings, does it my dear?" asked Lady Harrington from her place on the settee, interrupting Sarah's hurried explanation.

"We're just doing up the gown, my lady! Thank you for your continued patience!" called Sarah, in a sing-song tone that belied the frantic conversation between the two friends. Charlotte unfolded the letter quickly and read it, still unsure why Sarah had decided to deceive one of their wealthiest and most loyal customers. It read:

*Dear Lady Harrington,*

*Please forgive me for the timing of this letter. I know that nothing I can write here will excuse my absence today, but please understand that I mean no disrespect to you, nor to Lord Harrington.*

*I write to you with my parents blessing to tell you that I must request more time before I travel to London to meet your son, Lord Dorset. As I respect the wishes of my parents as well as their judgment, please understand that I have no objection to our intended courtship and hope dearly that said courtship will lead to our betrothal.*

*Unfortunately, my young cousin, who lives with my family as my father's ward, has taken ill. I'm afraid I must remain at home until the doctor assures us that she is well—my parents shall join me in London once she has made a full recovery.*

*I will look forward to your response, and thank you for your kindness and understanding during this trying ordeal.*

*Yours faithfully,*

*Miss Tabitha Crampton*

*Balfour Manor*

"Don't you see, Lottie?" asked Sarah, as quietly as she could without the countess hearing. "Tabitha won't be joining us today! And I don't know what I was thinking, but you look so beautiful in the gown. I just thought we could have a bit of fun and pretend that you're Quality for a few minutes," Sarah said with a giggle, clasping a hand over her own mouth as she did so. Charlotte's mouth fell open; she and Sarah enjoyed joking with each other, but they had never taken part in such an obvious falsehood.

"Sarah, someday you will pay for this jape," said Charlotte.

"It shan't be today; I will wait until you least expect it before I strike. Until then, let's get this over with." She couldn't name what had possessed her to go along with Sarah's ruse, but with no small amount of unease, Charlotte chose to indulge her friend just this once, consequences be damned. Sarah had a rather alarming flair for invention, and Charlotte hoped that her friend could use it to talk them out of any real trouble that may arise should "Tabitha" materialize inside the shop over the next few weeks.

Charlotte estimated that they could gain Lady Harrington's approval of the gown and send her happily on her way within the next quarter of an hour, at most. With a deep breath, she nodded to her friend; Sarah held aside the curtain so that Charlotte could return to the platform. Lady Harrington clapped her gloved hands at the sight of her.

"Oh, Tabitha, my *dear*! You look marvelous. I know I haven't seen you since you were a small child, but I can't believe how you've grown. And of course, I had to bring you to Beaumont's—as you can see, her work is second to none," she said, taking in the detail on the bodice of the gown. "Miss, you were quite right to change the underpinnings. Her *assets* are showcased here at their absolute best," Lady Harrington said to Sarah, a blush rising on her cheeks.

Before either Charlotte or Sarah could say anything, the countess continued. "Now, *dear* Tabitha, you must change out of this gown so that I can take you back to Stapleton for tea. My son Nicholas is eager to meet you, I'm sure! Miss, please have the gown wrapped and boxed straight away. I shall send a footman to fetch it later," she added, to Sarah. Both Charlotte and Sarah looked at the countess, mouths agape and eyes as round as saucers, stunned.

*Tea. With Lord Dorset. Right now.*

What a *dreadful* miscalculation. Charlotte felt sure in that moment that she should walk out of Madame Beaumont's and never return, because she would absolutely be dismissed for this indiscretion. She would have to answer to her mother in heaven for betraying the kindness of Madame Beaumont, but it quickly occurred to her that after this day, Saint Peter would not accept her at the pearly gates even if she begged. If she and Sarah were lucky, they would survive the rest of the year with their meager nest egg, but she doubted they had enough for both food and coal to get through the next winter.

"Come along, Tabitha, quickly now! I'll be perusing the new samples downstairs while I wait for you to change. The carriage is waiting out front for us," said Lady Harrington to the two silent women still frozen before her.

"Of course, my lady," replied Charlotte as she came out of her trance, dipping into a stiff curtsy as the countess turned toward the staircase to the first floor. Once she was sure that Lady Harrington was out of hearing distance and that she and Sarah were firmly behind the heavy privacy curtain, Charlotte turned to Sarah, her mouth set in a firm line and her heart beating out of her chest with fear.

"What on Earth am I to do now?" asked Charlotte, not sure if the tears welling in her eyes were from fear or from anger with her friend.

"You will go to tea, of course!" replied Sarah casually. "I will fetch some clothes for you from last year's samples. I have seen the viscount before; he is quite handsome. Just let Lady Harrington do all the talking. You know she usually does anyway." She had clearly lost her mind. Charlotte thought fondly of committing her to Bedlam—maybe then she would see reason.

"The viscount could be the most handsome man in London, but it doesn't change the fact that I have lied to the Countess of Harrington and am now expected to continue this lie for an afternoon at her home. What am I to do if her daughter attends this tea? The countess clearly doesn't know me from Adam, but Lady Emmeline is *our age* and will certainly remember me from the near thousands of times I have measured her every limb!" replied Charlotte, in a single, frantic breath.

"Charlotte, he *is* the most handsome man in London. You can play at being his future wife *and* have a posh tea at the same time," said Sarah, helping Charlotte out of the lavender silk for the last time.

"You've missed the most important part of my previous statement, Sarah. You know Lady Emmeline will give me away the moment she sees me. This is preposterous!" Sarah ignored her friend's desperate pleas and disappeared behind the curtain, leaving Charlotte in her underclothes. When Sarah returned with a simple but finely made sky-blue day dress and a tastefully coordinating pelisse, Charlotte had given up hope of ever passing another happy day in her natural life.

Sarah helped Charlotte dress quickly, smoothed her friend's hair, and fastened a pair a delicate kid skin gloves at Charlotte's wrists in silence—a rarity between the two women. Only when she had finished did Sarah speak again.

"Charlotte, you and I..." She stopped to consider her next words before she went on. "You and I have a comfortable situation. We are lucky ones. But has it ever occurred to you that there are aristocratic men and women swanning all over London who could buy and sell our entire lives without a second thought? I've heard there are gentlemen who go to their clubs every night to gamble away sums five, even ten times higher than what we have saved. It means *nothing* to them. The ladies who come here for their clothes spend more than our combined yearly wages just on stockings alone! Can you blame me for getting excited because you might experience that life for an afternoon? I thought maybe you could pretend, just for today." Sarah's eyes filled with tears. "When you come home after, maybe you could tell me all about it. We might not get another chance," she added, sadly. Charlotte's heart broke at her friend's words, even if they were in no small way manipulative.

"Of course, I'll tell you about it. Now help me down to the first floor before I change my mind."

# Chapter 3

Later in life, when Charlotte looked back on the carriage ride from her place of work to Stapleton House, she remembered few particulars. How had she made it from the shop to the carriage without being seen by her coworkers or Madame Beaumont? She did not doubt that Sarah had spun some elaborate tale, but Charlotte did not have an answer. When she took the liveried footman's hand and entered the coach, could she have guessed that the coming days would change the entire course of her life? Considering that at the time she assumed she would be thrashed to the point of death for even attempting such a scheme, she could not.

Charlotte had never been inside such a lavish conveyance. As she sat across from Lady Harrington in the spacious compartment, she spread her hands over the lustrous upholstery covering the plush cushions. She had heard ladies in the shop complain of unbearable carriage rides countless times before, but she felt sure that none of these ladies would have survived the journey via mail coach Charlotte had made from her boarding school in Sussex to London as a young woman if *this* was what they considered uncomfortable.

"So, you see, my dear, we simply *had* to have you over for tea to meet my darling Nicholas." The countess had been speaking almost constantly since the carriage left Madame Beaumont's, but only at the mention of Lord Dorset's first name did Charlotte begin listening in earnest. Charlotte bit the inner edge of her lower lip, trying to focus her attention on Lady Harrington rather than her frantic thoughts and rioting pulse.

*You must listen to the woman if you're to learn who you are supposed to be.*

Charlotte knew from novels she had read that if one were captured behind enemy lines and held for interrogation, it was best to stay as close to the truth as possible without revealing sensitive information—this made it somewhat easier to lie to one's captors creditably. Since this would certainly not do in Charlotte's case as she knew nothing of "Miss Tabitha Crampton" aside from her name, and that the honest truth of her own identity was not an option, she chose to say as little as possible about anything at all.

"It was so kind of you to invite me, my lady. Please accept my sincerest gratitude," she said, hoping to avoid the topic of Miss Crampton's betrothal to the viscount. This tactic failed immediately.

"When your mother and I were girls together, we rather fancied that we would have children who would wed because it would mean we could become sisters ourselves in a way, via the suit," said Lady Harrington. "I'm so thrilled that it seems the great dream of our girlhood is coming true!"

"Is that so? What a delightful story. Mother never told me," replied Charlotte. The words felt strange in her mouth, and foreign as she said them aloud. That familiar pang of sadness leapt in her stomach.

*Remember: You are Tabitha Crampton, and her mother is alive.*

"Yes, your mother is as close to me as a natural born sister, Tabitha. We had such a happy childhood, playing together. And once we grew and were presented at court, I couldn't have asked for a better friend to accompany me to all of those endless balls. We had such fun in those days, as I'm sure you will have with your friends during the season," said the countess.

"Yes, indeed. Such fun," replied Charlotte with the warmest smile she could muster. She had never dreamed of attending a ball. She had never even learned to dance; the headmistress at the Waverly School for Orphaned Girls thought it impractical to teach the next generation of scullery maids how to waltz.

"Of course, you must have heard, we shall be hosting a ball at Stapleton when your parents arrive, and you simply must attend in the lavender gown, my dear. I will not accept no for an answer, and I have no doubt that my Nicholas will dance every dance with you, as I am sure that he is to fall deeply in love with you at first sight!" she added, barely stopping for breath.

"That sounds lovely," replied Charlotte, knowing full well that she had no intention of falling in love with Lord Dorset (a man whose profligate reputation preceded him), and no intention of attending the ball at Stapleton, as it would surely be attended by the *real* Tabitha, as well as her parents. To avoid telling further lies, Charlotte decided to avoid discussion of the ball altogether and moved to change the subject. "Will Lady Emmeline be joining us for tea?" she asked, hoping to determine just how many minutes of life she had left.

"Well, I should think that is unlikely seeing as she is traveling in the lake district with her aunt and uncle presently. I believe I explained that to you in my most recent letter, did I not?"

*Oh, no.*

"Oh, how silly of me. Yes, of course you did, my lady. Please forgive me. I must be tired from the morning," Charlotte said, hoping she had not revealed herself. Lady Harrington pressed on.

"Yes, I'm sure you have had much to do these days. Tell me, are you still studying music? Your mother told me years ago that you had a real gift for the pianoforte," said Lady Harrington. Charlotte had seen a pianoforte in person only once, when she was sent to assist with a delivery of clothing and accessories to Lady Jersey's townhome. She had been asked to wait for her ladyship in a receiving room with one of the ornate instruments tucked neatly into a corner. There was absolutely no way she could pretend to play if pressed.

"My mother has exaggerated, I'm afraid. I only had a few lessons as a child, and have not played in many years. I was not at all suited to the instrument, it seems," replied Charlotte, grasping for words. She breathed a sigh of relief that this reply seemed to satisfy the countess as the carriage slowed. They had arrived.

The carriage door opened and a footman helped the countess down from her seat. Charlotte followed her, wishing with all her might that a chasm would open in the earth beneath the grand steps that led to the wide oak front door of the home, swallowing her whole and ending this farce. If she were to die in that moment, she vowed that she would haunt Sarah until the end of time for masterminding this foolish scheme.

Charlotte followed Lady Harrington through the large front doors and into an entryway that was easily three times the size of the small flat she shared with Sarah, with ceilings more than twice as high. It seemed to be constructed almost entirely of marble, with large, smooth columns in each corner, lavish furniture lining the space, and arrangements of vibrant hothouse flowers displayed prominently. While Lady Dorset moved through the space unmoved by its grandeur, Charlotte was breathless. She barely even noticed that yet another footman had helped her out of her borrowed pelisse, gloves, and bonnet and had whisked the items away to some unknown room for safekeeping.

"Follow me, Tabitha. I shall ring for tea and send for my son. What a delightful afternoon this shall be," said the countess with a girlish smile as she led Charlotte down a grand hallway. They entered a sun-lit parlor with six towering French doors situated along the length of the room that opened onto a lush garden. The parlor was decorated in soft blush-colored fabrics that seemed purposefully coordinated with the flowers that were just beginning to bloom in the garden outside.

Charlotte tried desperately to memorize every detail to report back to Sarah, from the likely hand-painted wallpaper (citrus trees and peafowl over a cream-colored background) to the towering mantlepiece (stunning plaster scrollwork inlaid with yet more marble). In her wildest dreams, she could never have conceived of such a fine home, and could only imagine that it had been built and decorated at great expense.

Charlotte turned in place, slowly taking note of the opulence surrounding her. Her memory drifted to the town-home where she had lived with her mother as a young girl. She knew that they weren't poor then, but nothing compared to the startling affluence of Stapleton House. She let her mind wander further, to her final conversation with her poor mother.

Charlotte didn't like to think of her mother as she laid dying in her dark bedchamber, but she had never forgotten what she had told her then, her voice a weak rasp.

"I cannot protect you any longer. You will go away to

school, Celeste will care for you when she can, and you can earn your living in her shop when you are of age. Your father is not a bad man, but do not try to find him. He lives in a different world, one that we cannot ever hope to join. I'm ashamed to tell you that he does not know of your birth, and I hope that you can forgive me. It isn't fair, but neither is life, my darling."

A startling thought gripped her then, out of the darkest corners of her mind.

*Does my father live in a house this grand?*

Charlotte took a seat on a low sofa next to the countess and held her breath as the household staff entered with the tea service. Each silver tray was laden with finger sandwiches, scones, dainty bite-sized cakes, small pots of clotted cream, strawberry jam, and piles of biscuits. The tea cups placed before them were made of bone china so fine that it was almost transparent; Charlotte knew with certainty that she would chip the delicate gold-plated edge if she dared to take a sip. She prayed for strength, and begged God that the countess would not ask her to pour. The sheer decadence was beginning to overwhelm her.

Behind them, one of the large garden doors opened. Charlotte's skin warmed at the sound.

*What a curious sensation.*

She felt a large presence behind her and had the strange impression that a pair of probing eyes were fixed on the back of her neck, appraising her, assessing her value as though she were a mere porcelain figurine. How was she supposed to continue with this absurd plan? She had half a mind to stand and run away as fast as she could, but something she could not name rooted her to her seat. She wasn't sure she could remember the way through the enormous house even if she had tried. Just as she began to panic in earnest, a rumbling, *male* voice interrupted her thoughts.

"Good afternoon, Mother. Shall we get this over with?"

Dorset had spent the last hour strolling through his parents' extensive gardens. The fresh air had done him some good, although he supposed that purging behind the hedgerows was to thank for his improved condition. He found his mother waiting for him in the parlor, along with Miss Tabitha Crampton, the woman his parents would have him court and marry if they had their way.

When he stepped through the exterior door, Dorset couldn't see her face clearly, but when the woman finally turned her face to him, he was rendered speechless. Her skin was luminous; her lips were a vibrant shade of pink he had never seen before. Her cheeks blushed to a *delicious* shade of peach as they locked eyes. He longed to reach out and touch her, to feel for himself if she was a living, breathing woman or a painting by a Dutch master, propped up in a chair by his mother as a joke.

"Nicholas, don't stand there with your mouth hanging open like a fish! Come here so that I may introduce you to Miss Tabitha Crampton, daughter of Baron and Lady Balfour. She has come all this way to meet you, darling, and you stand there gawking as though you've seen a ghost!" He could always count on his mother to fill silences, and this was no exception. She went on, as though she did not require breath. "Tabitha, you must forgive my son, I have been told that he was feeling unwell earlier this morning," added the countess. Dorset approached them and gave a small, gentlemanly bow to the stunning creature he now knew was Miss Crampton, his intended bride. After bending to kiss his mother on her cheek, he offered Miss Crampton his hand. Reluctantly, she placed her hand in his; her skin felt like the finest French silk.

"Miss Crampton, it is a pleasure to make your acquaintance," he said, pressing a gentle kiss to her knuckles while keeping his gaze directly on her stunning face.

"Thank you, my lord. I assure you the pleasure is mine," she replied, turning away from him nervously.

*Damn.*

He was riveted by her beauty, so much so that he had forgotten all about his mother and father's marriage plot. Lady Harrington wasted no time reminding him as he lowered his large frame onto the empty seat on the delicate settee, just beside Miss Crampton.

"Nicholas, Tabitha and I have just come from Beaumont's. They have made her the most stunning gown I have ever seen, and she is to wear it to the ball your father and I are hosting. She shall be the talk of the *ton*, I am sure of it!"

"I do not doubt it, Mother," he replied, accepting a cup of tea from a servant. The hot liquid restored his sense—she may be the most beautiful woman he had ever seen, but he was still firmly against marrying. He needed to make his boundaries clear, quickly. "Unfortunately, I shall be unable to join you at the ball. I have a matter of business to attend to and shall be out of town," added Dorset, unable to meet his mother's eyes. He couldn't help but notice that Tabitha did not seem disappointed by this news; in fact, she seemed positively terrified in general. About what, he could only guess, but he imagined that his mother had been spinning tales to her all day.

"Business? Nonsense! What business could you possibly have outside of London during the *season*? You will attend the ball, and it is my wish that you shall escort Tabitha," said the countess, with a smile. His mother spoke with firm conviction, no doubt believing her word final. The three of them sat in strained silence as Dorset tried and failed to come up with another, more believable excuse. This tea was spinning out of his control far too quickly, although he should have known that his mother would be a step ahead of him where the ball was concerned. The matter was settled for now—he would have until Lord and Lady Balfour arrived to excuse himself as Miss Crampton's escort. Dorset carried on, attempting to lower Tabitha's expectations.

"Certainly, Mother," he replied, before turning to Tabitha. "You mustn't believe a word my mother has told you. She loves me far too much for my own good, and believes foolishly that others will do so as well, if only she can convince them." He smiled to himself as he added sugar to his tea.

"Now, *darling* boy, do not be modest. Why just the other day, Lady Westingham herself told me of how your advice to her husband, *the Marquess* of Westingham, had proven correct —their daughter's dowry is now among the most *substantial* in town, thanks to your ingenious mind for speculations."

While he had wished to change the subject from balls and romance and marriage, this was not a conversation he would entertain. Even worse, his mother spoke of his investments, schemes he had studied and prepared for years to ensure their returns worth the risk, as a mere hobby. The truth was, he had dedicated himself to the study for years, and so ardently that he had built himself a fortune that rivaled his father's holdings. Dorset was not bluffing when he had told his father that morning that he did not need their money.

"My mother exaggerates, I'm sure. I have been known to dabble in the markets, but I am sure the Marquess had matters well in hand all on his own," he replied. Dorset knew better than most that his mother, like all ladies of London, adored gossip, and thought it best to distract her before she inquired as to why Westingham had found himself so short of blunt that he could not marry off his eldest. Besides, as future earls did not generally partake in actual work, Dorset did not wish to linger upon the subject any longer. Thankfully, the ladies had already moved on.

Dorset watched Tabitha's delicate jaw and neck as she continued to converse with his mother, committing her lines and shades to memory. Something about her made him feel compelled to chop down a great oak tree and build her a sturdy home with his bare hands. This woman was soft and untouched by the world, a world that Dorset knew all too well to be cruel and dangerous for young, attractive ladies. Silently, he appointed himself her protector, knowing that if she attended his parents' ball, the other gentleman present would rip each other apart to get a piece of her. In his younger days, Dorset would have pursued her himself, for nothing more than the thrill of the conquest.

*If I cannot, no one can.*

"Tell me, sweet Tabitha, how is your mother enjoying her life in the country house? I have so missed her since your father gave up their house in town but I know that she must be well settled by now," said the countess, the tea in her cup surely cold and forgotten. One never lacked for conversation when she was present.

"Mother is quite well, my lady. Of course, she misses you terribly, but she has plenty to keep her occupied. She has just begun a new needlepoint," replied Miss Crampton. The end of every phrase she uttered seemed to twist upward, like a question. Why did she sound so unsure?

"Needlepoint! I should think not!" replied his mother, shocked. The girl looked stricken. She set her tea cup down hastily, the gilt china clinking as she did so.

"I beg your pardon, my lady?" she asked, the color in her cheeks rising. Dorset wasn't sure what had prompted his mother to dispute Tabitha's claim, nor did he understand why she was so shaken in response, but he did wonder if he could commission a portrait painter to find the correct shade to emulate that tempting, peachy flush.

"Tabitha, *dear*, your mother has *not* taken up needlepoint since we, as girls, decided one day to climb a tree on her parent's land in Surrey. She took a tumble and broke her pinky finger, which we *of course* tried to keep a secret, because we were terrified of her governess, who would surely have given us a thrashing for having done something so foolish in the first place. I'm sure you have heard this story many times, but as we did not call for a doctor to set the bone in time, your mother could never use the finger properly again, and always found needlepoint particularly painful," said the countess, incredulous that her friend's own daughter seemed to be hearing this for the first time.

"Oh, yes, of course. How silly of me. Perhaps she had decided to give it another attempt," replied Tabitha. Now visibly nervous, she looked everywhere around the room except for at his mother. Dorset tried to change the subject to save her from the countess's wrath, to no avail.

"Mother, I'm sure Miss Crampton did not mean to offend you. Let us not dwell on it," he said.

"Hush, Nicholas. Tabitha, I daresay your mother has not made another attempt, and I am surprised you would suggest such a thing. I shall be writing to her this afternoon to ask her myself!" she replied, reaching for a cake. At this pronouncement, Tabitha seemed to shrink into herself. This would not do.

"Miss Crampton, where are you staying while you're in town?" asked Dorset, hoping to change topic to a neutral subject, and to take the reins of conversation from his excitable mother. Tabitha's eyes went wide at his question, and she seemed unable to answer, frozen to her seat. Surely, he had said something wrong. In a feeble attempt to play protector, he went on. "My sister, Lady Emmeline, is traveling at present, but when she returns I'm sure she would like to make your acquaintance," he said, searching for a subject that would calm Tabitha's rapid breathing. Once again, he had failed.

"That is very kind of you, my lord. I shall look forward to it," she replied, just above a whisper. The poor girl was practically holding her breath and looked ready to faint. Anyone could plainly see that she was an unwilling participant in their parents' arrangement. Dorset had no intention of forcing any woman to do something against her will, even if it was something as innocent as afternoon tea; he would absolutely not let his parents force the girl into a marriage. He made a note to raise this objection with his father, who, as though summoned by Dorset's own thoughts, entered the room.

"Please forgive my lateness, I had to settle a matter with my solicitor," he said, striding through the room. The earl was as tall as his son, and though he was softer around the middle and had a head full of salt and pepper gray hair, his eyes shone with a youthful glint; the years had been kind to him. He leaned down and pressed a kiss to his wife's hand before he addressed Tabitha.

"Good afternoon, Miss Crampton," he said, dipping his head to her. A scowl clouded his gaze as he considered the girl. The Earl of Harrington was not as forthcoming with conversation as his wife, but he was rarely at a loss for words and often commanded any room he entered. Nicholas could not help but notice that in this moment, as his father regarded Tabitha for the first time, he seemed without words, just as Nicholas had been when he first entered the room. The main difference was that the earl did not seem as thoroughly beguiled by this woman's stunning beauty as Dorset had been. On the contrary, he seemed confused by her very existence, and for the life of him, Dorset could not figure out why.

"Father, I was just telling Miss Crampton that I should like to introduce her to my sister when she returns," said Dorset, trying to salvage some semblance of polite conversation at this disaster of a tea. Much to his mother's chagrin, he was not an observant churchgoer, but in this moment, Dorset prayed to God for guidance.

*What must I do to save this poor woman from our family?*

"A capital idea," replied the earl, who sipped his tea. Any sense of suspicion that Dorset had read on his father's face the moment before was gone, replaced with placid civility. "Miss Crampton, you honor us with your visit today. Tell me, what do you think of my son?" Leave it to his father to get straight to the point. Tabitha coughed suddenly—the forward question had taken her by surprise.

"Forgive me, my lord, we have spent just a few minutes in each other's company. Surely, you must not expect me to give you an answer," she replied, her tone clipped. Dorset admired Tabitha's response, knowing that most young ladies would be either too eager for the earl's favor and would reply with flattery, or would be so flustered by his directness that they would whither under his stare. Tabitha did neither—she held her ground. She turned to Dorset then, and he couldn't help but smile at her. The corner of her mouth twitched just barely, but he sensed that she wanted to smile back.

"Oh, Tabitha, ignore my husband. He is *far* too direct for his own good," said the countess with a laugh. If there was a deity in heaven, his father would steer the conversation away from courting and marriage and continue talking until it was time for Tabitha to take her leave.

"Yes, apologies, Miss Crampton. You must forgive me for being anxious to see my son happily settled," said the earl, who seated himself on a chair next to his wife. Dorset was so embarrassed that he wished to melt into a puddle at that moment. He guessed, based on the flush in her cheeks that had now spread to her ears, that Tabitha also wished for bodily evaporation. He wasn't sure if it came with age or if it had happened to them from the moment he was born, but Dorset had long suspected that his parents no longer possessed the capacity to display tact.

It was a shame that he had given up on marriage entirely—Dorset gave his parents credit for their choice of daughter-in-law, and knew that even though he could never make her a decent husband, at least his bride would have been stunning. Dorset folded his hands in his lap and dug his thumbnail into his opposite palm, reminding himself that successful marriages weren't built on looks alone, and that he was unworthy of this woman.

"Nicholas! Have you lost your hearing, my son?" His mother's exclamation interrupted his thoughts. It was time to end this tea and send this woman back to her family, before he decided that his parents had been right about her all along.

"I'm sorry, Mother, I am still feeling rather unwell. I'm afraid I must return home. I should never forgive myself if I were to pass my illness to anyone present," he said. The earl raised a skeptical eyebrow in response, but thankfully, said nothing.

"Oh, dear!" replied his mother, reaching for a bell. "Shall I send for the doctor? I must say that you do look rather pale this afternoon. We shall have you attended to at once!"

"No! No, please. I shall be much more comfortable at home, and I assure you that I shall send for a doctor once I arrive there," Dorset replied, finally seeing a light at the end of this painfully awkward tunnel. He turned to Tabitha, who gazed back at him with a pleading look in her eyes. She was clearly as desperate to escape this parlor as he was. "Miss Crampton, I would be happy to escort you home, if you wish," Dorset said, knowing that a private carriage ride was not entirely appropriate, but wishing with all his heart to steal a moment alone with her so that he could explain himself.

"Absolutely out of the question!" said Lady Harrington, dashing his hopes for a quiet rendezvous. "Nicholas, have you forgotten your manners? You must not be alone with Tabitha without an escort. She shall take our carriage back to her relations' home and I will not hear otherwise."

"Of course, Mother," he replied, standing now to take his leave. Tabitha did the same. They seemed to both understand that if they did not escape now, they would be trapped for further questioning indefinitely.

"Thank you so much for your hospitality, my lady," said Tabitha, with a curtsy.

"Allow me to show you to the carriage," said Dorset, eager to remove this poor woman from the room before anyone could protest.

"Thank you, my lord," she said. Dorset was called "my lord" by any number of people he came into contact with on a daily basis, but something stirred deep within him at the sound of the possessive words on her lips. He didn't know where the feeling came from, but he wanted so badly to be *hers*. How was this possible after only knowing the woman for the time it took to drink a cup of tea?

They made their way to the grand entry room in silence. He glanced over at Miss Crampton, and noticed that she was walking with her head held high and eyes straight ahead. Anyone else might assume that she was fine, but he noticed that she was taking shallow, quick breaths, the pulse point on her neck fluttering just below her skin. She was a wild animal, ready to spring out of her cage.

A footman produced her gloves, bonnet and pelisse, helping her don the items before they exited the door. Dorset watched her button the front of her pelisse at her chest, with deft, skilled movements, and he imagined those same fingers undoing the buttons on his coat, and then his waistcoat, before moving to the fall of his trousers.

*Christ, Dorset, control your thoughts.*

It was time to deposit the woman in a coach before he

began something that would delight his parents but that he would surely regret—courting her.

They walked down the expansive stone steps where the carriages stood waiting, offering the freedom for which they were both desperate. Dorset thanked his maker that his parents had bid them goodbye from the parlor, rather than following them out to see them off.

"Please, allow me to apologize for my mother and father. I'm afraid they may have made promises to you on my behalf that I cannot keep," Dorset said. Miss Crampton turned to him; he could see questions forming in her mind, and moved to speak again before she could protest. "You must know, I have no intention of marrying—"

"Lord Dorset, please—" She moved to stop him, but he went on. He couldn't let her leave today without making his intentions, or rather his lack of intentions, clear.

"Miss Crampton, I understand that you have come here at great personal inconvenience just to meet me. If my father is to be believed, which I'm not entirely sure he is, your parents have agreed to our suit. Forgive me, but I could sense your trepidation during tea and I'd like to set you at ease before we part today," he said. Her eyes were downcast; he resisted the urge to reach out and tilt her chin up as he went on. "I will not marry you. Please do not leave today assuming otherwise."

Her breath caught. For the first time since they left the parlor, she met his eyes. He again noticed the color rising in her cheeks as she spoke. "My lord, you seem to be operating under a delusion. For you see, it is *I* who will not marry *you*. Good day."

She moved toward the carriages, but Dorset stopped her with a firm hand at her elbow, spinning her back to face him. Once again, he had intended to calm her and had failed.

"Miss Crampton, please, I did not mean to upset you. You must understand that while on paper I can have no real objection to our potential marriage, I cannot in good conscience go through with it. I would make a dreadful husband."

She shook herself free of his grasp, and backed away from him, inching ever closer to the carriage behind her. "Of that, my lord, I have no doubt."

Dorset exhaled a chuckle at this response. He supposed that as he had just said the words aloud, he could not be offended by her response. Just as it did before, her honesty charmed him.

"In that case, let us part today as friends. I meant what I said earlier. I would like for you to meet my sister," he said with a smile, reaching out a hand to help her into the carriage. She regarded his upturned palm with uncertainty before taking it. Even through their gloves, he could feel her warmth.

"I would like that very much, my lord," she replied, her green eyes darkening as they held each other's gaze. Surely it was a trick of the light, as the sun was lowering in the sky. After a silent moment, she turned and entered the coach.

Dorset wasn't sure when he would see her next. He knew that he shouldn't even want to see her again. The thought alone left him bereft, desperate for some excuse to place himself in her path.

*I cannot marry her.*

*She is too pure for a scoundrel like me.*

*Em would love her.*

Emmeline would be home from her trip within the week. If acting as chaperone to them both was the only innocent way he could stay by Miss Crampton's side, then so be it.

He watched the carriage trundle away down the street until it had disappeared around a corner, and he told himself a lie.

*That woman is not for me.*

## CHAPTER 4

Charlotte felt certain that she had never told so many lies in a single day. The final falsehood was to a coachman; she told him that she had forgotten her reticule at Beaumont's, and asked to be taken there rather than her home. She was certain that Tabitha Crampton was not planning to stay in a Cheapside walk-up garret flat when she came to London, and knew that her cover would be blown if she showed members of the Stapleton household staff where she lived.

It was growing dark when she exited Beaumont's via the staff entrance, once again restored to her own clothes and identity. Sarah's shift had ended, and a fresh team of seamstresses were busying themselves at their stations in the back rooms, preparing orders for the following day. Thankfully, Madame Beaumont had adjourned to her penthouse on the top floor of the building for the day; if Charlotte and Sarah had been dismissed, they wouldn't have to face the news just yet.

She and Sarah usually journeyed home in a hack, but Charlotte feared that they couldn't spare the expense if they were both out of work come the morning. It took Charlotte nearly an hour to walk home; she had never taken the journey alone, and was well aware that as an unaccompanied woman, she was a prime target if she wasn't careful. No man she passed on the street was to be trusted. Her very existence was proof that gentlemen were no better than common men, and were often worse. Charlotte knew that she should remain vigilant until she was safely behind the locked door of her home.

Her mind wandered as she walked. Her surroundings now on the darkened streets of London were so different from the opulence of Stapleton House. Is this what her mother meant when she told her that her father was from a different world? She hadn't given him much thought as a child, for she didn't miss the man. Her mother and Madame Beaumont had filled her days with all the delights and wonder that the backstage of an opera house can provide a young girl, and after her mother's passing, she had been sent off to the boarding school straight away.

Only as an adult did Charlotte learn that aristocratic men in London used visiting opera companies to find companionship that their wives either would or could not provide, selecting a new background dancer or ensemble singer as though from an auction catalog. In return for their ruination, these women received financial protection. Had her father tempted her mother in this way? Charlotte wondered what riches the man could have offered to get the most talented soprano in London to his bed, only to disappear like a wisp of smoke on a breeze after she fell pregnant. She thought of her mother's beloved amethyst and diamond earrings that Madame Beaumont kept locked for Charlotte in the shop's underground safe. Were mere baubles enough to tempt the woman Charlotte remembered as the epitome of grace?

And to think, if the man had taken responsibility for his actions, if he had actually cared for her mother, Charlotte wouldn't be traipsing through the muddy streets of Cheapside back to her shared flat in a derelict building. Maybe, if Charlotte had the benefit of her father's largess, she could afford to get Sarah a new pair of glasses, for the ones she had were no longer strong enough thanks to the endless hours of lacework they did by candlelight.

She didn't know if the man was still alive, but it was more than possible—in fact, it was probable. As anger and confusion built in her heart, Charlotte wished with everything that she had that she could show him just how her life had turned out. She wanted to make him feel even a fraction of the grief she had endured, and she wanted him to know the reality of what it meant to carve out a living as a single 28-year-old woman without hope of finding a husband.

Finally, she reached her building. Her feet and back ached as she climbed the stairs and unlocked her door with the key she had been clutching in her fist, a makeshift and thankfully unnecessary weapon. Sarah sprang upon her before she could even close the door.

"Lottie! You survived! Let me take your cloak. Sit down by the fire; I will bring you some bread and cheese, and you must tell me everything. What was their house like? Was the viscount as handsome as I remember? Are you in love?" Charlotte collapsed into a chair and closed her eyes. She knew Sarah was energetic, but this line of questioning was decidedly unwelcome.

"Sarah, I am exhausted. Apparently, living the life of the idle rich is not as relaxing as it would seem," Charlotte said, accepting a plate from her friend. "I'll start at the beginning. My dearest friend hung me out to dry and sent me into the lion's den, totally defenseless," she added. Sarah gave Charlotte her sweetest smile in response.

"You were absolutely not defenseless. You are the cleverest person I know. I wouldn't have sent you into that carriage if I didn't think you could manage yourself," said Sarah. Her words were kind, but they did not change the ordeal that Charlotte had just been through.

"Well, let me give you the short version. I bungled my way through even the simplest conversations, because as luck would have it, the countess is very close with the woman's mother. She asked me *questions*, and every answer I gave was wrong! The earl seemed to know that I was an imposter, and Lord Dorset looked as though my very presence made him ill. Oh! Did I mention that he intends to introduce me to his sister, Lady Emmeline? If we can somehow keep this charade from Madame Beaumont's attention, it will be a miracle, but none of that will matter the next time Lady Harrington and Lady Emmeline come in for a gown only to put two and two together," added Charlotte. She could feel her pulse quickening at the thought of losing their positions.

"Charlotte, I took care of Madame, you don't have to worry," replied Sarah. How could she be so calm? It was maddening.

"What do you mean I don't have to worry? What did you tell her?"

"I simply told her that Lady Harrington had asked for your special assistance at her home, and that it was *possibly* because she saw how lovely you looked in the gown, and I *might* have insinuated that a certain viscount had taken a fancy to you," Sarah said.

"What? A *certain viscount*? Sarah, I told countless lies today, but none of them were as harmful as yours," replied Charlotte.

"Well, at least I saved our jobs," said Sarah, as unruffled as ever. "You know that Madame Beaumont will never discuss such matters with the customers. And besides, it will be the Harringtons' problem when the real Tabitha arrives and she isn't half as lovely or charming as you are, and Lord Dorset will realize that he can't live without you."

*Was she always this exasperating, or had Sarah recently suffered a head wound?*

Charlotte rose and went to their bedchamber to change out of her work dress. Her corset was digging into her skin through her chemise; she had suffered through enough discomfort for the day. Sarah followed close behind with a candle, peppering her friend with question after question as Charlotte slipped into her worn linen nightrail and tied on her dressing gown behind a screen.

"Tell me about Dorset, Lottie. Is he as tall as they say he is?" asked Sarah.

"Sarah, please keep in mind that Lord Dorset and I did not fall in love today, and we will likely never engage socially again thanks to my status as a parentless, common spinster with a trade, and his as a titled future peer. And no—he's taller than I expected."

"Taller! I knew it. Tell me more. What did he smell like?"

"His scent? I am sure that I do not know!" Charlotte had become an expert liar since she woke up that morning—Dorset smelled like warm cedar and rich leather; decadent and wealthy. She kept this to herself.

"What else? You promised to tell me all about it, remember?"

"I did, didn't I? The house was quite grand. Our entire flat could fit inside the foyer, and I suspect that the walls in the hallway were papered with damask silk—" Sarah raised a hand and stopped her before Charlotte could continue.

"Yes, yes, that all sounds fine, but I want to know about Dorset. Did he charm you?"

"Sarah, I'm sure I don't have to remind you that its *Lord* Dorset to us, and no, I wouldn't say that he charmed me. In fact, he declared outright that he has no intention of marrying Miss Crampton at all," she replied. Her friend smiled.

"Yes, yes, Lord Dorset it is—although I've heard ladies in the shop calling him 'Lord Corset' when they think no one can hear." Sarah clapped a hand to her mouth to suppress a giggle before she went on. "Imagine, just for fun, that you were a lady, and you met him purely by chance. Would you let him court you?"

Charlotte bit her lower lip and furrowed her brow in thought. She shouldn't encourage Sarah, but there was no harm in wondering. "I don't know. The entire time I was there, I kept wondering about..." Charlotte stopped herself. If she said the words, she would be forced to have a conversation she didn't feel ready for.

"Wondering what? How to nick a miniature without anyone noticing?" asked Sarah, giggling some more. Charlotte failed to find the humor in the situation.

"No, not that. I just couldn't help but wonder if my father is as rich as the Dorsets—if he lives in wealth and comfort but my poor mother died after bearing his unclaimed child." Sarah didn't respond. Charlotte could feel her sadness growing harder in her heart, turning to something darker, angrier. How could he have left them, when even on her deathbed, her mother claimed that he wasn't a bad man? Had she loved him?

"It doesn't matter, anyway. And besides, Dorset stated without question that he is uninterested in courting me, so we needn't discuss such things," she said.

"No, he said he isn't interested in courting *Miss Crampton*. Its not the same," said Sarah with a devilish smile.

"You're right, it isn't the same. He isn't interested in courting and proposing to a proper, scandal-free lady. I, on the other hand, was born a scandal and shall die an unmarried commoner because of it. And besides, I will not fool myself. As handsome as he is, I cannot expose myself to the charms of a wealthy gentleman and suffer the same fate my mother did, twenty-eight years ago."

"So, you admit that he's handsome?"

*Blast.*

With a simple slip of the tongue, her private thoughts had been revealed. Sarah had a talent for getting people to share more than they intended; Charlotte wasn't usually susceptible, but she was exhausted, and her small but comfortable bed was beckoning. She closed their bedchamber door to keep the heat in and watched as Sarah climbed into her own bed opposite from Charlotte's before she extinguished the candle.

Maybe it was the exhaustion that caused her to say aloud what she did next, or perhaps it was the nascent speck of fury that had settled deep in her chest while at tea that afternoon. Charlotte didn't know for sure, but she now knew what had to be done. She had too many unanswered questions, questions that she had not known to ask as a girl clutching her mother's weakening hand as she watched her slip away.

"I have had enough interrogation for a single day. Goodnight, Sarah. I hope you have a nightmare as chilling as the one I have just survived. In the morning, we can set about figuring out how to do the impossible."

"Impossible? What do you mean?" asked Sarah from her bed in the darkness.

"Yes, and I have no idea how to begin, but I'm certain I'll require your help. I want to find my father."

It had been three days since Miss Tabitha Crampton had invaded Dorset's world. He wasn't sure if it had been his father's declaration (marry her *or else*), his mother's insistence that he escort the woman to their upcoming ball, or his pronounced nausea at the time, but thoughts of Tabitha swam in his head from when he rose at his usual hour of eleven o'clock in the morning until he went to bed well past midnight each night.

He thought of how she faced his parents during tea, her spine straight and gaze unwavering, even though she was obviously there against her will and deeply uncomfortable.

He thought about the slope of her neck, and wondered what it would feel like to run a fingertip over the skin there.

He thought of her raising a teacup to her lips to drink her tea. In all his years of chasing after women, he had never before been jealous of a damn teacup.

When he couldn't shake the image of Tabitha's flushed cheeks from his mind, Dorset turned to strenuous physical activity. On the day after the tea, he had ridden his fastest horse out of town and over hill and dale, driving the great beast harder and faster as he went, letting the harsh wind whip at his face. When he returned home, both he and the horse were exhausted. Thoughts of Tabitha remained.

The next day, he entered the London Fencing Club determined to take on all challengers. He sparred for hours, until his trousers and jacket were soaked with sweat. Dorset's muscles ached with each lunge, and yet he did not cease until his foil snapped. He exited the sparring area, tore his mask from his head, and knew that again he had failed, for Tabitha remained.

On the third day, he decided to take a more literal approach to memory loss: pugilism. After a punishing hour with the heavy bag at his boxing gymnasium, an opponent had approached him for a friendly match; the gentleman was stockier than Dorset but less experienced. Dorset won easily in two rounds, but not after taking a jab or two to the ribs, and another well-placed right cross. It wasn't enough; Tabitha remained.

Dorset awoke the following day aching from head to toe

and sporting a rather ghastly bruise around his eye. He hauled himself out of bed and dressed with the help of his concerned valet; Dorset's clothes were expertly tailored to his body, but they had never struggled so much to get his trim waistcoat and jacket on over his stiff shoulders.

He sat down to eat breakfast and mindlessly leafed through that morning's paper, freshly ironed by his butler. Dorset couldn't focus on the printed words. His horse, the hours of fencing, the punches he took: all had failed to rid him of his fixation. He couldn't beat Tabitha out of his own mind, so he decided to give his exhausted body a break—it was time for a steam.

Thankfully, he didn't have far to go. After a short walk through Mayfair, Dorset found himself in the changing room of the Turkish bath on Jermyn Street, gingerly removing his clothes before wrapping a plush towel around his waist. He heard the door to the changing rooms open as someone entered, and swore under his breath; he was not in the mood for conversation.

*So much for private relaxation.*

"Nicky! Where have you been hiding? I haven't seen you at the club in four days."

With a sigh of relief, Dorset turned slowly on the spot and found himself face to face with Lord Richard Markby, the eighth Duke of Sutton—his affable friend and, more often than not, partner in crime. They had known each other since they were boys—if Dorset couldn't sweat out his current dilemma alone, Markby was the only person he would tolerate. He hadn't seen the man since their ill-fated night of indulgence, but as usual, Markby looked perfectly at ease and no worse for wear.

"Markby, thank God it's you. I was worried I'd have to exchange pleasantries and discuss the weather," said Dorset, reaching for another towel and draping it around his neck.

"I think we dispensed with social niceties back at Eton, wouldn't you agree? Besides, when two friends are as close as we, they can sit in comfortable silence all day," replied Markby, shucking his own jacket. "Here for a steam, or were you just planning to stand around naked in the changing room?"

"You see right through me, old friend."

"I'd take offense at your use of the word 'old,' but you're two months older. I won't hold it against you."

"How gracious of you," said Dorset, holding open the changing room door for his friend, now similarly outfitted in terry cloth towels and leading the way to the wet steam room frequented by London's most fashionable gentlemen. They stepped carefully around dozing men draped over marble benches, red and sweating. Thankfully, a private alcove was available.

"Tell me, where have you been since last week at White's? I was about to send out a search party," said Markby as be blotted a towel over his glistening brow.

"I haven't been missing, I just needed a break from the club. I didn't recover well from the last time you saw me."

"I don't doubt it. I matched you drink for drink and spent the next 12 hours over a basin. I had to give the housekeeper a pay rise when she threatened to give her notice. I'm not sure that we weren't poisoned."

"It was one for the books, wasn't it? I don't think I've ever felt that sick, although the events of the day after only made it worse," said Dorset. He took in a deep breath of the warm, damp air.

"Come along, unburden yourself to your oldest friend. You don't disappear unless something's really bothering you, and judging from the bruise under your eye and that you seem to be unable to walk normally, I'd say it has something to do with a woman."

"Right again. Is it that obvious?"

"Do you mean to tell me that you've been holed up with a mistress since I last saw you? I didn't think Geneviève was back from Austria until next month," said Markby.

"No, no, we ended things before she left. Let's just say I did not want to tie myself down to just one opera dancer, and she didn't agree with my line of thinking," replied Dorset, realizing just how little his friend knew of his new moral backbone. "This woman is different—different in that I've decided I can't pursue her, but I'm not sure that any other woman will do now that I know she exists." Markby turned to him with a look of stunned horror.

"My God, Dorset. What are you saying?"

"I'll start from the beginning," Dorset said. "My parents sent for me just hours after I left you at White's. I stumbled into my father's study, still drunk and growing sicker by the second. He told me that he and my mother had arranged my marriage to a respectable young lady, and that I was to get down on one knee and beg for her hand or be cut off." Rather than reply, Markby let out a low whistle. "Here's where it gets tricky: I had sworn off marriage and women that very morning. I'm newly celibate, you see. I'm a terrible rascal, as you know, and I simply can't bear it any longer."

"Ah, I see. You've reached your limit. I can respect your abstention, but I fear there are depths I have not yet plumbed. Forgive me if I soldier on in the name of depravity." Markby's appetites were legendary.

"You're forgiven, of course. Go forth and do your worst to all womankind, if you must. Just get their permission first."

"Dorset, you know I never force women. Don't be crass," Markby said, offended at the very thought. Unlike others in their social circles, Dorset and Markby were firmly against coercion.

Dorset went on, sweating profusely now. "My newfound moral fortitude is only part of the problem. You see, I met the woman, grew infatuated with her at first sight, and now I can't marry her because I have vowed to myself that our licentious bloodline will end with me. Its all over before it could even begin, but I can't stop thinking about her."

The two men sat in silence for a few minutes, losing themselves to the heat of the room. Dorset changed position and felt beads of sweat trickle down over his chest and abdomen. He felt more limber already, and he wondered if confessing his feelings to his friend had helped, or if the steam was sweating the pain and confusion from his body.

"Let me get this straight—you're prepared to be cut off from your family fortune even though you've met your match, all because you can't stomach the thought of fathering another generation of Dorsets?"

"That about sums it up," Dorset replied. "I've invested well enough that I do not need my family's money, and I've lived my life to this point in pursuit of my own selfish pleasure. God forbid I make another me. I just wish I'd never met the woman. I can't get her out of my head."

"Tell me about her. Describe the siren who has brought the great 'Lord Corset' to heel," Markby said, looking concerned now.

"Her name is Tabitha Crampton. I had never laid eyes on her before—I take it she stays mainly in the country, and although I estimate that she is older than twenty-five, she has not yet had a season."

"Never heard of her. I'll admit, I'm surprised that a meek country mouse could turn your head."

"Markby, you wound me. You know that all women turn my head, and that is precisely the problem. But this one is certainly not meek, nor mousy, and I fear that she has changed everything."

"Well, it would take one with sharp claws to snag you, Nicky. But you're still set against courting her?"

"Dead set against it. She deserves so much more than I can give her."

"We both know that's nonsense. You're as rich as Croesus, and women across London are desperate to get you in their beds to see if you live up to the scandalous rumors. I'm constantly disappointing the ones who have already had the pleasure, and if I'm being totally honest, it's starting to hurt my pride, Dorset. I shall thank the Good Lord in church next Sunday that you've reformed and won't be in my way any longer."

Dorset chuckled at this. He knew his friend was just trying and make him feel better. It didn't change the fact that he was pining for a woman he barely knew and would never have.

"She sounds lovely. My condolences to you both on the premature death of your courtship. Although...a thought has occurred to me," said Markby, grinning mischievously. Dorset didn't know what his friend would say next, but he didn't care for the look on his face.

"What? Out with it—"

"Calm down, Nicky," Markby replied, cutting him off. "I've always admired your remarkable taste. From your home, to your clothes, to your women. I don't doubt that this Tabitha is a treasure—"

"She is not 'my woman,' Markby," Dorset snapped, not liking where this was going.

"Ah, wonderful. Then you won't mind if I court her?"

*Traitor.*

"You wouldn't."

"I would! From your description, she is an uncommon beauty with a brain in her head and in the market for a husband. With my parents gone and no heir to my title, I've been feeling a pull toward the altar. Why not give it a go with Miss Crampton?" Dorset had been resting his hands on his towel-covered lap; he knotted them together to keep from wringing Markby's neck.

"Absolutely not. Markby, there are far too many witnesses here, otherwise I would throttle you for even suggesting it," Dorset said, rising from his reclined position and trying to calm his breathing. Markby had the nerve to simply smile back at him, as though he hadn't just decided to throw their decades-long friendship down the drain and court the only woman Dorset had ever considered marriageable.

"Well, if you don't want me, your nearest and dearest, courting her, then you know the solution, don't you?"

*Clever bastard.*

"Court her yourself, you blasted idiot," said Markby, settling back against the cool marble and closing his eyes, a smug smile playing across his face. Dorset got up from the bench they were sharing and adjusted the towel around his waist, resisting the urge to take the one around his neck, twirl it into a tight, soggy rope, and snap it at his friend's chest, as they had when they were boys in school.

"Damn you, Markby. I will."

# Chapter 5

"Ouch! Watch where you put those pins, Lottie!" Charlotte and Sarah had been hemming Lady Marchbank's newest gown in the back room of Beaumont's for the better part of their morning. It was simple work they had done thousands of times before, but Charlotte's mind was elsewhere, and she had forgotten to warn Sarah about a straight pin she had placed deep within one of the folds of satin. "You're awfully distracted this morning. Want to talk about it?" asked Sarah.

Charlotte did not want to talk about "it,"—not today, and not ever. In this case, "it" happened to be Nicholas Felton, Viscount Dorset, and Charlotte feared what would happen if she admitted aloud that she had been consumed with thoughts of both seeking revenge on her absent father, and of him. If an aristocratic man was to blame for the course of her life, why couldn't she stop imagining what it would feel like to be held in the arms of one of the very same?

Charlotte had intended to keep focused on gathering what information she could, finding any clue that would lead her to her father's identity. Instead, her mind wandered as she sewed to thoughts that she shouldn't entertain.

Thoughts of Dorset's strong grip as he helped her into his parents' carriage.

Thoughts of the trim cut of his finely made coat, and how it skimmed perfectly over his broad chest and sculpted shoulders.

Thoughts of his playful, private smile after she told him she would never marry him.

That was just the problem: Why should she have fond thoughts for a man so above her station that she would likely never see him again outside of her capacity as a seamstress? Maybe he would come into the shop someday to purchase gifts for his mother, sister, or more likely, *his wife*. Perhaps he would ask her opinion on the cut of a sleeve, or a sweep of a skirt. The truth was, he could walk in at any moment, and Charlotte knew in her heart that he wouldn't give her a second thought.

The only reason he had even spoken to her at his parents' home was because she had lied about her true identity, and because she was outfitted in beautiful clothes that she could never actually afford. And besides, if he did recognize her in her plain work dress and apron rather than the aristocratic costume she had worn the other day, he would know instantly that she had lied to him.

And yet, no matter how hard she tried to clear her mind and focus on the great expanse of salmon-colored satin before her, she could not stop thinking of him. Charlotte had felt sadness and grief in her life, but she had never felt unrequited yearning. Was this what it felt like? A deep, unfulfilled ache in her chest?

She had experience, of course; she had no reputation to protect, and it had been thrilling to steal moments alone with the young stable hand at her boarding house in the year before she left for London. That was nothing more than a fleeting dalliance between two teenagers—she didn't miss the boy when she left Sussex on the mail coach, even if she missed the things he did to her body. Whatever it was at the time, it had not prepared her for this new feeling, this grief for a relationship that would never exist.

"Charlotte, talk to me. Please." Charlotte looked up at Sarah and saw genuine concern in her eyes. Between her dark mood and her earlier confession that she wished to seek out her father's identity, Sarah had seemed worried for her. It was enough to push her sadness over the edge, and before she knew it, a tear rolled down her cheek.

"Oh, Sarah. Everything has gone wrong," she said, setting down her pin cushion and reaching for a handkerchief in the pocket of her apron. "I'm such a fool. I know that it can never happen—it's completely hopeless," she said, dabbing at her eyes.

"What's hopeless? The hem looks just fine so far, and we have plenty of time to finish. I'm sure Marchbank will love it—"

"No, no, not the hem. I have to confess something to you, and you must promise you won't make fun." Sarah raised her right hand as though she were swearing an oath in front of a magistrate.

"Charlotte Price, I solemnly vow that I will not mock you for any reason for the rest of our lives. Now, tell me what's wrong before I start to genuinely worry."

As they continued to sew, Charlotte told Sarah that despite his emphatic declaration that he would never marry her, and her agreement, and the fact that none of it mattered anyway because she wasn't actually Miss Tabitha Crampton, Charlotte was besotted with Dorset, and therefore was devastated that she would never have him.

"So, you see, I might be a woman of advanced age, but I'm

concealing a silly schoolgirl fixation on a man who doesn't know I exist. If you're any kind of friend, please help distract me so that I can get through the rest of this day without giving him another moment of my time," Charlotte said.

The weight on her chest lightened at the confession, even if she knew that it was frivolous nonsense to begin with. Sarah set down her needle and thread and reached over to Charlotte, clasping Charlotte's hands in hers. They both bore the telltale needle pricks and callouses—the marks of women who worked with their hands for a living. How the Dorsets hadn't noticed her scarred hands and thrown her out of their home, Charlotte couldn't guess.

"Oh, Lottie. You're not silly, you're human. Any woman with eyes in her head would be taken with him, and you got to spend an afternoon pretending to be his bride. Please, don't be so hard on yourself. Now, I'll race you around the rest of this hem; let's see how quickly we can finish up and get onto the next one," said Sarah, just as Polly, a young girl who had just started apprenticing, burst into the room.

"Sarah, Charlotte! Madame needs you right away—a very fine lady has come into the shop and she's with Madame now. She wants to speak with the both of you, something about a gown from last week," Polly said.

"Thank you, Polly, we'll come at once," said Sarah, rising from her stool. "We had so many ladies in the shop last week. Do you know who it is?" she asked. Sarah's tone was nonchalant, but unease began to build in Charlotte's chest.

"It's Lady Emmeline Felton, and she told Madame that she's looking for a girl named Tallulah. Or no, maybe it was Twyla, I can't remember—" Charlotte held up a firm hand, silencing the girl.

"Tabitha. She's looking for Tabitha."

*So much for putting Dorset out of your mind.*

Charlotte turned to Sarah, and went on. "Well, Sarah. The

jig is up. Let us begin our march to the gallows." Polly looked at Charlotte like she was speaking another language, but it was no use explaining to the girl what they had done. "You'd better fetch Miss Crampton's letter to show her, don't you think?" asked Charlotte. Sarah pulled it from her apron.

"I've got it here. After you, Polly," Sarah said. Charlotte and Sarah followed the girl through the private hallway from the back room to the showroom floor.

There, they saw Madame Beaumont, in her usual feathered turban, chatting happily with Lady Emmeline, who looked as chic as ever. Her light brown hair was twisted up in an elegant knot and tucked under a tasteful bonnet, tied with a jade green ribbon that coordinated beautifully with her gown and shawl. Both women turned as they heard Charlotte and Sarah approach.

"*Alors,* here they are. Lady Emmeline, you remember Charlotte and Sarah. They assisted your mother last week with Miss Crampton's gown. I will leave you in their capable hands," Madame Beaumont said.

"Thank you, Madame Beaumont. I am sure they will be a great help to me," replied Lady Emmeline. The two women exchanged kisses on both cheeks, and Madame Beaumont swept from the room with Polly close behind, flashing Charlotte and Sarah a knowing look as she did so.

*Lord, help us.*

"Good afternoon, Lady Emmeline. How may we help you today?" asked Charlotte, eager to get to the point so that she could begin a life of crime to keep their fires lit.

"Good afternoon. Madame Beaumont tells me that you assisted my mother last week when she came in to purchase a gown for Miss Tabitha Crampton. Is that correct?" Lady Emmeline asked.

"Yes, my lady. We had the gown sent to Stapleton House that very day. Is something the matter with it?" asked Sarah.

Charlotte knew that the gown was utter perfection—this conversation was almost certainly related to the woman and not the dress.

"No, no, I'm sure the gown is fine. You see, we are having trouble getting in touch with Miss Crampton. She joined my parents and brother for tea that afternoon and left in one of our carriages. I meant to call on her this morning, but she did not leave her direction. The footmen said that she instructed them to bring her here after the tea, as she had forgotten her reticule, and she did not allow them to stay and see her the rest of the way home. Do either of you know where I might find her?" Charlotte took a deep breath.

*The truth will out.*

"My lady, I'm afraid we have some explaining to do. Sarah, I think it's best if we start with the letter," said Charlotte. How she managed to keep her voice steady was a mystery.

"I agree," replied Sarah. She handed the small envelope to Lady Emmeline, who was regarding them with watchful suspicion, not unlike young Polly a few minutes earlier.

Charlotte and Sarah stood silently, as still as stone, while Lady Emmeline read the letter. Once she had finished, she folded it carefully, returned it to the envelope, and slipped it into her reticule before she spoke.

"I think it would be best, if you both agree, that we discuss this in private. Is there a changing room available?" she asked.

"Of course, my lady. Follow me," said Sarah. The three women went up the grand staircase to the fitting area, where one of the fitting rooms stood empty with the heavy curtain tied back. There were other customers about; they would have to be discreet.

After they entered the small space, Charlotte untied the curtain and secured it on the other side, blocking them from view. Anyone watching would assume that Lady Emmeline was here for a fitting, and nothing more. For the moment, it was the perfect cover.

Lady Emmeline regarded the two seamstresses with an unreadable gaze; Charlotte couldn't tell if she was going to report them to the authorities or invite them over for another tea. Thankfully, she didn't keep them in suspense long.

"I take it, from this letter, that the woman who had tea with my family last week was not actually Miss Crampton. Is that correct?" Charlotte and Sarah spoke at the same time in response.

"Yes, my lady."

"Before I make any assumptions regarding what actually happened, I'd like for you both to give me a full account, if you don't mind," she said, her face as still and calm as a lake on a clear spring morning. Sarah stepped forward.

"First, let me say that this was entirely my idea. Charlotte is not to be blamed for any part of this," she said, hurriedly. Charlotte turned to Sarah and smiled—she was a good friend.

"Lady Harrington ordered a ball gown for Miss Crampton, but unfortunately, we did not have the lady here to measure," said Sarah.

"That sounds like something my mother would do," said Emmeline with a smile. "Please, go on."

Sarah began to pace the room. "As luck would have it, the measurements that Miss Crampton provided to your mother via post were nearly the same as Charlotte's, so Madame Beaumont decided that we should fit the gown to her. We were doing final alterations on the gown in advance of your mother's appointment on the day in question."

"I see. Things are slowly becoming clear," said Lady Emmeline, turning her gaze to Charlotte.

*She knows.*

"Charlotte was modeling the gown one last time for Madame when your mother arrived—she was a few minutes early for her appointment, you see," said Sarah, her brow furrowed. "The letter from Miss Crampton had arrived just minutes before. One of the apprentices, knowing that Miss Crampton's appointment was set for that very hour, opened the letter. Once she read the letter, she found me straight away," said Sarah.

"As Sarah said, the countess arrived early for her appointment, and she saw me on the platform in the gown," said Charlotte, giving Sarah a reprieve. "No doubt, she recognized the design from Madame's original sketch, but she did not recognize me. Before I knew it, she had approved of the gown and was whisking me away to Stapleton House for tea, believing me to be Miss Crampton."

"Is that so?" asked Lady Emmeline. She scanned Charlotte from head to toe and back again, which made Charlotte feel exposed, as naked as the day she was born. Clearly, she did not see how her mother had mistaken this seamstress for a baron's daughter.

"It's true, my lady. Charlotte looked so beautiful, and knowing that Miss Crampton would not arrive as scheduled, and once your mother thought Charlotte was Miss Crampton, I thought it might be a laugh to go along with it. You must understand, Lady Emmeline, we had no idea that your mother would insist on bringing Charlotte home to meet your brother. That's when it all went pear-shaped," said Sarah. Charlotte held her breath; all their cards were on the table, as it were, and now they were at Lady Emmeline's mercy.

"This is quite the tale. First, let me tell you with all sincerity that I believe it. Secondly, I believe absolutely that you meant no harm. Whether or not harm has been done is a question for another time. I have a feeling that Miss Crampton will not be thrilled by the impersonation." Now it was Lady Emmeline's turn to pace the small fitting room.

"Please accept my deepest apologies, my lady. Your family

showed me great hospitality that day, and I will never forgive myself for lying to them," said Charlotte, eyes downcast. She chose to conceal the fact that it was the Dorset family's immense wealth that had inspired Charlotte to track down and shame the man who had impregnated her poor mother.

"Thank you for apologizing, Charlotte. I have a feeling that sitting through that tea was punishment enough for your actions," Lady Emmeline replied. When Charlotte looked up and met the lady's eyes, she was smiling. "Let me ask you this, Charlotte—what did you think of my brother?"

*Oh, dear.*

"Your brother? Well, by his own admission, he was unwell that day, and he told me emphatically that he had no intention of courting me—or, Miss Crampton, I suppose," Charlotte said. The rising blush on her cheeks was betraying her true thoughts.

"Yes, I'm aware that he took some sort of ill-conceived vow of celibacy that surely will not last. Men can be so tiresome," said Lady Emmeline, with a sigh. Charlotte did not understand what she was getting at, and wished she would make her point plain. "But tell me honestly, and trust that you have my strictest confidence: Did you like him?"

Charlotte knotted her hands together and looked down at her feet. When she spoke, her voice was barely above a whisper. "Yes, my lady. I liked him very much."

Sarah came to Charlotte's side and put an arm around her waist. They had behaved like fools. Why wasn't Lady Emmeline hauling them up in front of Madame Beaumont and demanding their dismissal?

"Well, that makes things interesting, now doesn't it?" asked Lady Emmeline.

"I'm afraid I don't understand your meaning, my lady," said Charlotte. Desperate confusion had set in.

"Allow me to explain. I had a chance meeting this morning

with Lord Markby, a friend of the family. He reported in confidence that my brother has confessed to him that he is beside himself with longing. He has thought of nothing but the lovely 'Miss Crampton' since the day he met her, and has resolved to court her, if only to protect her from the ravenous masses of lordlings who will surely be tripping over themselves to do the same."

*How is this possible?*

Charlotte gripped Sarah's hands in her own and held in a breath as Lady Emmeline went on. "I knew from the start that something about this confession was amiss. You see, I made Miss Crampton's acquaintance last year while I was traveling through her part of the country. To say she was unpleasant is an understatement. She had not a lick of sense in her head, and cared only for putting myself and others in our party down as though her cruelty passed for wit or cleverness. The woman is so disagreeable that I fear she has no redeeming qualities whatsoever," she said, pausing before she went on.

"My brother's description of his 'Miss Crampton' is so unlike the woman I met. I do not believe it possible that she has changed her character and appearance so completely in so little time. It does not surprise me in the least that she would fail to appear at a prearranged appointment. I'll admit that I'm surprised that she even sent word at the last minute, although I suspect that the woman's mother wrote the letter to cover for her."

"My lady, if you don't mind my asking, did Lord Dorset describe Miss Crampton to Lord Markby?" asked Sarah.

"Indeed, he did. My brother, who has had no shortage of female attention since we were youngsters, with all the sincerity he's capable of, said that she was the most singular beauty he had ever encountered, and that he is desperate to see her again," she replied.

Charlotte's mouth dried at this admission. He was still

thinking of her. The pit in the center of her chest was widening. Would she fill it with affection for the man whose face she saw every time she closed her eyes? Or with the growing, simmering hatred she felt for the man whose face she might never see?

"Lady Emmeline, please. Tell me no more. You must know that we can never meet socially," said Charlotte. She needed a way out of this fitting room, quickly.

"I'm not so sure about that, to be honest," Lady Emmeline replied. She was smiling warmly at Charlotte now; it almost put her at ease. "Thankfully, my family is rather well connected and well-liked throughout the *ton*, despite my mother's occasional lack of conversational discretion. I feel certain that we could protect you from any real scandal. Let me be clear that my motives are entirely selfish. I would much rather see my brother married for love to a seamstress than to a ghoulish fortune hunter with bad manners."

Charlotte had tried her best to listen to Lady Emmeline, but she found herself unable to focus after the words "married for love to a seamstress."

"What exactly are you suggesting, my lady?" asked Sarah.

"I'm suggesting that we extend your scheme for just a little while longer. Lord Markby has opened his country estate for a short while, and has invited a small party. I was rather hoping that the two of you would join me. Charlotte, you carry on as Miss Crampton, and Sarah, you pose as Miss Crampton's maid," said Lady Emmeline.

"Forgive me, my lady. What exactly is the purpose of this?" asked Charlotte. Her pulse was rioting now; she never dreamed that she'd be asked to a country estate to pass the time with Lady Emmeline and her ilk. She couldn't bear to entertain the thought, for there was no way that Madame Beaumont could do without her and Sarah this far into the season. Like all the other seamstresses, they often took home embroidery work to complete at night, and their absence would not go unnoticed.

"The purpose, my dear girl, is to force you and my brother together without the meddling influence of my parents so that I may secure myself a sister-in-law who I actually enjoy spending time with."

*Impossible.*

Charlotte and Sarah looked at the lady, stunned, not unlike the twin looks they had given the countess when she had announced that it was time to depart for tea at Stapleton House.

"I warned you that my motives were selfish, didn't I? Leave everything to me. I'll tell Madame Beaumont that I require your special assistance, and I will cover your wages while we're away," she said. Charlotte was beginning to see that Lady Emmeline could be just as persuasive as her mother.

"That's very generous of you, my lady, but Charlotte will need a wardrobe if she's to pass as a lady. We could use samples from the storerooms, but Madame will certainly notice that they're gone," said Sarah. This conversation was getting quickly out of hand. Charlotte feared what would happen if Sarah and Lady Emmeline were left to conspire without a voice of reason.

"Wardrobe shall be no problem. I'll place an order myself before I leave today. I know that between the two of you, you can perform the necessary alterations," said Lady Emmeline. She and Sarah were growing excited now; Charlotte needed to step in.

"Wait just a moment, please. My lady, I cannot in good conscience allow your brother to court me if he thinks I'm someone else. I'll admit that I've never before been in this posi-tion, but I feel certain that this shall end in disaster," Charlotte said, straining to keep her tone calm and respectful.

Lady Emmeline stepped forward and took Charlotte's

hands. Her smile was radiant; Charlotte could not help but feel soothed even as she knew without a doubt that she was being influenced. "You're right, Charlotte. It very well might end in disaster, but think of how sad we'll all be if we do not try. Let me take care of the particulars. Sarah will perform splendidly, I'm sure, as she seems to have a knack for this sort of thing. You have almost nothing to worry about, aside from revealing your true identity to my brother as you see fit."

"Oh, is that all? And all this time I was thinking it would be difficult," said Charlotte, bitingly. She would never dare speak to a customer in this tone, but she felt sure that they were well beyond the boundaries of social order.

"Lottie, I'm sure that Lady Emmeline would never ask you to do something you didn't want to," said Sarah.

"Quite right, Sarah. I would never force your hand, Charlotte. And please, I think we are all friends here. I insist that you both call me Emmeline," she said, as though it was commonplace for ladies to befriend seamstresses.

"Wouldn't it be lovely to take a holiday? Dorset is just a bonus. I'm sorry, my lady, I mean, Emmeline—*Lord* Dorset is just a bonus. And Lottie, maybe we could use the library there to conduct that *research* that you mentioned the other day."

Sarah and Lady Emmeline turned to her with pleading looks, not unlike children begging their mother for a sweet. Charlotte couldn't deny that the thought of seeing Dorset again soothed her heartache, just a bit. And she supposed that a ducal library would be beneficial, even if the only helpful book was the moldering copy of Debrett's gathering dust on those ancient shelves. She couldn't believe what she was about to say, and yet the cosmic powers of longing and desire loosened her tongue.

"When do we leave?"

# Chapter 6

"Come on, Dorset, we're nearly there!" Mere days following their sojourn to the Turkish bath, Dorset found himself on horseback, trailing behind Markby, who was riding ahead of him on an impressively built bay mare through the countryside. At some point between Dorset's confessions to Markby in the steam room and a bracing dunk in the facility's cold plunge bath, Markby had convinced Dorset that some fresh air was just what they needed.

After another quarter of an hour, they approached Sutton Abbey. The sprawling neo-gothic manse was one of Markby's many entailed haunts, but most notably was the seat of his dukedom, inherited following the death of his father, the previous Duke of Sutton.

They slowed their horses from a canter to a trot as they neared the house. Rows of servants awaited their arrival on the front steps, and as they made their way past the sweeping lawns and up the finely kept gravel drive, a groom and stable hand met them to take their horses.

"I've put you in your usual room, Nicky. Fourth floor, opposite end of the hall from mine," said Markby.

"You never did tell me who else is joining us. It can't be just the two of us and Emmeline, can it?" asked Dorset as he took in the looming façade of the great building. It seemed a terrible waste to open the place up for just the three of them, although Markby wasn't one to shy away from extravagance.

"No, no, of course not. Lord and Lady Heathcote arrive this evening. And, I'm told Emmeline is bringing along a friend," he replied casually.

"Told by whom?" asked Dorset. He didn't like it when his friend and his sister spoke privately, if only because it made it harder to keep tabs on their schemes. Markby didn't have any siblings by blood himself, but Dorset liked to think that he and Em had filled the roles of brother and sister admirably— that Markby and Em regularly had a lark at his expense was an unfortunate byproduct of their friendship.

"Em herself, of course. We do talk about things other than you, Nicky," he replied, with his trademark half-smile.

"A chilling thought."

Dorset followed as Markby greeted the servants. His butler, who looked as old as the house itself, addressed them with a restrained nod. Cobwebs showed more emotion.

"Your Grace. Lord Dorset. Your valets arrived earlier today by coach and have readied your rooms. I'm told that baths have been drawn for you both in your respective quarters."

"Thank you, Hanson. They probably smelled us from a mile off and put the kettles on," said Markby. Dorset had a feeling that Hanson, who was seemingly growing grayer and frailer by the second, would never get used to his youthful, jovial employer; he raised the corner of his mouth just one millimeter in response.

As soon as Dorset closed the door to his suite's sitting area, he stripped off his clothes. His valet wouldn't thank him for leaving them in a pile on the floor, but he was desperate to be rid of them so that he could sink into a hot bath. His private water closet was through the bedchamber, and in it he found the large copper tub full almost to the brim with steaming water.

With a firm grip on either side of the tub, he lowered himself down. Dorset relaxed into the water with a groan, silently thanking Markby's housekeeper for anticipating that he would need this so badly. As he cleaned himself, he wondered who Emmeline was bringing along—she was well-liked and had many friends, so there were any number of ladies she had to choose from.

*Unless...*

He didn't want to get his hopes up, but he let himself fantasize that Em had successfully found Tabitha Crampton, loaded her into a carriage, and would deliver her here to him, tied with a satin bow. He had told Markby everything about his fixation upon the lady, and had no doubt that Markby had likely delivered that information straight to his sister—including the small detail that Miss Crampton had, upon leaving his parents' home, disappeared into the crowds of London. He was starting to think that he'd dreamt her.

The bath water began to cool, and Dorset felt his fingers pruning as he lingered in the water, imagining Tabitha here with him. His cock stirred and stiffened at the thought as he closed his eyes and let his mind wander. He stroked himself slowly from root to tip, imagining what she tasted like, what sounds she would make as he slowly teased and tempted her to ecstasy.

He would take his time with her, learning her every curve and contour before lavishing her with pleasure. His hand was a poor substitute for her touch, but he continued stroking himself as he felt his release building. He visualized her writing beneath, above, and beside him—and started to lose control.

*Every desperate kiss.*

*Every moan, needier than the last.*

KNOCK, KNOCK, KNOCK.

*Fuck.*

"What is it?" Dorset growled, furious. He had been on the brink of release, but now that his erection was flagging, he could think of nothing other than murdering his intruder.

"Pardon the interruption, my lord. I've set out your evening clothes. I'm told drinks will be served in the lounge while the duke awaits the arrival of Lady Emmeline and her party. Dinner shall be served after the ladies have arrived and changed."

It was his valet, doing his job as brilliantly as always. Unfortunately, the timing of this intrusion was painful indeed. Dorset gritted his teeth before he spoke.

"Thank you, Stilton. I'll be out in a moment." He dried hurriedly and donned his dressing gown before joining Stilton in the bedchamber.

Dorset slapped on some cologne and dressed mindlessly, slipping into his shirt, trousers, and waistcoat with Stilton's practiced help. As the valet tied and pinned his cravat, he gazed out of the large window above the dressing table that looked out over the sweeping drive at the front of the abbey. In the distance, a carriage came into view.

*If only she was in that carriage...*

Although his aching flesh had been left unsatisfied, his mind was still occupied with thoughts of Tabitha. He had to pull himself together; after all, he was celibate now, wasn't he?

*Not a chance.*

He watched as the grand carriage that he recognized as one from his parents' home pulled to a stop in front of the house. It was laden with so many trunks and boxes that it was no wonder that it had taken them so long to arrive. Em always traveled with an extensive wardrobe, but Dorset guessed that this was at least twice her usual amount. Either she was planning some kind of exhibition during their short stay, or she had other fashionable ladies in tow.

Emmeline exited the coach with the help of a footman and smoothed her skirts before turning back to say something to whomever was still inside. Just then, a slippered foot peeking out from just below a skirt appeared at the top of the carriage steps. Another footman came forward and offered his hand—the lady inside placed her hand in his and leaned forward, just far enough for Dorset to see the long, elegant line of an alabaster neck and a tastefully done mound of sable waves pinned up under a stylish bonnet.

*It can't be her.*

The lady exited the carriage fully, but turned her head back. Was she considering escape?

As she turned, Dorset could see just a sliver of a peach-colored cheek from under the brim of her hat.

*Impossible.*

Dorset cleared his throat. "Stilton, did my sister's maid happen to tell you who she had decided to bring as her guest?" He tried and failed to keep his voice steady when he asked. He knew he sounded nervous, but God knew that Stilton had seen him in far more compromising conditions—so what if his man caught him absolutely gobsmacked over a woman?

"Yes, my lord. Fiona did mention that your sister intended to bring Miss Tabitha Crampton. I am told she is a lovely young woman, but you have met her, have you not?" replied Stilton, casually. Dorset grabbed his evening jacket and was halfway across the room and nearly out the door before he replied.

"Indeed, I have."

~

"Don't worry, Charlotte. You'll do splendidly." That was what Emmeline said to her as she hesitated getting out of the carriage upon arrival at Sutton Abbey, and Charlotte repeated it silently to herself in her head as she was shown to her bedchamber in this towering country estate. It was every bit as grand as Stapleton House had been, and felt at least fifty times as large.

Their journey to Sutton Abbey had been a long one, but it gave the four women inside (Emmeline, Charlotte, Sarah, and Emmeline's maid Fiona) plenty of time to prepare. The carriage, weighted down with a staggering amount of clothing—for both Emmeline and Charlotte—had gone slower than Charlotte thought was possible; making the journey on foot would have been faster.

As they trundled at a snail's pace on the road to Sutton, Emmeline had told them that she had worked out the room arrangements with Markby beforehand: Emmeline would be at the far end of the hall next to Markby's room, and Charlotte would be in the next room down, next door to Dorset. The other guests of Markby's would be staying on another floor.

Charlotte had never had a private bedchamber before, much less one with a private water closet. The plush carpet matched the linens and drapes on the four-poster bed, which matched the curtains and the upholstery on the chairs—everything was done up in the most beautiful shade of blue, like a clear sky in summer. It gave Charlotte the feeling that she was living in the clouds, and on the fourth floor of the towering abbey, it was nearly true.

She was idly inspecting the set of brushes and combs laid out on the dressing table when she heard a light knock at the door. It was Emmeline, now relieved of her traveling cloak, hat, and gloves, and Sarah, who looked the very definition of a proper ladies' maid.

"We thought it might be a lark to get you ready for dinner all together!" said Sarah, with her usual enthusiasm. "Fiona's just gone down to the wine cellar to fetch us a bottle and some glasses."

"Yes, I thought it completely unfair that we'd miss out on pre-dinner drinks just because that carriage ride took so long," said Emmeline as she settled herself on a chaise lounge by the fire.

"I suppose a little liquid courage couldn't hurt," replied Charlotte as she unpinned her bonnet in front of a mirror. "Although, I must say, without the earl and countess here, I have a feeling this will go much smoother than the first time I attempted to be Tabitha. At least no one here but you has ever met her."

"Quite right. You can just be yourself, with a few aristocratic adjustments," said Emmeline, kicking her shoes off and putting her feet up to warm them. Charlotte still had no idea how she should explain her true identity to Dorset. She hoped inspiration would strike her soon; maybe the chef had prepared some and it would be served with the cheese course.

Fiona rejoined them carrying a tray with a bottle of wine and glasses, which she set down and began serving straight away.

"Thank you, Fiona. Allow me to propose a toast. To Charlotte and Sarah: May this be the first of many successful adventures," said Emmeline, smiling from behind the lip of her glass.

"Hear, hear!" responded Sarah, beaming. The ladies clinked their glasses and each took a sip. "Oh, dear, look at the time. We've got to get cracking if you're to be ready in time for dinner."

It was decided that Fiona should style both Emmeline and

Charlotte's hair while Sarah went to fetch their gowns and accessories for the evening—since Sarah was not a trained ladies' maid, it made much more sense that they play to her strengths. Charlotte sat down at the dressing table first, and Fiona set about removing her hair pins and brushing out her long waves.

"The wine is delicious, but I don't think I'd like to go back to that wine cellar again, my lady," said Fiona. She began to twist and pin sections of Charlotte's hair in the latest style.

"Did you see a ghost or two? There have been so many generations of Suttons, I'd imagine that a few of Markby's forebears are still hanging around the place," replied Emmeline, still lounging by the fire.

"I didn't exactly see one, my lady, but I *felt* them. It was so cold and dark. The housekeeper told me that the latch on the door is broken. I was scared half to death that I'd be locked in and never heard from again!"

"Nonsense, Fiona, you know that I can't live without your services. I would have found you at once," said Emmeline, rising now as Sarah returned with their evening clothes and a trunk full of accessories.

With her hair now finished, Charlotte joined Sarah behind the dressing screen and began putting on her costume for the evening, starting with a finely spun chemise, followed by silk stockings, a beautiful embroidered corset made in France, underskirts, and lastly, a silk gown in a fetching shade of dusty rose. Sarah stepped back, folded her arms across her chest, and regarded her not as a friend, but with the frank appraisal and impersonal detachment of a dressmaker.

"You look lovely, but it's not quite there. I know just the thing!" She rifled through her bounty of trims, stockings, gloves, and feathers before she drew out a length of fuchsia ribbon. "We should highlight your waist with this," she added. Sarah tied the ribbon around Charlotte's waist, forming a bow at her back. The effect was immediate, and Charlotte admired the hourglass illusion in a full-length mirror next to the dressing table.

"You're right, it does highlight how constricted I am in this corset. If I faint at some point, you must blame the French," said Charlotte.

"I have a feeling that a certain notorious gentleman staying just down the hall would be happy to relieve you of this problem," said Sarah. Charlotte opened her mouth to scold her friend, but Emmeline spoke up before she could.

"Pardon me, but while I am certainly a willing participant in this plan, I would rather not know what goes on behind closed doors between my brother and Charlotte's corsetry." Sarah suppressed her trademark giggle.

"Please forgive Sarah, Emmeline. As you know, she speaks before she thinks," replied Charlotte. She settled herself down on the chaise lounge that Emmeline had just vacated.

"That might be the understatement of the year!" said Emmeline from behind the dressing screen. When all four women burst out into laughter, Charlotte began to feel truly at ease; the disastrous tea that began this charade was a fading memory.

Once Emmeline had dressed, the two women left the safety of the bedchamber and started down the flights of stairs to join the gentlemen. Charlotte wasn't exactly afraid, but she had the distinct impression that whatever happened, there was no turning back now. She might return to her garret apartment with Sarah and their lives sewing dresses by candlelight for the Quality of London, but something fundamental, buried deep within her, had shifted. Maybe it was the company, maybe it was the wine, maybe it was the clothes she wore now as armor. Everything had changed.

## CHAPTER 7

Dorset accepted another cocktail from a passing tray in the drawing room. Now that he knew Tabitha was here, he felt wild and desperate. He needed something to distract him, something to help him calm his racing thoughts. Unfortunately for Dorset, this reprieve would not come, for just as he turned to ask Markby yet again if he'd known that she was coming and kept it from him, the ladies appeared.

"Markby, darling, you're looking well," said Emmeline as she entered the room ahead of Tabitha. Emmeline offered her hand to Markby. If Dorset hadn't been so consumed by the sight of his deepest desires before him, looking lovelier than he thought possible and literally tied with a bow, he might have noticed that Markby took Emmeline's hand kissed it with a ravenous look of longing in his eyes. No, Dorset did not notice a lot of things, but how could he with Tabitha just feet away?

Without thinking, he crossed the room to her and spoke. "Miss Crampton, I was told my sister was bringing a friend with her to join us. What luck that friend is you. I was beginning to fear we would never find you again." He took her hand

and kissed it. The sensation sent a jolt of energy from his lips throughout his whole body—he noticed that she seemed to shiver under his gaze.

*Had she felt it, too?*

"Lucky is right, my lord. You must thank Lady Emmeline, for she knew just where to look to find me," she replied, smiling. He smiled back at her, and for the first time since they had parted at Stapleton House, he felt the warmth of the sun on his skin.

"Markby, allow me to introduce Miss Tabitha Crampton. Miss Crampton, please meet my friend, Lord Markby, the Duke of Sutton." Tabitha dipped into a small curtsy as Markby bowed to her.

"Miss Crampton, pleasure to meet you."

"Likewise, Your Grace," she replied.

"I must insist that you call me Markby," he replied, all charm and hospitality. "You'll find over the course of this visit that I am not particularly 'graceful,' and the only people who address me with such formality are either in my employ or are preparing to request a favor."

Further acquaintances were made between the ladies and Lord and Lady Heathcote before Hanson entered to announce that dinner was served.

"Your Grace—"

Hanson hesitated when his eyes landed upon Tabitha, for just a moment. The man recovered quickly, but even the slight crack in his usually flawless façade was astounding to those used to his unchangeable stoicism. He cleared his throat.

"Apologies, Your Grace. Dinner is served."

They entered the dining room and found their seats, no doubt prearranged by Emmeline with the staff. She had inherited their mother's flair for influence, but with a healthy dose more subtlety. She would make her future husband very powerful one day, Dorset was sure of it.

Dorset was seated with Lady Heathcote on one side, and Emmeline on the other. Tabitha was directly across from him, between Lord Heathcote and Markby. In hindsight, it was a wonder any food made it from his fork to his mouth; he felt flustered and half hard, like a boy of thirteen struggling with new, unnamed carnal urges. Lady Heathcote broke his concentration when she addressed Tabitha.

"Miss Crampton, Emmeline tells me that you are quite close friends. How is that you've come to know each other?"

Tabitha paused before answering, no doubt deciphering just how much she should reveal about the calamitous tea at Stapleton House. "Our mothers are very dear friends. As I'd never had a season myself, my mother and Lady Harrington agreed that I should come to London and stay with relatives. Luckily, Lady Emmeline found me and has rather taken me under her wing," she replied.

*Clever girl.*

"How wonderful," said Lady Heathcote. "I must say, the two of you look a picture in your gowns. Emmeline is always clothed in the latest fashions; no doubt she has counseled you on your wardrobe." No one offered compliments and insults in one breathless phrase like English ladies, and Lady Heathcote was one of the best.

"Indeed, Lady Heathcote," replied Emmeline, casually. "Tabitha's taste is second to none, and I have consulted her and her alone when it came to ordering new gowns this year. She practically had to drag me to Beaumont's to remake all of my old things. I was beginning to look dreadfully out of date."

"Well, I always go to Griming's. I find French dressmaking rather risqué, you know," replied Lady Heathcote. She was clothed from neck to floor in heavy, dark wool—the word "conservative" didn't fully cover it. If pressed, Dorset would have called her frock a shroud.

Tabitha was maintaining her composure admirably in the

face of Lady Heathcote's veiled attacks, but Dorset could sense from her arched brow and tight-lipped half-smile that she had heard enough.

"I assure you, my lady, Beaumont's offers a vast variety of options for women, both young and *old*. I'm certain there would be something there that would suit your more traditional tastes and still be considered *à la mode*. Why, just the other day, we clothed an entire family of ladies, from young girls just out of the nursery, on up to their grandmother," Tabitha said coolly. Like a skilled pugilist, her jab had landed. Lady Heathcote reddened from the high neck of her shroud to her scalp.

"Forgive me, Miss Crampton—when you say 'we' clothed them, what exactly do you mean by that?" asked Lord Heathcote. Tabitha looked over at him with alarm.

Dorset was loath to admit that the man had made a point; this didn't make sense. How did a woman from the country who was so isolated as to reach what Dorset guessed was her mid-twenties without a season know the inner workings of a London-based dressmaker's shop so intimately?

"Apologies, my lord. I am simply devoted to the staff there—they save me the chicest designs in return for my exclusive patronage." Tabitha took a deep drink of her wine and looked over at Emmeline.

"You know how ladies are, Heathcote. Heads always so full of nonsense, we barely know what we're saying," Emmeline said with the wave of a hand.

"Indeed, Lady Emmeline," replied Lord Heathcote with a smile.

*Idiot.*

With Tabitha's connection to her favorite dressmaker no longer in question, the group passed a pleasant meal. Before he knew it, Dorset was left alone with Markby and Lord Heathcote to take brandy and cigars while the ladies retired to the salon. He had never questioned this practice before, but tonight it seemed a rather archaic tradition—now that he knew where to find her, he didn't want to let Tabitha out of his sight.

Markby and Heathcote had been deep in conversation about the dangerous implications of a new worker's suffrage petition recently submitted to parliament by local farmers, but Dorset found the topic impossible to follow. Shaking himself from his thoughts of Tabitha, he realized that his friend was probably bored beyond belief; he cleared his throat and prepared to give Markby a reprieve.

Thankfully, a footman stepped in before Dorset could think of something to add to the conversation regarding the plight of the suffering lower and middle classes—it was time to rejoin the ladies. Dorset wasn't sure how he would manage it, but he had a singular goal as they stubbed out their cigars and made for the door. He needed a private word with Miss Tabitha Crampton.

Charlotte knew that aristocratic women were tiresome; she had probably measured, clothed, bustled, and trimmed more ladies of the *ton* than anyone in this house other than Sarah. What she hadn't considered was how nasty they could be to each other under the guise of polite conversation.

She realized that as a member of the working class, Charlotte was invisible to these ladies—worthy of neither their polite attention, nor their scorn. What surprised her was that even now as she masqueraded as Tabitha, Lady Heathcote had circled her like a shark in bloody water.

Emmeline was fluent in this snakelike parlance, and had gracefully borne the brunt of Lady Heathcote's attention. In truth, Charlotte had stopped listening some time ago, and had excused herself from the seating area they shared to examine the paintings that hung from ornate gold frames on nearly every available inch of wall space.

As she regarded a portrait that she assumed was of the earthly form of one of the spirits now haunting the wine cellar, the gentlemen rejoined them. She turned to find Dorset coming straight for her.

*Good Lord.*

He had been ill the day they met. His skin was gray, he'd had dark smudges under his eyes, and he seemed nauseated by the very air around him. Now that she was seeing him at his finest, hearty and hale, she wasn't sure she could suppress her reactions to him. She wasn't even sure that she wanted to suppress them. She was starting to *flutter.* Charlotte never fluttered.

His skin was smooth and golden; he practically glowed from within, the effect only strengthened by his smile as he approached her. As he stepped ever closer, she had to lean her head back to maintain eye contact with him. It was such a stark difference from her usual position, hunched over a bit of lace embroidery as she worked late into the night by candlelight. She could get used to this new view.

"Miss Crampton, I haven't had a chance to tell you how pleased I am that you've joined us for this little sojourn," he said, leaning casually against a bookshelf next to the portrait she'd been admiring. He crossed his arms over his broad chest, and Charlotte let her eyes dip to his muscles there, so visible through his finely tailored coat. She suddenly decided that if she could choose her own passing when her time came, she would request death by crushing embrace.

"I should admit that I took some convincing. But you know Lady Emmeline, when she sets her sights on something, the rest of us are at her mercy," she replied. Dorset replied with a quiet laugh, little more than an exhalation. His blue eyes sparkled.

*Sapphires.*

"I certainly do."

Suddenly, it had grown unbearably hot in this room, but Charlotte wouldn't have left his side if she had been paid two hundred pounds.

"Come, Dorset, Miss Crampton! Join me in a game of Hearts!" said Lord Heathcote from across the room. He was settling in at the card table with a deck in hand.

Without breaking eye contact with Tabitha, Dorset spoke. "Heathcote, you know I detest playing cards. I'm sure you can play as a foursome." His gaze was searing through her; if anyone looked over at them now, there could be no mistaking his intentions.

*Could there?*

Taking his hint, Markby and Emmeline joined the Heathcotes at cards, leaving Dorset and Charlotte to themselves. They each took a glass of champagne from a footman and settled in on a low settee away from the card table, near an exterior door propped open to cool the heat in the room.

"I can't shake the feeling that I owe you an apology, Miss Crampton. I behaved abominably when we first met. I can't imagine what you must think of me," Dorset said. He was right. The things she was imagining were not proper in the least.

"You don't owe me anything of the sort, my lord. I was not quite myself that day, I'm afraid," she replied, more to her champagne glass than to him. She wasn't yet ready to explain to him the full truth of that statement.

"Well, in that case, I insist that you call me Dorset. We've been through too much to stand on ceremony," he replied. This man was too handsome for his own good; the planes of his face seemed predestined to reduce Charlotte to a stammering ninny. She decided then that his jawline should be classified by Scotland Yard as a deadly weapon.

"I'll drink to that," she said, without thinking. He smiled fully now, his teeth a white flash between his full lips as he gently clinked his glass on hers. He held her eye contact as they each took a small sip. Charlotte's stomach dropped—she had moved from mere flutterings to a full swoon.

He set his glass down on a low side table and took Charlotte's as well, leaving them mostly full. He stood and offered her his hand, which she took without question before he spoke.

"You know, I find that the fire in this room is rather too hot for my liking. Would you care to take a turn with me in the garden?"

"I quite agree, it is stifling," she replied, following him out into the night without a care in the world.

*What will Lady Heathcote think of this?*

*Blast Lady Heathcote.*

Dorset offered her his arm, and Charlotte took it. She thrilled at the touch, even through layers of fabric. His dark dinner jacket was beautifully made, but Charlotte knew that even bespoke tailoring couldn't make up for the formless, sedentary figures so common amongst gentlemen.

The arm underneath her hand was strong, no doubt honed to sculpted perfection through hours of physical movement. This man was active and alive; Charlotte's pulse thrummed as she realized that while she was no waif, he was almost certainly strong enough to lift her clear off the ground.

They walked in silence through the stone portico and out onto the grounds, beneath the night sky. The full moon lit their path from the house to a grand rose garden, not yet in bloom this early in the year. As their silence stretched on, Charlotte began to grow nervous; how on Earth was she supposed to reveal herself to him without ruining everything? As she contemplated this, Dorset spoke.

"Do you mind if I ask you what may be a rather personal question?"

*It depends on both the question and who you're asking.*

"Not at all. If I find it objectionable, I won't give you an answer," she replied, hoping that her tone sounded lighter than she felt. Thankfully, Dorset chuckled quietly.

"Fair enough. How is it possible that you haven't yet had a season? As the daughter of a gentleman, surely you would have been out by now." Charlotte released her hold on his arm and stepped away from his warmth. Something in her instantly regretted the action, but she needed space from him to gather her thoughts.

*I haven't had a season because I'm the child of a dead opera singer and a gentleman who compromised her and then abandoned her to her fate. Earning a wage dressing ladies like your sister doesn't leave much time for a presentation at court.*

Charlotte walked on with her back to him, and felt his gaze sear the exposed skin between her shoulder blades. She knew he wouldn't accept a flippant response to such a direct question, and she was growing tired of playing Tabitha. It was too difficult for her to remember the half-truths she had already told, and she wished more than anything to be done with them.

*Tell him before it's too late.*

"I'm afraid there isn't a simple explanation," she said, turning back to face him. Dorset was three rose bushes away, standing tall in the moonlight with his sinewed forearms folded in what Charlotte now considered his trademark stance. He stood still, immovable, while a gentle breeze rustled the leaves around him. Although his body appeared as still as a bronze statue, his facial expression belied the questions no doubt on his mind.

*You can't build a relationship on lies.*

*You won't have a relationship at all once he knows the truth.*

"I fear that if I tell you the truth, you will despise me for it," Charlotte said. Was this the first honest thing she had said to him since she had pronounced unequivocally that she would never be his wife?

He stepped toward her, closing in. When he was within one rosebush, he spoke.

"As someone despised by many, I consider myself an expert. What you say may be true, but you don't seem to possess the necessary qualities for true contempt," he said. He was close enough now that she could see his eyes darkening, even in the soft moonlight. His gaze trailed down to her lips. Without thinking, she moved closer.

"Is that so? What, exactly, do I lack?" She bit her lower lip and waited for him to reply, her breath quickening. She was teetering on the precipice of lie and truth, and the wait was tortuous. She wanted some indication that he wouldn't hate her once he knew her real name, that he would continue looking at her as he was now: like she was a five-course meal set at a table for one, and he, a man starved.

He stepped close enough that the shining toes of his boots nearly touched the hem of her gown.

"First of all, your manners are impeccable. You couldn't offend a living soul, although I expect Lady Heathcote felt your rebuke quite keenly at dinner," said Dorset. His voice was low, private. Charlotte felt her cheeks burning as she remembered dressing down the lady who dared question Madame Beaumont's supremacy in the realm of London fashion.

"I can't help that she seems to have rather conservative tastes, can I?" Charlotte asked, smiling.

"Certainly not, and you have no idea how glad I am that you and Lady Heathcote are not in agreement. I have half a mind to write a letter to Madame Beaumont personally thanking her for her efforts." His eyes dropped from her mouth to her exposed collarbone, and then lower still.

He stepped closer now. Her skirts nearly enveloped his legs. Charlotte was breathless with anticipation—was it because she was about to reveal the truth to him, or because he was about to kiss her? She wasn't sure, but she knew without a doubt that she could not let him proceed while thinking she was another woman.

As she struggled to calculate her next move with the scent of his woody cologne clouding her judgment, the cold night air decided to make the choice for her; what had been a gentle breeze plunged in temperature and picked up speed at just the same moment. A chill ran down her spine, and goosebumps swept across her exposed arms and chest.

"You're cold. Allow me," Dorset said, his voice a rumbling whisper in her ears. With two large and blessedly ungloved hands, he pulled her to his chest and held her there with an iron grip. As though it were the most natural thing in the world, he wrapped one arm around her waist and ran his other hand back and forth over her exposed back and neck before tucking an errant wave of hair back behind her ear. Warmth bloomed deep within her and spread over her skin. "Do you want to go back inside?"

*Never.*

"No. What I must tell you should be told in private," she replied. She spread her hands across his broad chest and grasped the lapels of his jacket desperately. His next words were a growl.

"I'd hoped we were done talking," said Dorset. He raised a hand to her cheek and ran his thumb over her bottom lip; a groan escaped the back of his throat as he did so. The combination of the sound and his touch thrilled Charlotte. She had lost all sense, but she didn't miss it in the least.

Lifting her chin, Charlotte closed her eyes and parted her lips.

*Finally.*

"Tabitha," he whispered, brushing his mouth over hers.

*Absolutely not. He'll kiss me as Charlotte or not at all.*

"Wait!" said Charlotte, cursing herself, both for going this far and for stopping. Dorset stepped back but kept his hands on her waist.

"I'm sorry, we shouldn't—"

"No, you don't understand," Charlotte said quickly, cutting him off. "There's something you should know."

"I'm all ears," he said, suspicion blooming on his handsome face as his smile faltered. He would hate her now, she was sure of it. Charlotte closed her eyes and tried as hard as she could to picture him just seconds earlier, when he had looked at her with wild, unslaked thirst.

*This was a disaster from the beginning, and I have no one to blame but myself.*

"I'm not Tabitha Crampton."

# Chapter 8

Dorset felt his face turn to stone, his lips set in a thin, rigid line. He released his grip on her waist and stepped away from the soft, warm curves of her. She remained in place, her eyes downcast. His next utterance was barely audible, for she had knocked the wind out of him with her confession.

"Explain."

"You must understand, I never meant to deceive you. Things got rather out of hand when your mother insisted that I come to tea, and then your sister found me and she was very convincing," she said. Dorset realized now that he did not know her true name, and despite his confusion and mounting distrust, he needed to know what to call her.

"Your name," he growled. "Tell me your name." She lifted her gaze and met his eyes. A single tear glimmered in the moonlight as she spoke. Her voice was clear and strong, and somehow Dorset knew that what she said next was the absolute truth.

"My name is Charlotte Price. I'm a seamstress at Beaumont's. I can't seem to stop thinking about you. And you'll never understand how sorry I am that I lied."

*That makes two of us, Charlotte Price.*

Dorset wasn't sure that he could withstand another moment alone with Miss Price now that he knew her true identity, but he considered next move carefully. For the second time that day, he had teetered on the razor thin edge between longing and satisfaction only to be denied by forces beyond his control. This mounting frustration clouded his judgment; he swayed on his feet as he felt his pulse pounding throughout his every limb.

He took a deep breath, ran his hands through his hair in frustration, and resolved to go straight to bed—alone.

"Miss Price, it has grown late. Please allow me to see you back to the house, where I will bid you goodnight." He offered her his arm, but she did not move from where she stood. By refusing to hear any further explanation from her, he had drawn a hard line between them, and as they stood in still silence for the next moment, Dorset felt that line grow to the size of a chasm.

"No, thank you. I'm quite enjoying the fresh air," she replied with a distinct quiver in her voice. What kind of gentleman would he be if he left her alone and weeping in a garden in the dark of night, even if she had attempted to seduce him with a false identity and what he guessed were his sister's clothes. He would deal with that sister in the morning, after he had time to sort out the hurt feelings and the endless questions clouding his mind.

"I cannot leave you here alone—it is almost midnight and I am responsible for your safety." Anger flashed in her eyes, highlighted by the tears that fell silently down her cheeks, flushed with that same shade of peach that had so beguiled him the first time they met. It seemed it had been Dorset's turn to say the wrong thing.

"You think you're responsible for my safety? You forget, *my lord*, that I'm an orphaned commoner who has lied to you from the start. I don't deserve such kind attention and I don't possess any virtue worth protecting. Please, do us both a favor and leave me here. Make any excuse for me that feels appropriate—I trust you can come up with something convincing."

Dorset flinched at her pointed use of his title. How had this gone so wrong?

"Goodnight, Miss Price." He bowed to her and turned on his heel, marching back to the house with determined strides. Each footfall seemed to echo through the silent garden where he had just abandoned the first woman he had ever considered courting respectably.

*She lied to me. Why do I feel in the wrong?*

Drawing on his childhood years spent as Markby's hide-and seek-partner, Dorset found a side entrance into the house and made his way to a service stair that led directly to the landing at the top of the stairs outside his bedchamber. The less the rest of the group knew about what he had just learned, the better.

After shucking off his evening jacket and waistcoat, Dorset poured himself a generous measure of Scotch from the decanter near the bedside. He took one sip of the searing, peaty liquid and then another before setting his glass down on the mantel and crossing his arms over his chest, staring deep into the dancing flames at his feet.

*She's a seamstress. A seamstress named Charlotte Price. A seamstress named Charlotte Price who lied, with the help of my sister, to gain...what exactly?*

Dorset rather suspected that he would never know the entire truth, but he hoped that Emmeline could shed some light on this whole affair, and soon. Had Em been tricked as well, or did she know the truth of the woman's identity from the beginning?

He began to pace, wondering if this beautiful seamstress from his mother and sister's particular favorite dress shop had taken them all, or if she had simply hoodwinked him. Had his parents known about this? Was everyone else in this cavernous manor in on the joke and laughing at him over cards in the salon somewhere below where he stood?

Hours passed. Dorset remained stationed in front of the now-dimming fire. He had long ago run out of whisky, but somewhere between his fourth glass and the fifth, he had resolved to leave Sutton Abbey and return to town at first light.

*What about Miss Price?*

Was she pacing in front of her own fire now that she had confessed all to him? Was she asleep in her bed? Emmeline had certainly dressed her appropriately for dinner, but had she thought of her night clothes as well? Were those night clothes fastened with common buttons, or were they tied with fine silk ribbons?

*Get ahold of yourself.*

The woman had lied to him about her identity, but Dorset still couldn't master his longing for her. He should have known when she followed him out to the garden that all of this was too easy, too perfect. Ladies didn't appear out of thin air at one's parents' home for tea and disappear like steam from a kettle only to reappear at one's friend's country estate just in time for dinner and a clandestine stroll in the garden. Even still, he wanted so badly to know what it felt like to undo the hairpins securing the chignon at the nape of her neck, and to watch those dark waves tumble down over her shoulders before he wove his hands through them and claimed her once and for all.

With thoughts like these, Dorset knew he would not drift off to sleep anytime soon. He slipped his ink-colored dressing gown over his shirt and trousers and lit a candle before he crept noiselessly out into the hall. Moving carefully through the darkness, he navigated the still and silent passages and stairways down toward the kitchens, below which he knew he would find the wine cellar. He wished with all his might that it housed something strong enough to quiet his rioting mind for at least a couple of hours.

He felt delirious when he reached the kitchens and located the landing that led belowground. Centuries of diligent servants and midnight wanderers had smoothed the stone stairs down to a lumpy slope; he took each step carefully. Was it a trick of the dim candlelight, or was the heavy, oaken door at the bottom slightly ajar? Dorset rubbed and blinked his tired eyes before he stepped closer. No—he could see now that the door was open.

He considered that a footman probably forgot to close the door after dinner service that night, and had decided to mention it to Hanson the following morning when he heard faint footsteps coming from the other side.

*I suppose I'm about to catch the culprit in the act...*

With his candle raised, Dorset approached the door and pushed its heft to the side with one arm. His candle cast the cellar in a dim glow, and as his eyes adjusted, he could just make out a figure before him.

"What are you doing out of bed at this time of night—"

"Oh, thank *goodness* it's you! I heard you on the stairs and thought you were a ghost!"

Dorset stopped short just inside the doorway, the rest of his rebuke forgotten as he realized just who he had found lurking in the dank, dusty cavern.

Charlotte Price.

～

After several hours of tossing and turning in the largest, most comfortable feather bed she had ever had the good fortune to have all to herself, Charlotte decided to give up on sleep entirely. She was sure that her insomnia was some kind of punishment for her trickery; she didn't feel right staying in a bed fit for a queen now that she had revealed herself to Dorset and had ruined their evening.

*Not just an evening—I've ruined everything.*

With candle in hand, Charlotte clutched her loaned dressing gown tight around her shivering body and set out into the darkened halls to find the library. She wasn't sure where it was located but she thought maybe if she found it and the copy of Debrett's Peerage almost certainly housed within, she could start narrowing down the search for her father from every gentleman to ever live to a specific group of a few hundred men based on their age and proximity to London. It was a gargantuan task to be sure, but why wait for morning when there was a very real chance that she and Sarah would be escorted off the premises the next morning and sent back to Cheapside?

With her candle burning low, Charlotte had wandered through a music room, two large halls, a billiard room, what she guessed was the breakfast room, and a cavernous ballroom with four crystal chandeliers before she found what resembled a butler's pantry, and finally the kitchens and their gardens beyond.

She was growing colder now, and had nearly given up on finding the elusive library when a narrow staircase off the kitchen leading down belowground caught her attention. This must be the entrance to the haunted wine cellar that had so chilled Fiona.

Had she ever seen a wine cellar before? Definitely not, but why not take the chance now? Taking care not to slip on the timeworn limestone, she inched along the passage with one hand on the wall beside her. The great arched door at the bottom of the stair wasn't locked, but she wasn't sure she'd have the strength to open the latch and move it aside with one hand.

With great effort, she opened the door just wide enough to squeeze through. A blast of frigid, earthy air blew out what was left of her candle, leaving her in complete darkness and at the mercy of the spirits within. A chill went down her spine at the thought.

*Ghosts aren't real. But if they are, maybe I can ask how Mother is doing.*

Did she hear footsteps above her? She hoped so—maybe the owner of said feet had a candle and could lead her back to the bed she never should have left. Charlotte cursed herself and her decision to find the library at this hour, in a strange, gargantuan home.

The steps grew nearer now, and her heart leapt into her throat. Darkness seemed to choke all sound from the room; her pulse rioted with anticipation.

*Please let this be a friend and not another disaster...*

She took a deep breath as the door she had struggled to inch open was pushed aside with laughable ease by a solid, satin-clad arm.

"What are you doing out of bed at this time of night—"

It was Dorset, hair rumpled and in his nightclothes. She exhaled with relief and spoke before he could continue.

"Oh, thank *goodness* it's you! I heard you on the stairs and thought you were a ghost!"

He squinted in the dim light. Realization dawned slowly —she watched as his brow furrowed, then relaxed into a look of pure confusion. It was obvious that he was here looking for something, but he hadn't expected to find her.

"Miss Price? Is everything all right?" he asked, his tone hesitant and impersonal, so different now than his low whispers in the rose garden, whispers that felt like vibration on her skin more than an audible sound. He stepped closer to her as though he still didn't believe that he'd found her there.

"Yes, everything is fine. I'm afraid I couldn't sleep, so I went exploring. Then my candle went out and I was just about to panic when you came in."

"I see. Well, I'll light yours with mine and then see you back to your rooms," he said, not meeting her eyes. His tone was clipped, and his body language guarded. He declined to explain why he too was out of bed and wandering the halls, but she knew better than to ask. Any familiarity between them had vanished the moment she spoke her real name in the garden.

"Thank you," Charlotte replied, feeling a chill now from both the air and the man in the room.

Just as Dorset stepped toward her and reached for her candle, the room shook with a resounding thud accompanied by another rush of air. Charlotte gasped. The door had closed behind him.

Blessedly, Dorset's candle remained lit; he handed it to Charlotte and then turned and tried to open the door without success. His shoulders slumped, and he let his head fall against the solid, immovable oak.

When she spoke, Charlotte addressed the back of his head; his sandy brown hair was askew. She longed to rake her fingers through it.

"Oh, dear. Fiona told us earlier that the latch is faulty. Are we stuck?" she asked quietly. She knew that Dorset was upset with her, and rightly so, but the chill had numbed her feet and she wanted badly to get back to the safety and solitude of her bed. She could wonder about what exactly his hair felt like from beneath the sumptuous down counterpane that awaited her four floors above them.

"I'm afraid so, Miss Price," he said without turning.

"Please don't call me that. No one does," Charlotte replied, barely above a whisper. He offered no response to this request before he turned and scanned the walls above their heads, at last finding an oil lamp on a high shelf. He lit it with his candle and then set both down on opposite ends of the shelf, casting the space in a faint, flickering glow.

They were surrounded by large oak barrels, endless racks of dusty bottles sealed with wax, and some pieces of discarded furniture, likely stored here for repair at some point but long since forgotten. The ceiling was lower than Charlotte expected, and she noticed that vines and twisted roots were growing through cracks in the walls.

The air was so cold that they could see their breath as they stood in silence. He wouldn't look at her, and yet she was unable to take her eyes off of him.

Charlotte opened her mouth to speak, but he silenced her with a raised hand. "Don't. Please don't explain. We'll be here until the servants wake, and we need to keep warm until then," he said, eyeing a discarded sofa in a corner. "This will have to do. I'm afraid we don't have a choice."

After giving the cushions a thorough shake, he slipped off his dressing gown and held out a hand to Charlotte. Did he expect her to share the sofa with him? The thought of his body heat tempted her, but he was so angry with her. Surely, he didn't mean to share this makeshift bed for what remained of this disastrous night. She remained where she stood a few feet away.

"Miss Price," he said, his tone impatient, "you will catch your death in this cellar if we are not careful." His tone was firm, but he still wouldn't meet her gaze. She wanted him to rage at her, to show some sign that he felt something, anything, about what she had confessed earlier.

Still, she did as she was told, and took a seat on the sofa. Without speaking, he wrapped his dressing gown around her shoulders and tied it around her waist, taking care to pull the lapels close around her neck. The smooth, warm fabric smelled like leather and cedar. A deep breath transported her back to their first meeting; she shivered at the thought.

"Won't you be cold?" she asked, wondering why he was showing her such kindness.

"I'll be fine," he replied, dragging a ragged-looking wing-back chair from a corner and placing it opposite the sofa. He took a seat facing her, stretched his long legs in front of him, and crossed them at the ankles before crossing his arms over his chest and leaning his head back. He looked exhausted.

A moment passed before either of them spoke. Dorset broke the silence with a question she didn't expect. His voice, usually so resonant and assertive, was quiet in the large cellar.

"Why did you do this?"

"I thought you didn't want me to explain," she replied.

"I've changed my mind."

Charlotte told him everything, from the first dress fitting to her arrival at Sutton Abbey, leaving out the details regarding her chemical attraction to him. As there was no longer hope of a connection between them, it didn't seem vital to raise the point. To his credit, he listened without interruption, but she could not read his expression. She took a deep breath and went on.

"I thought that I might be able to learn something about my father's identity. It sounds preposterous to say it all aloud, but that's what I hoped. Maybe in a record book somewhere, or an old letter, there would be some mention of my mother that could help me."

He sat quietly for a moment before he spoke. "It's certainly not impossible, although I suspect we would have more luck if we asked the older members of staff for some advice on where to look. Markby is the only one of his kind since his father died two years ago, but Hanson has been with the family since time immemorial."

*"We" would have more luck?*

"Do you mean to help me with this? I rather thought you hated me," she said.

"As I told you in the garden, I don't think it's possible to hate you," he replied.

"I didn't mean to take advantage of your kindness. And I really am quite fond of you," she said. Charlotte wasn't sure where she had found the courage to speak so plainly, but one didn't always find oneself wrapped in a man's dressing gown and trapped in a wine cellar without distraction. Why not speak only the truth?

"Fond?" Dorset smiled. "I don't think anyone's been fond of me before. I'm a *scoundrel*—haven't you heard the rumors?"

"Of course I have, Lord Corset," she replied, teasing him. "Tell me, how did you earn such a prestigious title? Is the land entailed, or did you win it all over cards?"

*Finally, a smile.*

"Those days are behind me, mind you. I'm quite reformed," he said.

"I assure you that I won't be offended," she replied. For the first time since they had left the salon for the garden earlier that evening, Charlotte felt their easy conversation and his good humor return.

*Thank God he doesn't hate me.*

"As long as you won't be offended," he said, sitting up now and leaning forward on his knees. This brought him closer to Charlotte, although he still towered over her place on the low sofa. "I had spent an evening with a young lady who was particularly *satisfied* by my company," he said, an impish grin spreading across his handsome face.

"I see," replied Charlotte, with an arched brow.

What would she give to know exactly what he had done?

What would she give to trade places with the lady in question...

"Although this lady and I did not have plans to meet again, she felt rather possessive, and decided to stake her claim, literally. She took the pieces of a corset I had ripped in two, had them strung up on a pole, and planted it in the front garden outside of my townhome. Her flag flew for hours before the staff noticed it and removed it. The name has stuck ever since."

"A corset, *ripped in two*?" asked Charlotte, aghast. "What a waste of material and craftsmanship."

"Correct, a dreadful waste. For the record, I did replace said corset and sent a note with my apologies."

"It's the least you could do, I suppose," said Charlotte. Even with Dorset's dressing gown pooling around her, she felt as cold as ice. Try as she might, she could not suppress a violent shiver, and she pulled the fabric closer to her chest. "I want you to know something," she said, her teeth beginning to chatter. Concerned, he leapt to his feet and hesitated for only a moment before he knelt before her.

"Are you sure? You're shaking like a leaf," he said. He reached for her and began running hands vigorously over her arms to warm them. She melted into his radiant warmth. They were face to face.

"Is the wine cellar not a sacred chamber?" she asked, trying not to lose herself to the feel of his large, strong hands. The heat was beginning to spread.

"Of course it is," he replied, his voice lower now. He slowed his hands but did not rise.

"I wouldn't have done any of this if not..." She stopped, unsure of how to finish the statement she had started.

"If not for what?" he asked. That low, humming whisper had returned, and Charlotte's body responded with a hum of its own, deep in the pit of her stomach.

"If not for you. I wanted to see you again. I could think of nothing else."

He moved his hands from her shoulders, slowly up the sides of her exposed neck, and then took her face between his palms. A flush spread over her cheeks as she closed her eyes, unable to look into his serious gaze for even a second longer.

"Charlotte, I'm going to kiss you now. Is that all right?" he whispered, his mouth nearly touching hers. She thrilled at the sound of her name on his lips and opened her eyes to meet his.

"Yes," she said. His eyes darkened and dropped to her mouth as he threaded a large, confident hand through the tousled hair on the back of her head.

He gently tugged her hair to angle her face below his before he kissed her, thoroughly. She reached for his shoulders and fisted the fine fabric of his shirt there as he parted her knees and moved between them, bringing their bodies closer.

When she opened her mouth to his searching tongue, he groaned with satisfaction. His hands trailed over her entire body, somehow covering her everywhere at once. How did he manage this?

His skilled mouth trailed down her throat; she couldn't help but let her head drop back as she succumbed to the sensation. If this was a kiss, she had never been kissed before this moment, had never known the pleasure of a man's touch. A boy's? Certainly. But never a man so practiced and capable.

"Charlotte," he breathed into her neck. "If only you knew," he said, still lavishing kisses upon her flushed skin between the words. "If only you know how desperately I wanted to find you. I thought you were lost forever," he said, his pace quickening as he trailed back up to her needy, kiss-bruised lips.

Each kiss acted upon Charlotte's senses like a drug. She gripped his strong shoulders, and returned his passion with her own, losing herself to the moment. But even then, as he joined her on the sofa and pulled her into his arms, a quiet voice of reason sounded in her head.

*Ours is not a love story.*

Dorset sensed her hesitation.

"What's wrong?" he asked, his brow tightening.

"Nothing...nothing's wrong," she replied. "Except, in a way, I am lost forever. I meant what I told you that day, after tea. I cannot marry you." He let his head dip, their foreheads touching. He spoke to her through downcast, hooded eyes. His lashes were thicker and more lush than the mink Charlotte had trimmed Lady Fairbank's cloak with last winter.

"I will admit that I had something other than marriage in mind at the moment," he said, smiling now. "Besides, I'm not sure we could get a special license at this hour."

Charlotte grinned. "You think you're so clever, don't you," she said, playfully swatting at his broad, warm chest. He caught her hand in his and gripped it tight before raising her open palm to his mouth and kissing it. When he spoke, his low voice was barely audible even in the still silence.

"You're right. I know."

With those quiet words, he had confirmed what Charlotte knew was true: There would be no courting, no balls, no church bells. Her heart ached.

Dorset reached out with one strong, warm hand and brushed the back of his fingers across her cheek. "Peaches," he whispered.

"I beg your pardon?" she breathed, her cheeks burning under his velvet touch. He drew a gentle thumb across her bottom lip, his eyes focused only on her swollen mouth as he went on.

"Your cheeks, when you flush. They're the color of ripe peaches." He paused, but held her gaze as he trailed a lazy hand from her knee to her mid-thigh. Charlotte knew that to disrobe in this frigid cellar would be foolish indeed, but she cursed the layers of fabric between his hand and her sensitive skin there as he gently gripped the curve of her thigh.

*We only have tonight.*

Dorset's eyes darkened as he pulled her in once more, kissing her more slowly now. His pace was lazy, decadent, *sinful.* Warmth coiled through the pit of her stomach and settled lower. Charlotte ground her knees together in a feeble attempt to sate the growing desire that he stoked like flames with each drag of his tongue across hers.

"It's not just your cheeks. Your lips are the same shade, so tempting," he whispered, directly to those same lips. His hands trailed up her thighs and over her stomach, settling on her heavy, aching breasts. He teased and pinched, working her to the point of madness while maintaining his steady, slow rhythm.

Charlotte's breathing was unsteady. Any sense that she'd been cold when she entered the cellar had dissipated, and she knew she had Dorset's passionate attention to thank. Even in the low light cast by the candle and oil lamp, she could see the evidence of his desire for her straining through the front of his trousers. When she reached down and palmed his rigid length through the fine cloth, he drew in a ragged breath of his own.

He swore under his breath, his voice like gravel. Charlotte felt like the most powerful woman in all of Britain.

"Charlotte, I've decided that I must return to London first thing in the morning—" Dorset stopped before he went on. He let his head drop to the back of the sofa and his eyes flutter shut as she continued to drag her hand slowly back and forth across him, attempting to take his full measure through his trousers.

"I know, it's all right. We only have tonight," said Charlotte, finishing the sentence he had started and stopped as she felt him stiffen further beneath her touch.

"Not 'only,'" he growled. Slowly, he sat up, grinning like a tomcat with a mind for mischief before nuzzling into her neck and gently biting the delicate skin where her neck met her shoulder. "We have tonight."

He nipped her neck again before he went on. "Let me see if my theory is correct," he said. "I suspect..."

*Kiss.*

"...that you taste like a ripe, juicy peach..."

*Bite.*

"...and I won't leave this cellar,"

*Lick.*

"...until I find out for myself."

He meant to taste her, and she knew that he didn't mean any of the numerous places he had already feasted upon with his kisses. Still, she wanted to be sure.

"You haven't an answer?" Her vision swam. Dorset smiled down at her and placed a single, long finger upon her lips. She kissed his fingertip but did not look away from his playful, sapphire gaze.

"Not here, darling."

*Yes, please.*

Dorset laid her back against the seat of the sofa. Starting at her feet, he slowly gathered up the yards of fabric covering her legs. Inch by inch, he meandered and roamed, taking his time as though they wouldn't have to make their escape before sunrise and find a way back to their beds without being seen. For a moment, Charlotte believed it too.

She was bare to her thighs now, though she felt stark naked under his hungry stare.

"Are you cold?" he asked, as he settled himself on the dusty ground at her feet. Charlotte shook her head but said nothing aloud. He parted her legs at her knees before pushing the layers of dressing gowns and nightrail up higher, to her navel, exposing her fully. His mouth dropped open in awe at the sight before him.

Without taking his eyes off of her body, he unfastened the fall of his trousers. His cock, thick and ridged and as hard as steel, bobbed out from behind the fabric. He stroked himself lazily as he addressed her; Charlotte's mouth watered at this erotic display.

"Has anyone done this for you before?"

"Yes," she replied, on a shaky breath. A stable boy, long ago. Nothing more than a distant memory of the smell of horses and bits of hay clinging to her hair and clothes. Nothing at all like this, like Dorset. Charlotte was straining to control herself, so desperate now for the release that he promised.

He clenched his jaw as he ran one gentle thumb through her folds and up over that sensitive ball of nerves at her center as he touched himself. She gasped. "Charlotte," he growled, "tell me if you want me to stop."

"You have to start first," she said, unsure if she could withstand the torture of waiting for another second. He barked out a laugh in response.

After hooking one trembling leg over his shoulder, Dorset set about his task. He circled her center with his tongue while he gently pressed one of those wicked fingers into her opening. The overall sensation sent stars through Charlotte's line of sight; she couldn't stop herself from arching up toward him, desperate.

This must be what it felt like to drown in a whirlpool. A swirling tongue, and a swirling finger worked in concert to a dizzying degree. The staggering pleasure radiating from her core pulled her under, and Charlotte didn't fight it.

*I'm so glad I got out of bed.*

She was on the edge now, dangerously close to coming unraveled on Dorset's sensuous tongue. He soldiered on, pressing another finger inside of her.

With the increased pressure, Dorset brought Charlotte to

the very edge of her being. He seemed to revel in her, responding to each of her moans and whimpers with his own. She never dreamed that a man would take his own pleasure at the same time that he worked tirelessly in pursuit of hers; it was intoxicating.

*His reputation is well earned.*

Charlotte trembled and cried out before she reached down and grasped the back of his head, desperate to increase the pressure. He groaned into her as she did so; the sound of his hand working his own flesh sent her careening over the precipice.

Pleasure she had never felt radiated through her limbs as she slowly, slowly returned to herself. They were both breathing heavily now, sweat clinging to their skin despite the cold. Charlotte watched as Dorset leaned back on his heels, stripped off his rumpled shirt, and used it to clean himself, discarding it before righting his trousers and fastening them once again. Naked to the waist now, he pulled her from the sofa and into an embrace, the scent of her still lingering on his lips as he spoke.

"The servants will wake soon. It's time I returned you to your bed, Peaches."

# CHAPTER 9

Dorset didn't sleep a wink after he returned Charlotte to her room. A lucky change in humidity had loosened the door, allowing them out of the cellar and above stairs without notice. He assumed but did not care that a scullery maid or two may have spotted them as they dashed through the halls, hand in hand, just before dawn. He'd left her at her door with one last kiss. They didn't bid each other goodbye; no tears were shed.

As soon as he had seen her standing alone and shivering in the cellar, his anger had dissipated in an instant. He believed her explanation, and he hoped that she would be able to find some evidence of her father. If some tenuous attraction between them was the means to her ends, he didn't mind being the object of that affection. God knew Dorset had used thinner excuses to justify a dalliance or three in his past.

*You fool, it wasn't just a dalliance.*

He didn't dwell on where the thought had come from, but it took him by surprise as he strode down the wide steps in front of Sutton Abbey toward his waiting horse, saddled and made ready by one of Markby's impeccable men. This wasn't the time to entertain frivolous thoughts, to yearn.

*Gentlemen do not yearn.*

He took a deep breath of the cool morning air as be approached his waiting mount. As he exhaled, his breath visible in the chill, he made a silent vow. "We had our night. I will be free of her by the time I return to London, so help me God." From behind him, a familiar voice interrupted his thoughts.

"Don't leave, Nicky," said Markby said. It was unlike his friend to be awake at this hour, but it seemed Markby had received and read the note Dorset had slipped under his door just minutes earlier. Written in haste, the note simply said that he had been called back to town. "Heathcote can't shoot worth a damn, and Em seems rather preoccupied, don't you think? She's dreadful company. She keeps going on about researching something in the library. It sounds like a damned bore."

Dorset turned and saw Markby in his dressing gown, his fair hair in disarray, rubbing his eyes against the slowly rising sun. So much for slipping away without notice, without real explanation. He didn't wish to expose Charlotte to potential harm, but more than that, he wanted to remain in her confidence.

"I'm afraid I don't have a choice. Keep a sharp eye on Heathcote if you hand him a gun." Dorset stepped into the stirrup and swung his other leg over the side of his horse. "Have Em bring my trunk back, will you?" he called down to his disheveled friend.

"I should toss it in the river! At least explain yourself," Markby replied.

"Let's just say that things between Miss Crampton and I are no longer cordial and therefore I must take my leave."

*Not exactly a lie.*

"Cordial? Don't serve up hogwash and expect me to eat it."

"I'll tell you my side when you return to town, but take my word that I cannot and should not stay," said Dorset, feeling badly for leaving but knowing this was the only way forward. Now that he had known the pleasure of Charlotte's company, he needed to begin to forget her for good. Even now, he felt her shape as she curved closer to his embrace, heard the desperate sounds that had escaped her throat as they'd kissed.

"Fine, fine. Away, you three-inch fool," shouted Markby, sullen and already turning back toward the house and most likely bound back to his bed.

Dorset gripped the thick leather reins and turned the horse toward the drive, ready for the long day of riding ahead of him. He had made it just a few yards before he remembered the cellar door incident and called back toward the house. "Markby! The wine cellar door was left ajar last night—best have someone alert Hanson," he said, just before picking up speed to a trot.

Markby waved to him in acknowledgment. If Dorset had lingered for just a moment, less even, he would have seen Mrs. Browne, Markby's housekeeper, join the young duke in the towering doorway at the top of the steps. Indeed, if he had chosen to stay rather than flee that morning, he would have heard Mrs. Browne explain to Markby in frantic tones that Hanson had in fact taken ill the night before, due to a great shock.

"A shock?" asked Markby, wishing he could go straight back to sleep but doing his best to attend to the task at hand the way a good head of household should—the way his father had before his death.

"That's just the thing, Your Grace. Before we could get him to sleep, he kept going on about having seen a ghost. He swears it, on his life he says," replied Mrs. Browne, wringing an embroidered handkerchief in her pale hands. "It seems to be the young lady, Miss Crampton. He has sworn, to me, to all the boys who got him to his bed, and to the doctor in the night, that she's the ghost of a woman—a woman he knows to be long dead, mind you—who once passed through here, in your father's time. We can't get him to make any sense," she said, without pausing for breath. "Mary from the kitchens sat up with him all night, and they say he's awake now. We've tried to get him to take some broth and settle, but he insists on seeing you directly, Your Grace."

"Well, let's not get him out of bed. If it's as bad as you say, I must go to him at once," Markby replied, growing concerned. He had solicitors and men of business who assisted him with the handling of his vast estate, but losing Hanson would be a blow. The man had encyclopedic knowledge of the Sutton Dukedom—knowledge that would be lost forever without his presence in these halls.

He followed Mrs. Browne down to the servant's quarters, well below his own. Each person they passed, some children as young as ten or twelve, dipped into a curtsy or a bow before hurrying back to their work. No one met his eyes. He hadn't walked these halls as a grown man, nor as duke. The ceilings were lower than he remembered, but the clean, polished floors gleamed underfoot, just as they had when as a child he would slip down to the kitchens in search of a bite to eat, or mischief —often both, with Dorset and Emmeline in tow.

At last he reached Hanson's private bedchamber, a luxury provided only to him and Mrs. Browne as the senior-most members of his staff. Still, it was small enough to fit inside of Markby's closet stories above them.

"Your Grace, at last," said Hanson. His voice was shaking. The elderly man looked small and unwell confined to his brass bed. A chair materialized behind Markby next to the bedside, and he took it.

"Mr. Hanson, you've given us all quite a scare. What seems to be the matter?" asked Markby. He tried to maintain his usual jovial tone; based on the ashen looks from Mrs. Browne, Mary from the kitchens, and the two assembled footman who were no doubt "the boys who got him to his bed," he wasn't sure he had succeeded.

"The matter, Your Grace, is that last night when your Grace and your guests were seated for dinner, I saw the face of a ghost in this home. I would have sworn to it on my mother's Bible. Only upon waking this morning have I realized what this portends."

"Hanson, I hold you in the highest esteem. I have never met a more serious man, and indeed I hope I do not in all my days. But a *ghost*?"

"Not exactly, Your Grace. I have no doubt that the woman in question is very much alive. I believe that she is the daughter of a woman once acquainted with your father, an opera singer by the name of Catherine Price."

"Do you mean Miss Crampton? I'm not sure that's possible, Hanson." Didn't the woman have parents in Derbyshire, both of them alive, well, and acquainted with Lady Harrington? Markby was growing more confused by the moment, but Hanson pressed on, resolute.

"Please, Your Grace. There is no doubt in my mind. I will venture to explain if your Grace does not mind if I speak plainly about your father's affairs—affairs of a personal nature," said the man, proper even now as the two men, employer and employee, sat with each other in their night-clothes. Markby would have laughed at the sight of them if Hanson hadn't mentioned his late father.

"By all means, proceed."

"I'm sure I don't need to remind you that your father, tragically widowed after the passing of your mother during your birth, never remarried and lived the rest of his days as a widower," said Hanson quietly.

"Unfortunately, you do not. Please skip to the part of the story that explains how a ghost found herself at my dinner table last evening," said Markby. He didn't mean to be impatient, but any mention of his late mother twisted something deep within his chest. What love would he have known if she had survived? Was it his fault she had died that night, surrounded by Britain's finest doctors?

"I'm afraid I cannot explain how she came to be here, Your Grace, but you must believe me that the woman who calls herself 'Miss Crampton' is the exact twin of this Catherine Price, who passed from this life eighteen years ago. The late Miss Price was an accomplished performer, beloved for her talent. I met her a great many times as a guest of your father's, and I could not forget her face if I tried, it is so burned into my memory. When I saw that same face again, as young and as vibrant as the last time I laid eyes upon it nearly three decades ago, I knew it must be an apparition. I realize now that this cannot be. As I swore to those assembled here last night that I saw a ghost, I would swear with absolute certainty in front of God, my country, and Your Grace that the woman Lady Emmeline brought here as her guest is the daughter of Catherine Price." Hanson spoke with absolute conviction as the color rose in his face. He began to cough. Mary rushed to his side with a glass of water.

"So, we have an imposter," Markby said. "It wouldn't be the first time, I'd imagine. I'll discuss it with Lady Emmeline; there may be some explanation." The duke was unsure why Hanson had taken to his bed over such a matter as this.

"Please, Your Grace," Hanson said. He tried feebly to sit up, but the heavy blankets over his lap held him in place. Mary mopped his pallid brow with a cool, damp cloth. His dark eyes, surrounded by papery skin, bored into Markby's; it sent a chill down his spine and reminded him not a little bit of the late duke's discerning gaze. "The explanation is this: Catherine Price, may God rest her soul, was your father's mistress, after your mother's death. Sometime near the end of their relations, rumors spread that she fell pregnant. Please understand that I do not make the following claim in jest, and that I believe we can locate proof if we search through your father's personal letters. The woman claiming to be Tabitha Crampton is your half-sister."

# Chapter 10

*~~Lord Edward Dinsdale, 2nd Earl of Cheltenham~~ (too young)*
*Lord Phillip Rossmoor, Viscount Herringbone*
*~~Lord Gregory Argyle, 8th Duke of Hertfordshire~~ (too dead)*
*Lord George Bredon Wimsey, 14th Duke of Denver*
*Lord, Jesus Christ, deliver me from this endless search...*

"Charlotte, did you get that last one?"

Emmeline's voice shook Charlotte from her trance. From her station at a writing desk near a window inside of Sutton Abbey's cavernous library, where she was supposed to be listening and copying down the many names Emmeline read aloud, Charlotte had been tracing a rain droplet as it slid down the pane beside her. It was a dreadfully cold day; the moors beyond were shrouded in a low, dense fog.

"Yes, it was Argyle, wasn't it? I've crossed him off," Charlotte said. She pulled her shawl tighter around her shoulders and shivered. The warmth of the roaring fire at the other end of the room did not reach her place by the window. Emmeline regarded her with sympathy. All assembled—Charlotte,

Emmeline, and Sarah—were beginning to understand the enormity of their task, and to lose hope.

"Why don't I ring for some tea?" asked Emmeline, sensing that all three could use a bolstering. She rose from her place and crossed the room to the bell. Sarah regarded the open copy of Debrett's with utter defeat in her eyes and sighed.

As she stared down at the growing list of names of men who may or may not have impregnated her mother based only on the loosest criteria, Charlotte thought she might burst from the staggering mix of emotions roiling somewhere inside her rib cage. She felt hopeless, for apparently there had been more peers of the realm over the past forty years than she thought possible, each a candidate for fatherhood until she consulted medical records—records she wasn't sure she would find, nor access now that she had revealed her identity. She felt exhausted thanks to the previous night spent without sleep. But most of all, she felt the keen sting of loss—the loss of the man she had taken fully into her confidence just a few hours before he had left her, for good.

*Lord Nicholas Felton, Viscount Dorset*

*I should cross him out, as well. Reason: class divide.*

Charlotte ached for him. She didn't want to, but how could she help it? For a fleeting moment, they had been close. Who had given him permission to be so charming when he should have raged at her? And why did Charlotte allow herself to melt like butter in a hot pan when he gave her just a morsel of his attention?

The answers to these questions did not matter, because rather than stay here, Dorset had chosen to ride out into the frigid, misty morning, back to London and away from her. She should thank him for it, but she could not deny that his absence made her feel lower than she had the evening prior when he had left her alone and crying in the garden.

*At least we parted on good terms.*

Charlotte's thoughts now turned to her mother. Love affairs between so-called "Quality," as Sarah so often put it, and the common-born were never happy ones. Her mother knew this and had tried to warn Charlotte away from this very path in their final conversation. The vision of her mother, scared and withering upon Death's doorstep, flashed through Charlotte's memory. Once again, she heard that final warning, as clear now as she had that day at her mother's bedside.

"Your father is not a bad man, but do not try to find him. He lives in a different world, one that we cannot ever hope to join."

*Dorset lives in a different world.*

*One I cannot ever hope to join.*

*I let him seduce me in a wine cellar and leave the next morning without another word.*

That familiar anger, forgotten as soon as she had set foot on Sutton grounds, grew once more. Charlotte needed to focus on her task at hand: finding her father at any cost.

"Lottie, come sit with me by the fire," said Sarah, who had removed her eyeglasses and was rubbing her tired eyes. Charlotte joined her just as a tea service was brought in and placed before them. Visions of the Stapleton tea flashed through her mind, and she remembered the abject terror she had felt that day; the memory did nothing to help her general sense of unease, although she supposed she was no longer a lying imposter.

Emmeline poured three cups and returned the teapot to the tray before she spoke. "Well, it seems we have quite a way to go, doesn't it?" she asked, putting things rather lightly.

"Indeed, my la—" Sarah started. "I mean, Emmeline. Assuming the duke won't turn us out. Which reminds me..." Here it was, the moment of truth regarding Charlotte's attempt to tell Dorset the truth. Her stomach clenched as Sarah went on. "What did you tell Lord Dorset?"

For once, Sarah sat quietly and awaited a response. Charlotte took a sip of her tea and regarded both of her friends over the rim of her raised cup.

*I told him everything and then he ruined me in the basement.*

*It was marvelous.*

Charlotte cleared her throat and set down her tea. "It was simple; I told him the truth," she said, folding her hands in her lap.

"The truth? What did he say?" asked Sarah.

"At first, he was...displeased," replied Charlotte, taking another sip of her tea. The lack of detail flustered Sarah. Emmeline, opposite them, sat quietly and buttered a crumpet.

*And later, he was pleased, but best not mention that bit.*

"Displeased? You'll have to do better than that, Lottie. Are we getting tossed out today or not?" asked Sarah, growing concerned.

"Well, to be honest, I'm not sure that he told anyone else. You see, he left for town at dawn." At this, Emmeline raised a single eyebrow.

"At Dawn? Without going into detail, do you care to share how you knew of my brother's movements *before the sun rose?*" she asked.

"Not particularly," replied Charlotte, reaching again for her teacup. Sarah clapped a hand over her mouth to stifle her signature titter. "Although, I suppose it is possible that the servants who saw him off have alerted the duke by now."

"Shall I go pack the trunks then?" Sarah asked, rising from the settee. Before anyone could respond, they heard the distant patter of many hurried footsteps—yards away and growing closer.

"What on Earth is that clatter? Maybe it's time for Markby's calisthenics," said Emmeline.

"Strange that he performs them in the hallways, don't you

think?" asked Charlotte. The women cast each other uneasy glances. The steps were growing louder.

"And with an army by his side, to my ears. Is he riding a horse?" asked Sarah. All three rose and moved toward door, stopping before they reached it. The footfalls were frantic and seemingly all around them, from the halls beside the library as well as above them on higher floors. They could hear doors being opened and slammed, shouted orders from a male voice, and cries from the others in response echoing through the great halls.

"Not in the solarium, Your Grace!"

"I checked the ballroom! Empty, Your Grace!"

"Keep looking! I must find her at once!"

"Oh dear," said Emmeline, quietly. "Sarah, I think you suggested packing the trunks. Let us not delay—"

Before she could go on, the library door was thrown open. Markby burst in with footmen at his heels, red-faced, chest heaving. "Thomas, run and tell Mrs. Browne that I've found them," he said, his eyes fixed on Emmeline, Charlotte, and Sarah, his gaze deadly serious. They stood bolt upright and completely still, startled by the duke's sudden appearance in his dressing gown.

*Why is he still in his dressing gown?*

Emmeline stepped in front of Charlotte and Sarah and addressed their host with a gentle tone. Charlotte did not doubt that she had used this tone with him in the past, and with success no doubt. Nonetheless, she was afraid. She and Sarah had so far managed to escape any trouble with Madame Beaumont, but an angry duke would certainly mean the end of their employment.

"Markby, to what do we owe the pleasure? We were just doing a bit of light reading," Emmeline said, all innocence. He locked eyes with her and his breathing slowed, but the intensity of his stare did not wane. A small muscle in her cheek jumped—the only sign of nerves on her person.

"Em, you won't believe it," he said, his voice low. "We still have to find the proof, but I think it's true," he added, his voice cracking. Either Charlotte's eyes were playing tricks, or the duke was near tears.

"True? What's true, Markby?" Emmeline approached him and placed her hands on his cheeks, examining his face with not a small amount of concern. She placed the back of her hand across his forehead, checking him for fever. Without answering her, he shook free of her ministrations; for once, he was not here to speak to Emmeline.

Markby approached Charlotte, determined. From a respectful distance, he examined the planes of her face, the shape of her hair, plaited and pinned just an hour earlier by Fiona's expert hand.

*He knows.*

"Your Grace, I'm so sorry. Please—"

"No, you must let me explain what I've learned—"

He stopped her before she continued, but lost his train of thought immediately, his voice trailing off as he examined her. She wanted to explain everything, to unburden herself of all of her lies, just as she had to Dorset. She was tired of pretending, and it was becoming too complicated to keep track of who knew her as Charlotte and who still thought she was the unfortunate Miss Crampton. Even if it meant returning to London on foot immediately, she would tell him all and set herself free of this farce. As she searched once again for the words, he continued to stare at her with curious intensity.

Slowly, he stepped closer to Charlotte and took both of her trembling hands in his. A silent tear fell down one of his high cheekbones as he looked at her with eyes that were a bright shade of grayish green, just like her own. He dropped to his knees and buried his face in her skirts, crying openly now.

"Your Grace, is everything all right?" Charlotte asked nervously, bending to try and help the tall man back to his feet. She was no match for him. She looked desperately at Emmeline, who was in the doorway receiving whispered information from Mrs. Browne, and at Sarah, who was rooted to the spot where she stood near the fire, terrified.

Slowly, Charlotte sank to her knees, face to face with the crying duke. He took her by the shoulders now and addressed her at last. "Tell me your name."

"My name?"

"Yes. Your name, please," he replied, strength returning to his voice.

"My name is Charlotte Price," she said, just above a whisper. She had said the same words to another just hours ago in the gardens outside this very room. Charlotte steeled herself for a dressing down from yet another furious gentleman.

Curiously, as soon as she spoke her name, the duke's serious expression lifted—he looked into her eyes and smiled. It felt to Charlotte like the warmth of the sun; he was so handsome, and yet, something about his attention felt entirely appropriate and not at all romantic. It was as though a fond cousin or dear uncle had embraced her after a long absence.

*Nonsense, Charlotte. You don't have any cousins, nor uncles, so how would you know what it feels like?*

"Charlotte Price," he replied. "Do you have any family?"

"Family? Not exactly, Your Grace. My mother, Catherine, died of tuberculosis when I was just a girl. I never knew my father," she replied. Why did he seem so happy to hear this tale of woe from a woman he now knew to have lied to him? He pulled her into his arms and held her so tightly that she felt fit to burst.

"Miss Price, you will never know how joyful I am to hear this. I'm going to call you Charlotte from now on, of course. And you must come home and live with me at once, I won't hear a word against it—" Markby went on in this manner, speaking to her as though she knew anything at all about what he meant, until Charlotte could not bear to hear another word. With all her strength, she pushed back against his solid chest.

"Your Grace, please! I'm sorry that I have lied to you and taken advantage of your hospitality. I know that I am not worthy of your kindness but please, do not make fun of me." He continued to smile at her, a smile so bright that the light of it could grow roses in the dead of winter.

*Maddening.*

"I'm afraid I got ahead of myself. I tend to do that, you know. You'll see soon enough," he replied. "Charlotte Price, you are my sister. Well, half-sister if we're being technical, but frankly, I don't give a damn about the difference. I'm an orphan too, you know. And I was dreadfully sad about it until I heard that Hanson had seen a ghost, and luckily, that ghost is you! But you're not a ghost, are you? You're my sister, and I'm keeping you."

"Your sister?"

"Oh, Markby!"

"Lottie, don't you see what this means?"

All three women had cried out at once, but only Sarah got to the heart of the matter. "Your mother, and his father! Not just his father, your father, too! We don't have to search anymore." Sarah took the list Charlotte had made and tossed it in the fireplace with a flourish.

"We'll need to be smart about this, Markby," said Emmeline. "Of course, she must live with you, but we have to think carefully about how we will introduce her to society." She paced the floor now, not unlike the day that this plot had hatched in a fitting room at Beaumont's.

"Society? I don't think—" blurted Charlotte. Sarah interrupted her immediately.

"My la—excuse me, Emmeline? We'll need to make sure she knows how to be a proper lady. Dances, music, a wardrobe! There's much work to be done." Why was she siding with them? What was happening?

"Yes, certainly, Sarah," Emmelined agreed. "I'm afraid it's the end of your time as a seamstress, Charlotte. I'm sure Madame Beaumont will be thrilled with this news." It seemed that no one in the library that day cared to ask Charlotte what she thought of "this news," or what she wanted. She began to feel dizzy and uncomfortable in her borrowed clothes.

"Stop it! Everyone, stop!" She had shouted so loudly that all present ceased their frenzied activities at once. With every eye upon her, she addressed her brother.

*I have a brother?*

"Your Grace—"

"No! Call me Markby, or Richard, or Brother Dearest, anything else, I beg you."

"Fine, *Markby*. How have you come to know this information? And I believe you mentioned proof that exists. Do we have it?" asked Charlotte. She would not allow herself to hope that this was true until they had as much evidence as possible in hand. Becoming the long-lost sister of a duke would change every aspect of her life, and she wasn't yet sure if that meant for the better.

Markby proceeded to tell her Hanson's tale and offered to take her to him as soon as he was feeling well enough. As he went on, she began to feel more skeptical. It seemed possible that Mr. Hanson had known her mother, but that didn't immediately translate to the butler's knowledge of his employer's intimate relations as far as Charlotte was concerned. She needed evidence, and just as she opened her mouth to express this point, Markby continued on.

"As for proof, Hanson believes there exists correspondence between our father and his man of business that will explain all. Dash the letters, I don't care a bit. You are my sister, I would swear to it in church." Charlotte considered this before she spoke.

"This is all very exciting, but I must insist that we do not make any changes until we find these letters. I mustn't jeopardize my situation—or Sarah's, for that matter—all because Mr. Hanson recognized me and some correspondence from thirty odd years ago may or may not exist."

"Dear sister, I disagree wholeheartedly. Look, we've had our first disagreement as siblings, I never thought I would see the day!" Nothing seemed to dampen the duke's spirits. He practically twirled about the room with excitement, and both Emmeline and Sarah looked on with adoration. Charlotte closed her eyes and sighed.

"Again, I must insist. Now, if you'll please lead the way, I would like to speak with Mr. Hanson. Oh, and one more thing," she said.

"Yes, what is it? I shall grant my new sister anything she desires."

"Do not tell Lord Dorset."

# Chapter 11



"*...* And so you see why I *must* have you accompany me today to *Chez Beaumont*, I simply *had* to spend some time with my dearest and only son and find out if there was any truth at all to these vague rumors."

Just one day prior, his mother had asked Dorset to pay her a visit at Stapleton in the morning, after which she would bid him good day so that she could keep an appointment with her modiste in the afternoon. Still unused to rising early, Dorset offered to accompany her instead. He told himself it had nothing at all to do with the fact that her modiste was Charlotte's employer, and certainly even less to do with the fact that he could still recall the delicate scent of her skin, and how it felt beneath his touch.

*Skin you shall never be close enough to touch again.*

Lady Harrington had been speaking nonstop since greeting Dorset as he entered her carriage outside of his town-home, and she continued on as they arrived at the grand shop on Bond Street. After updating him on the latest mundanities of their peers in London, the countess reached her point.

There seemed to be whispers circulating regarding a long-lost Markby family member newly come to the fore, and she wondered if Dorset had the pleasure of making this person's acquaintance while away at Sutton Abbey.

It all sounded like nonsense to him, but what troubled Dorset was that what she called, "these vague rumors" seemed to have reached his mother shortly after he had returned, and they were rumors that he had not yet heard himself. It had been four days since Dorset had returned alone. In those four days, he had heard nothing of the fallout from Charlotte's confession, and, now that he really thought about it, nothing at all from Markby, nor Emmeline. He was certain that one or both would have alerted him to news such as this without delay.

"A relative? I think I would know if a Markby relation had come out of the woodwork, Mother."

"I'm sure you're right, Nicholas, which is why I thought to ask you in the first place," she said as she perused an array of trims available for the spring. "I must tell Lady Beauchamp that her ladies' maid's cousin, who is, of course, a kitchen girl at Sutton, was quite mistaken and to be more careful about what she tells her friends on her afternoon free."

"Certainly, Mother," he replied. Dorset followed his mother through the ground floor showroom as she fingered colorful lengths of velvet, satin, and brocade, chatting merrily with any available shop girl who would listen. With her attention temporarily diverted, he took the chance to take in his surroundings, to absorb the atmosphere where Charlotte spent nearly all of her days.

Did seamstresses work every day? Dorset realized then, as he passed a glass case full of pearls and crystals of various size for beading, that he had no idea. Surely, that would be tiresome indeed—one would need a day or two of rest to attend to one's home, or to attend church services if one did such things. Even Lady Beauchamp's ladies' maid's cousin had an afternoon free. Did Madame Beaumont allow Charlotte the same? He wondered where she lived, and how far her home was from his own. There was so much he wished to ask her, and he cursed himself under his breath as he realized that he would never again get the chance to do so.

They both knew the reality of their situation; the longer he stayed in her life, the harder it would be to say goodbye for good. As his father's only son, Dorset knew he would eventually have to marry and produce an heir. He assumed that Charlotte would marry as well—she was clever, beautiful, and skilled. A man could do worse for himself in terms of a wife.

*He certainly can't do better.*

The thought of her going to bed with another man, even her husband, made his fists clench and his heart beat faster. Dorset would have to learn to master this jealous impulse, for there would be no half measures, no side relationship outside of their respective homes. He would not make her a mistress, and he knew from hearing her speak so passionately about finding her scoundrel of a father that she would never consent to such an arrangement.

No; Charlotte was not a mistress. She was a queen, and Dorset hoped that with time the ache he felt deep in his chest when he thought of her, so pronounced now even after only one night together and four days apart, would ease. It was careless of him to have gone with his mother that morning, boldly entering Charlotte's domain after their agreement that no arrangement could continue. He was ashamed of himself, an intruder in her world.

"Nicholas, my *darling* boy, did I mention the letter I received from the Crampton Family just last week?"

*The Cramptons?*

"No, Mother, you did not. I trust that they are all in good health," he replied hesitantly. What had his mother told them after the tea? Did she know that Charlotte wasn't Tabitha, and that Tabitha would forever be found wanting through no fault of her own?

"Well, I had to write them once I spoke with your sister—of course, Emmeline has *all* the sense in the family and figured everything out like she always does—but as soon as she explained to me that there had been some mix-up with a rather pretty seamstress, I knew I had to write to them straight away. Poor girl must have been scared out of her wits, but of course, I do not blame her. She was simply doing as I asked, in a way, wasn't she? Although, I'm sure you'll agree that it all got rather out of hand, but no matter. I have apologized to the baron and he's accepted my apology in the response that I received just last week, and, thank goodness that he has. They have agreed to move forward with the suit between you and *sweet* Tabitha."

*Just as I suspected: As usual, Emmeline knew all.*

Dorset glanced from one side of his mother's face to the other, checking for gills. How did she go on in such a manner without once stopping to inhale? And what on Earth was he supposed to say now that he had developed serious unrequited feelings for that "rather pretty seamstress" who had been his for too short a time in a dank and dirty cellar? He wanted her in a proper bed, *his bed*, aboveground and near a roaring fire. There would be no need for layered dressing gowns to keep warm, no need to hurry up and finish before sunrise, and most importantly: no impending marriage to Tabitha.

"What would you say if I told you that *I* no longer consented to the suit?"

"Nicholas, you've been against it from the start, have you not? You made that clear to your father, at least. Let me simply remind you that this means a great deal to your father and I, and I shall reiterate what I told you that day: I'm sure once you meet *dear* Tabitha that you shall recognize her best qualities, and that you shall both live happily together."

"How can you be so sure when you yourself—by your own admission—could not recognize her in a crowded dress shop?"

"Oh, Nicholas, do not quibble with me. Join me upstairs this instant—I'm told that Tabitha, the *real* Tabitha, is trying on her gown this very moment. I shall introduce you myself."

Miss Crampton was here? Now? Dorset followed his mother up the grand staircase in a trance as he pondered how this was possible; knowing his mother and the lengths to which she would go to secure his marriage, this was not a coincidence. He had been tricked, for of course his mother would have known that he wouldn't rise early enough to join her in the morning, and he would suggest accompanying her in the afternoon instead. It occurred to him as he placed each careful step upon the sumptuous mauve velvet that passed for floor covering in this ostentatious establishment that the only woman who had been honest with him, and who seemed to care at all about his feelings throughout this charade, was Charlotte.

*If there existed any possible way I could make her my wife, I would take her to a Gretna Green blacksmith and marry her today.*

At the top of the stairs, beneath a glittering chandelier and admiring herself in a large, gilt-edge, tri-fold mirror, stood the elusive Tabitha Crampton. She was refined in every way—fair, unblemished skin, rust-colored hair twisted up and pinned to her head, her unsmiling mouth set in a perfect pout as she turned to regard Dorset, the man she expected to court and marry her. His mother approached with outstretched arms.

"Miss Crampton, allow me to introduce my son, Lord Dorset. What a pity that it has taken this long to meet!" The countess looked between them expectantly. According to her, this was the moment she was sure that Dorset was to fall madly in love with this stranger: first sight.

Ever the gentleman, Dorset reached for Miss Crampton's hand, sheathed now in a buttercup yellow opera glove that matched the evening gown she was wearing and that he did not doubt his mother was here to purchase. As briefly as he could while still maintaining the social niceties expected of him, he pressed his lips to her satin-clad knuckles. He knew immediately that this was a mistake—the last thing his lips had touched had been Charlotte's.

"Miss Crampton, it is a pleasure to make your acquaintance."

"At last, Dorset! I couldn't believe the farce that took place in my absence. I hope we can agree to forget all about it." Stifling a flinch at the familiar use of his name, Dorset strained to maintain a neutral expression. He did not like this woman, but he suspected it was simply because she was not the auburn-haired seamstress with pin-prick marks on her elegant hands and lips that tasted of peach fool. Nearly losing himself to the thought of those lips, he hesitated—just long enough for his mother to cut in before he could respond.

"Oh, *of course*, my dear. Consider it all forgotten! Tell me, do you like the gown?"

"It's lovely, although I'm not sure the color suits me," she replied, her gazed fixed on Dorset.

"Nonsense, you look lovely. Doesn't Miss Crampton look *lovely*, Nicholas?"

*Blast.*

"Yes, she looks lovely, Mother," he said. As his cravat grew tighter, Dorset could feel heat rising in his cheeks; frantically, he grasped for any believable excuse to run from this woman. Charlotte may have borrowed her name, but why did he have the distinct feeling that the real Tabitha was the one out of place?

Dorset needed to exit this conversation, and quickly. A quick glance around the fitting area did not reveal a single marked exit. He would have to retreat down the grand staircase and leave the same way he came.

"I overheard one of the girls saying something about another gown in lilac silk—or was it violet? Don't you think that would be better suited to my complexion?" she asked, idly fussing with a bit of ruffled trim at her neckline as she gazed at her own reflection.

"Oh, no, you *must* wear this perfect creation, Tabitha," replied Lady Harrington. "The color reminds me of daffodils, *such* a lovely flower, don't you think?"

"Yes, I suppose. What do you think, Dorset? Daffodils or violets?"

*Violets, of course.*

"The color is perfectly fine, Miss Crampton," he said, his tone a touch more clipped than he intended, but he could not hide his discomfort. "If you'll excuse me, I think I've taken up quite enough of your time here when you certainly have important sartorial matters to discuss. Mother, Miss Crampton. Good day."

With the slightest nod in the direction of the two women now staring at him, mouths agape and surely aghast at his abrupt departure, Dorset turned on his heel and headed for freedom before either could protest. He was down the stairs in an instant and found himself nearly running through the showroom, dodging what seemed like scores of ladies waiting for an audience with the famous modiste. He nearly trampled a young girl carrying bolts of vibrant fabrics piled high in her arms, but stopped himself just in time. After a rushed apology and refused offer of assistance, he could see daylight.

Dorset burst through the front doors of the showroom floor and out into the usual bustle of Bond Street. He couldn't take the carriage home—his mother had remained inside, no doubt attempting to soothe any offense he had caused, offense Dorset was sure had been great. He had run from the scene like a coward, but to spend even another second in Miss Crampton's presence felt like a betrayal.

He knew this was nonsense, a poor excuse for poor behavior. Charlotte probably didn't give a damn who he spoke to. She had made it clear to him every time they met that theirs was not a love story, and it certainly would not have a happy ending.

*If that's true, why don't I believe it?*

Dorset hailed a waiting hack and resolved to apologize to his mother as soon as he could, as soon as he was sure she was safely installed back in her own home and was no longer in the company of Miss Crampton.

He had the duration of the ride home to come up with the content of that apology, and after entering his home and dispensing of his hat and gloves, he made for his study where he intended to write it all in a letter for immediate delivery. His plans, however, were interrupted the moment he settled behind his large, polished oak desk. A swift and familiar knock at the door told Dorset exactly who waited on the other side.

"Yes, Barlow, come in."

Mr. Barlow, Dorset's butler, entered. "Pardon the interruption, my lord. His Grace, Lord Markby is here to see you," he said from behind his thick moustache. The man was a least two decades younger than Markby's Mr. Hanson, but he maintained the same placid gaze and unflappable constitution unique to only the best butlers in England.

"Yes, he is here to see you, and he has news!" His jovial voice preceded him, and even before he had finished the sentence, Markby nearly leapt into the study. Dorset caught a veil of disapproval shrouding Barlow's expression as he left the two men alone and closed the door. It was no wonder—Markby was unusually ebullient that afternoon.

"Back from the abbey, I take it? I am anxious to hear your news, but you should know that there are rumors spreading about you, Richard. Are the two related?" Markby folded his tall, lean frame into a chair opposite Dorset's desk and assumed his trademark casual slouch. He was beaming, from ear to ear.

"I don't care about rumors, Nicholas. I have a sister!"

"A what?"

"A *sister*."

"A sister? You don't mean Emmeline, do you? Is this some kind of joke?" Dorset was reminded of his mother's earlier statement regarding the recent discovery of another Markby. Could it be true?

"Of course I don't mean Emmeline, you fool!" Markby's sunny expression had faltered—Dorset didn't stop to ask why the thought of Emmeline as a sister so disgusted his friend.

"Damnit, Markby, explain yourself!"

"I still don't understand all the specifics myself, but I have a sister, I'm sure of it. She isn't so sure as I, and she won't accept me until we find the proof."

"Proof? How on Earth will you find that?" asked Dorset.

"It's simple, it's in the letters," said Markby, waving away the question as though the issue of parentage and the ramifications of this discovery upon his dukedom were nothing to be concerned with.

Dorset poured two glasses of whisky and handed one to his friend. "Where was she all this time? In the attic at Sutton?"

Markby smirked over the rim of his crystal glass. "Very funny, Nicky."

"What do you call this sister? I trust she has a name."

"Indeed, she does have a name, but I have sworn to her that I shall keep her a secret for now."

"A secret? Even from me?"

"Especially from you," replied Markby.

*From me? But why?*

There was only one person visiting Sutton Abbey during the recent days whose family history was in doubt, and who was there searching for answers. Dorset's gaze turned serious as realization—or was it hope—dawned. "Markby, why on Earth should her name be a secret from me, of all people?" As he shrunk under Dorset's steely glare, Markby fiddled with his cuffs and looked anywhere but across the desk at his friend.

"Well, it seems that I did promise her, and I'm trying to be a good brother. It's my first time, you know, and I'm afraid that I've already let on far more than she—"

Dorset cut him off with a swift pound of his closed fist atop his desk, which sent his ink pot flying and made a startled Markby jump in his seat. "Damn you, Markby! Tell me her name," he shouted.

"All right, calm down, Nicky. I'll tell you, but if she asks, you must make it clear that I was forced," Markby replied. He set down his glass just as Dorset raised his own to his lips, his serious blue eyes never leaving Markby's face. "As it happens, my sister is Miss Charlotte Price."

Shocked by this statement, Dorset coughed and sputtered and tried valiantly but failed to keep his swallow of whisky contained within his mouth. As he struggled with a fit of coughing made worse by the burn of dark liquor, Markby sent the young footman who had righted the ink pot for a glass of water, rounded the desk, and delivered a series of strong blows to his friend's back.

Slowly, Dorset returned to himself and regained his composure. To his credit, Markby said nothing as he processed the news, but Dorset needed further explanation, immediately. "How in the name of God did you come to discover this?" he asked, mopping his brow with a handkerchief and accepting a refilled glass of whisky from his friend.

With the patience of a saintly schoolmistress, Markby recounted the events in question, from a bedridden Hanson's claims of a ghost, to the ladies' unsuccessful library research mission, and to the eventual embrace of hopeful brother and reluctant sister.

"I can't imagine why she isn't as happy as I am. She has insisted on returning to work and keeping her garret flat with Miss Ludlow, her companion, until we can locate the letters in question," said Markby, bringing Dorset up to the present moment.

"Ever practical, that sounds exactly like Charlotte," replied Dorset.

"Yes, and it sounds exactly like my father as well," said Markby. "Hold on, just one moment. To me, she is Dear Sister, to others, she is Miss Price, but my hope is that will soon change to Lady Charlotte. Exactly when did you become so familiar with my sister as to call her by her first name alone?"

*Best not mention the wine cellar...*

"Think nothing of it, Markby. I shall address her however you see fit if the time comes. We parted as friends—and nothing more," said Dorset. Although he was leaving out certain details that implied a greater connection than mere friendship, what he said was true, and it made his heart ache.

"What do you mean 'if'? Of course, the time will come that you must see her. But first, I have to find the blasted letters that prove she's one of us. She won't even think about giving up her position until they are unearthed and deemed genuine."

Monied dukes such as Markby often fielded claims upon their family line, claims nearly always made with requests for funds of some kind. As the afternoon stretched to evening and the two men sat down to dine, it occurred to Dorset that the unique twist in this case was that for once it was the duke—

richer than the Queen and God combined—who was desperate to prove this relation, and not the seamstress who lived in poverty and embroidered lace by candlelight each night to afford coal for her fireplace.

"So, she's keeping her position? At Beaumont's?" asked Dorset, idly smashing a small roasted potato with his fork. He tried to sound as cool and unbothered as possible, but the words felt desperate and probing as he heard himself speak them. He twirled the fork in his hand, regarding the potato closely to avoid eye contact with Markby.

*How much coal could the silver from this fork afford her?*

"Correct. She has said she will not jeopardize her well-being if this is found to be a misunderstanding. But I wish she would just take my word for it and let me take her in," said Markby.

"That's the thing about sisters. They only do as they please. Best to learn that lesson early on," said Dorset, smiling. He was happy for his friend, who did not have a single close relation and had much to learn.

The afternoon whisky and the wines paired with his dinner were beginning to slow Dorset's thoughts. A hazy image formed in his mind of Lady Charlotte, perfectly turned out, a society darling beloved by the *ton*. The sister of the Duke of Sutton would have her pick of balls to attend, more dresses than she could wear in a month, the attention of any suitor she desired. His pulse quickened at the thought—there wouldn't be just "any suitor." As Lady Charlotte, only sister of his closest friend the Duke of Markby, she could be his without scandal.

*Lady Charlotte, would you do me the honor...*

"...so, you see why we have to find the letters. Mrs. Browne is leading them all on the hunt, and I've instructed them to check the tombs if they must..." Markby had been speaking, but Dorset was no longer listening. He had to get to Charlotte, to tell her that he knew. Did he dare to tell her how he felt?

"Do you happen to know where she lives?"

"Of course I do. Well, I've never been there, but she gave me her direction so that I can send word when we find the letters. When we returned to town this afternoon she had me take her straight to Beaumont's. She said something about wanting to spend some time organizing the stock rooms."

"Whatever for?"

"Apparently, its tedious work that none of the girls enjoy, but she finds that it quiets her mind to take inventory alone, after closing."

Dorset suppressed the jealousy he felt hearing his friend tell him something he didn't know about her. It was an irrational response—why was that becoming more and more common? He took a deep breath and rose from the table. He couldn't waste another moment.

"Richard, let me see you off. Surely, you'll want to be home if Mrs. Browne sends word that the letters have been found." Markby looked up at him with a confused expression. It was a rare night that didn't see the two men to their club for cards or billiards after a dinner like this one. Still, he did not protest.

"Indeed, I do," he replied.

Once Markby was safely tucked into his carriage, Dorset took the stairs up to his bedroom two at a time. He needed a fresh shirt, and a splash of cool water on his face. There was no time for a shave, and while that would have been his habit considering where he was headed and what he intended to do once there, he could not risk waiting another moment. Replacing his waistcoat and frock coat, he descended the stairs as quickly as he'd come and set out for the stables, where he found a stable hand to help him mount his fastest horse.

"Out wif 'is Grace again this evenin', milord?" asked the boy.

"Not tonight, Thomas. I'm going to the dressmaker's. And I intend to be late returning, so don't wait up."

"The dressmaker's at this hour? Wo'-ever for, sir?"

"She's going to make me a wife."

# CHAPTER 12

At last, Charlotte found herself dressed in her own clothes and back within the familiar walls of Beaumont's. Returning here had felt like coming home, back to her world where everything was certain—but on this particular evening, as she measured and cataloged bolts of silk, satin, and brocade spread around her on a large worktable in the center of the shop's basement storeroom, she couldn't help but let her thoughts wander to the corner of her mind where she had tucked away the memory of that one *blissful* and altogether too short encounter with Dorset.

*It might as well have been a dream.*

When she first decided to find her father's true identity, she knew the task was nearly impossible. What were the chances that she would find her first solid bit of information thanks to an elderly butler who remembered her mother's face? It was pure luck, but she couldn't ignore that something about it—possibly the duke's own excitement—felt genuine. Nevertheless, it wouldn't do to get her hopes up. She had asked Markby to bring her to Beaumont's straight away, hoping that she could consult Madame as soon as possible. As

Charlotte considered how best to raise the issue, Madame swept in, clad in a glittering purple abaya-style gown with matching ostrich feather trim, as if on cue.

"*Bon soir*, Charlotte. I see you have returned from your travels."

"Indeed, I returned earlier this afternoon. I assumed that there would be some new fabrics in to sort, and I see I was correct."

"*Oui*, the other girls do not enjoy this task as you do, *chérie. Dit moi*, how was your trip to the estate? Have you any news?"

"Yes, and I was hoping that you can help me understand it. The butler there, a Mr. Hanson, says he remembered Mother visiting Sutton Abbey years ago. He recognized me."

"I am not at all surprised. I have always told you that you are the exact image of her, so beautiful in her prime, before *la maladie* ravaged her." Madame Beaumont's eyes began to water, and her voice cracked. "*Désolée*, Charlotte. You know I do not like to recall those sad days."

"Nor do I, Madame," said Charlotte. She did not like to upset the woman who had cared for her for all of these years, but she couldn't avoid the topic any longer. "I don't wish to dwell, Madame, but Mr. Hanson has made rather a startling claim, and I cannot decide if I should trust this information. I would be grateful for your insight."

"*S'il vous plait*, go on."

"Mr. Hanson claims that letters exist, sent between them, that will prove that the late Duke of Sutton is my father, and the current Duke of Sutton, an orphan like me, is prepared to claim me as his sister straight away." At this, Madame Beaumont set down the bit of lace she had been examining and removed her spectacles.

"*Oui*, of course, your *maman* was dear to me then, but

remember, she kept your father's identity a secret from me as well. She had it in her mind that she was protecting him."

Why would the late duke have needed protection? From what Markby had told her on their carriage ride back to London, he was one of the most powerful men in England at the time.

"Like you, I am not entirely convinced. The duke, however, is thrilled, and wishes to publicly claim me as soon as possible."

"*Mon dieu*, Charlotte. You will be a lady!"

"Not yet, Madame. I have asked the duke not to act until the letters can be found."

"Don't be silly, pet. Think of the life that you could have, and with a family like never before."

"I quite like the life that I have now," said Charlotte, the heat in her cheeks growing as she went on. "And what if the letters are found, and they hold the proof that I am not who they say I am?" She was breathing more heavily now, clearly growing upset.

"Charlotte, what is it that you are hoping for? What would you like to happen?" It was the first time someone had asked her this since this entire debacle began. She felt her heart swell with warmth for the woman seated on the stool next to her, the best guardian and mentor she could have ever wished for.

"This has all happened so quickly, and no one will listen to me. When I began this search, I was so angry with my father. I'm not sure I'm willing to join his family, sight unseen, and only because they are landed and wealthy."

"*Oui, je comprend.* All you know is that you were left without a parent when your *maman* passed. But remember my darling, she always told me that he was a good man who tried to do his best, as she did. I believe that they loved each other," she said.

Charlotte looked down at the crimson satin in her hands and realized she had been wringing it out like a common, wet rag. The rich sheen of the fabric glinted in the low lamplight around them; it looked like thick, red liquid sliding through her fingers and pooling on the table.

*Blood.*

"Charlotte, do not work too late. These fabrics can wait until the morning, I am sure," said Madame, bringing Charlotte's thoughts back to the present. "But before you go, you should know that there is a customer upstairs who requires some assistance."

"A customer? At this hour?"

"*Oui*, he knocked on the front doors and was quite insistent. In fact, he requested your services, specifically."

"*He* requested them? Did the man give his name?"

"He is a gentleman, *chérie*, and no, he did not."

"Has he been waiting all this time?" asked Charlotte, her mind racing. She only knew of two gentlemen who would know where to find her place of work. One was her potential half-brother and the other...no. It couldn't be him. She would not let herself hope that Dorset had come for her.

Still, Charlotte stood and smoothed her skirts. "I suppose I should go and assist the gentleman?"

"*Mais oui*, Charlotte. I am retiring for the evening, but the charwomen are here, so you shall not be alone. Do not forget to lock the door behind you when you are *fini*." With a wink, Madame Beaumont swept from the room. Charlotte's stomach knotted and flipped; she knew that Madame would not leave her if she were unsafe, but she did not like surprises.

She made her way from the rather spartan storerooms and up to the ground floor, which was palatial in both size and decor by comparison. Luckily, the lamps were still lit, and all of the curtains were drawn. The charwomen who came in to clean after the shop closed to customers had set about their tasks. They took no notice of Charlotte as she stepped around their brooms and buckets.

There, across the room from her, was the gentleman in question. She could see his tall figure stooped over a display case, his greatcoat slung over one arm. The fine fabric of his dark jacket was expertly tailored to his broad, muscled back.

She would have recognized him anywhere. Dorset did not yet know she was there watching him—she held her breath in anticipation and took a moment to appreciate his obvious, visible strength. She felt that he could likely carry her a great distance without much effort, and for the first time, Charlotte wanted more than anything else in the world to test this theory.

She stepped toward him and immediately knocked into a hat stand, too entranced by his physical beauty to pay attention to her surroundings.

*There goes the element of surprise.*

Dorset turned and spotted her just as she caught the hat stand in mid-air, rearranging its contents and putting it to rights. He spoke, barely above a whisper, but the sound seemed to fill the cavernous room, drowning out the sounds of the vigorous scrubbing and sweeping happening around them.

"Good evening, Charlotte."

She felt a current zip through her body, from the tips of her toes to the top of her head. How had he made every hair on her body stand on end with just a whisper?

"Good evening, sir. To what do I owe the pleasure of this visit?" she asked, feebly attempting to sound professional. This was her workplace, after all, and they were not alone.

"Sir? I thought we were past formalities," he replied, stepping closer. Ten paces still separated them.

"I was told that a gentleman had requested my services. I'm simply being polite," Charlotte replied. She stepped farther into the room, coming even with the bannister of the staircase that led upstairs to the fitting rooms. Eight paces.

"Indeed, I did not know if I would find anyone here at this hour, but I was hoping that it would be you." Six paces. "And you, alone."

His deep voice rumbled through her. She moved ever closer, drawn to him like a moth to flame. Four paces now.

"Are you here for a fitting? I'm afraid we do not provide menswear or tailoring but I would be happy to refer you to suitable alternative if you'd like," she said. The bodice of her dress felt tight and constricting. As though he sensed it, his eyes dropped from her face to the curve of her breasts.

"I do not require a fitting, Charlotte." Only two paces separated them. They were at the foot of the stairs, facing each other directly. Any closer and they would be flouting propriety; Charlotte did not know the charwomen well, and she did not wish to give them fodder for the ceaseless Beaumont gossip mill. With no small effort to keep her tone as even and as chaste as possible, she went on.

"Oh? What *can* I do for you, sir?" At this, Dorset raised one roguish eye brow, looking as though he knew exactly what he required of her. He opened his mouth to respond, just a moment before Mrs. Kirby, the head charwoman, approached and broke in.

"Excuse me, Charlotte dear, and milord, but we're to beat the rugs tonight. 'Tis a dreadful, loud business, and will take up most of the room on this floor, I expect. Shall we wait until you've finished with the gentleman?"

"Wait? Oh, no, please don't wait, Mrs. Kirby."

"A'right dearie, but you'd best go up to the next floor lest you want to get covered in the dust. We've finished up there."

*The fitting rooms.*

"Thank you, Mrs. Kirby. Sir, if you would kindly join me upstairs," said Charlotte.

"Gladly, Miss Price." With a nod to the charwoman, Dorset followed Charlotte up the grand stairs. Quickly, Charlotte checked each fitting room and found that each stood empty.

They were alone.

In an instant, Dorset dropped his greatcoat to the floor, crossed the room to her, and took her by the waist, pulling her flush with his large, solid body. He spoke, his voice a whisper, his lips brushing hers. It was excruciating and thrilling all at once; Charlotte felt her knees weaken as she melted against him, desperate for his kiss.

"Charlotte, tell me that you've missed me." His lips were so close to hers, and yet so far.

"Of course I have, you fool," she breathed, sealing her mouth to his for the kiss that she had longed for since the moment he last left her side in the hall outside her bedchamber at Sutton Abbey. With practiced skill, he parted her lips with his own and returned her kiss with tender, searching strokes. Dorset's hands tightened around her waist as she gripped and pulled at his collar. As though linked, their breathing grew faster, more frenzied. With each caress, they grew frantic, desperate to consume each other.

As it had before, all of her sense deserted her. She did not care a bit that they had agreed to share only the night in the wine cellar and to part amicably. She did not care that her parentage was in question and that she would surely mire his name in scandal should they be caught. And least of all, she did not care that they were two unmarried people who should not be alone together under any circumstance.

Charlotte sighed against him, bewitched. She nearly cried out when Dorset broke the kiss and spoke.

"Are we alone?"

"Yes."

"Thank heavens," he said, bending to bury his face

between her neck and shoulder. Charlotte threaded her arms around his neck and ran her fingers through his thick, glossy hair, pleased that this time, she was the cause of its charming disarray.

Dorset kissed her neck just above the collar of her work dress, tutting with disapproval.

"What's wrong?" Charlotte asked. What could possibly be the matter aside from their disregard of all social convention and what would undoubtedly be her own future heartbreak when she finally accepted that this dashing, eligible gentleman with the wicked mouth and hands as strong as iron would not be hers?

"The collar of this dress is abominably high—I wish to register a complaint with the dressmaker."

"You're speaking to her, my lord. We make all our own dresses." Dorset groaned as he trailed the tip of his nose up the side of her throat, and higher to her earlobe. His warm breath on her skin sent a throbbing sensation through her that settled deep in the pit of her stomach. She shuddered with pleasure as he brushed his lips over the shell of her ear and whispered.

"It's just like you: prim and proper and correct. I withdraw my complaint."

"On what grounds, sir?"

"On the grounds that I will not allow another gentleman to see the skin below this point. It belongs to me, and exists only for my pleasure." At this statement, spoken barely above a guttural whisper, Charlotte nearly collapsed.

"And what about *my* pleasure?" He pulled back and raised to his full height, still holding her by the waist with a nearly bruising grip. Tilting her head back, she met his gaze. Dorset regarded her with a devilish look in his eyes, not unlike the one he gave her just before he had feasted upon her aching flesh in that cellar. She wanted him to do it again, and again.

"Peaches, I am a gentleman. Your pleasure is my responsibility. I would sooner die than disappoint you."

*This man will ruin me.*

*I wish he would hurry up.*

As though he could read her thoughts, Dorset slowly began backing her into the nearest cubicle, which stood waiting with its heavy curtain pulled to the side. Once again, they were found in the throes of passion but without a bed—the velvet-covered chaise propped against the back wall of the fitting room would have to suffice.

Charlotte turned from him and closed the curtain, securing it across the opening so that they would not be seen. Her skin was aflame, and her corset had somehow tightened itself upon her sensitive frame. She wondered if he felt the same—desperate to feel the air and her touch upon his skin.

Turning, she watched as Dorset removed his frock coat and sat down on the chaise like a king upon a throne, his eyes upon her with lupine intensity. He sat with his thick, muscled thighs set apart, so like a man. With one large hand gripping each of his knees, she sensed that he was struggling to maintain his control.

Neither spoke, and Charlotte was unsure how to proceed. She stood before him with her hands threaded behind her back, his face nearly level with her chest. If it weren't for her flushed skin and shallow breath, she appeared the picture of a proper seamstress in her gray poplin dress and gauzy pinafore.

"Do you feel constricted, Peaches?" Again, his voice rumbled through her like a passing wave.

"Yes."

"May I assist you?"

*Yes.*

She nodded in response.

"Turn around, darling."

Charlotte did as she was told, and soon felt the tie at her

waist loosen and fall away. She lifted her pinafore over her head and tossed it to the side.

"Is that better?"

"Not at all, in fact."

"What a shame," he replied. She turned to face him and stepped to within his reach.

"May I assist you with these buttons? There are a great many."

"Certainly."

Slowly, and careful not to pop a single one, Dorset unfastened each button from the top of her prim collar, down to her waist. It was strangely thoughtful of him—did he know that she only possessed the one uniform dress and that popping her buttons would mean lost work and wages? She had the infamous "Lord Corset," ripper of bodices and breaker of hearts, carefully undoing each fabric-covered dome button she had sewn on at the beginning of this year.

This reminder of her station ricocheted through Charlotte's mind like a rifle's report, threatening to quell the growing desire that radiated from her core to her limbs.

*No, not now.*

Dorset had finished with his task. With the sides of her dress now open, she removed her arms from the long sleeves and shimmied out of the garment at the waist, letting it fall around her feet. Charlotte stood before him in her corset, chemise, underthings, and stockings. His lips parted at the sight. He loosened his cravat and began to unbutton his waistcoat, never taking his eyes from her.

What was it that drew them together so powerfully? Now, just as she had each time they had been alone, Charlotte felt an insatiable need for him. She took him in, her eyes lingering on his thick, straining cock, trapped between his trousers and his thigh.

*He feels it, too.*

"Do you see what you do to me, Peaches?" Charlotte blushed at this direct question, and yet she could not look away.

"It's rather difficult to ignore," she replied, trembling. Dorset leaned forward, placed his hands at her waist, and drew her close.

Without turning her around or looking away from her face, he reached behind her back and unfastened the laces of her corset. She made no move to stop him, and let the boned prison fall away. Her nipples hardened to tight peaks, visible beneath her thin chemise.

"Charlotte, I know that we said we would part as friends, that we wouldn't do this again..."

"Yes, I remember," she replied, threading her hands through his hair once again as he rested his head against her stomach.

"It isn't gentlemanly of me, I know, but I do not wish to keep my word," he replied, leaning back and watching her through heavy, hooded eyes.

"What is it that you wish?"

"I wish for you to be bare to me except for your stockings. And I wish for you to do as I tell you, very quietly, so that we do not interrupt the rug beating."

Slowly, Charlotte gathered the hem of her chemise in hand and removed it, tossing it aside. After toeing off her slippers, she did the same with her pantalettes. Dorset leaned forward, mouth agape.

"Peaches, you are the most beautiful woman I have ever seen," he said, reaching for her and bringing her down onto his lap. Charlotte settled herself above him; he drew in a sharp breath as she moved over his solid length.

Charlotte wondered, as he licked his lips with those sapphire eyes riveted to her flushed skin, if he said that to every woman he took to bed. The attention certainly felt genuine, but this was a practiced seducer if one believed the rumors about him. Had she not asked him about his reputation directly? Though it was difficult to remember in that moment, with his hands trailing over her curves, she recalled that Dorset had made no attempt at rebuttal.

Despite the intrusive thought, Dorset's attraction to her made her feel wanton, powerful. She sighed as he kissed her neck and ran his hands up and down her back, settling them with firm pressure on her backside. Could she call this feeling "powerful" if he was the source? Was this confidence not something she possessed all on her own?

"Darling, you must tell me if you want me to stop," he said, more to the sensitive skin of her neck than to her directly. He seemed to love this part of her, and lingered there as she replied.

"Never," she said quietly, on a shaky exhale.

"I mean it: If you feel uncomfortable at any point, do not hesitate to tell me and I shall stop at once," he said clearly, even with his mouth full of her throat and his hands kneading the shapely flesh of her bottom. She couldn't help but rock against him, his hands guiding her as she did so.

Charlotte gasped as Dorset trailed his sinful mouth lower, to the aching tips of her breasts. He remained there, taking his time with her, allowing her to feel each sweep of his tongue and every squeeze of his warm hands to their fullest pleasure. The overall result was intense—she could feel herself softening where Dorset grew harder. She needed him out of his clothes, needed her skin on his, immediately.

She had his shirt off, over his head, and forgotten in seconds. Charlotte ran her hands over his shoulders and down over his chest, dusted with hair and radiating warmth. Leaning back, he allowed her eager hands to explore. He felt solid beneath her touch, but warm, and pulsating—as though ancient gods had breathed life into a marble statue carved to her exact specifications. Still perched on his knees, Charlotte trailed her fingertips over his toned abdomen and lower still, until they reached the waistline of his breeches.

She didn't doubt that the breeches in question had been tailored by the most skilled hands in London. She assumed they were made from the finest cloth available—price would not matter to a viscount. The buttons were horn, each sewn on by hand with care and attention. If she weren't nude and aroused beyond her wildest dreams, she could have estimated their cost more precisely—all she could manage in the moment, however, was that they were dreadfully expensive. Still, with all her knowledge of men's clothing and the hours it had taken to produce these pants, they were, at present, no better to her than the rubbish filling the bins in the alley behind the store.

Moving from his lap to the floor, Charlotte knelt between his feet and removed his polished boots, one at a time. From her place between his knees, she watched as he unfastened the fall of his breeches and slid out of them; unable to resist, she gripped the fabric and freed him fully. To Charlotte's surprise and utter delight, Lord Corset did not wear undergarments.

"Don't be afraid, darling," said Dorset. He looked perfectly at ease, reclined against the back wall of the fitting room, fully nude. Charlotte reached for his thighs and finally felt the warmth of skin, warmth she had so often imagined alone in the dark of night.

"I'm not afraid," she cooed, flexing her fingertips into his muscled legs. He groaned as she slowly kneaded his flesh, making her way up his legs and closer to his veined and throbbing shaft. She took it in her hand and stroked it slowly, its flushed skin like the thinnest velvet stretched taught over steel. He swore under his breath; he was at her mercy.

A bead of liquid formed at his tip as she continued to slowly work her hand over his length. Coming up on her knees, she tasted that salty drop, and then took the swollen head of him fully into her mouth.

"*Christ*, Charlotte," he rasped. His legs tensed on either side of her; every groan seemed to vibrate through her as she sucked, licked, and teased. After a time, Dorset sat up—with great effort, it seemed. She released his member from her mouth but continued to lazily stroke his slick length. He helped her to her feet, then placed her where he had sat just moments before. After a lingering kiss, he spoke, his lips so close to her own.

"Charlotte, you honor me with your attention, but ever since the cellar, I've thought of nothing else. I intend to taste you again," he said, his voice a low rumble.

"Please," she whispered. Their lips met as he eased her down onto her back before parting her legs. The last time he had done this, she had cried out in ecstasy. If she made a sound now, they risked discovery—and disgrace. Would she risk harming Madame Beaumont's spotless reputation for a few moments of fleeting pleasure?

"We mustn't make a sound," she said, as quietly as she could. He was kissing her neck now as he settled between her legs on the floor before her. Slowly, he made his way down to her aching breasts, to her navel, and finally, to her sex, swollen now with unsatisfied need. His beard, no doubt freshly shaved each morning, had won the day's battle. The grit of his skin against hers sent shivers through her body. Gently, he parted her folds, gleaming even in the dim light with evidence of her arousal.

"I think you'll find that it's *you* who mustn't make a sound, Peaches. I shall muzzle myself." And muzzle he did, starting at her opening before taking her engorged clitoris in his mouth and lavishing it with searing, unbearable strokes.

Charlotte clapped a hand over her mouth to keep from crying out. Just as before, she was consumed with pleasure, and it wasn't long before she felt her release building. Like crashing waves, the feelings overtook her; she lost herself to the pulses of her climax, hoping that no one below stairs had a moment to stop and wonder what the seamstress and the gentleman were up to.

As her vision returned, she propped herself up on her elbows and regarded Dorset, still at her feet on the floor, sitting back on his feet and stroking himself in earnest now. He held her eye contact with such intensity as he did so that she did not dare look away. Through gritted teeth, he spoke.

"In my coat pocket," he said, chest heaving now, "my handkerchief." Realization dawned and Charlotte scrambled to join him on the floor, where she found his coat discarded in the pile of their entangled clothes. Searching through the interior, she found the breast pocket and the handkerchief tucked neatly within, embroidered in one corner with a violet.

Quickly, Charlotte handed it to him and watched, transfixed, as he reached his own climax, spending into the handkerchief. She knew that they could not join without risking pregnancy, but she wondered how it would feel to receive his full size, and how the pulsations of his orgasm would mirror her own.

*You must never find out for sure, lest you suffer the same fate as your mother.*

The thought washed over her like a bucket of cold water, dropped from above without warning. She did not fear that Dorset would penetrate her against her will—she feared that she would beg him to, and would enjoy it so thoroughly and so often that the inevitable would happen: another baby, born on the wrong side of the blanket.

Dorset reached for her, and drew her into a crushing embrace. She must fight the feelings of warmth and comfort that she found here, in his arms. For while she knew that there was a glimmer of possibility that she was the half-sister of a duke and therefore much nearer to a respectable wife than she had been the last time they spoke, *he* did not know that. To him, she was still a seamstress of unknown birth.

Withdrawing from his arms, she reached for their clothes and began to dress. She knew her hair was mussed and surely, she bore the telltale signs of his beard against her cheek and lips. She would need to usher him out the back, and quickly.

"We must hurry if we're to escape notice," she said, hurrying into her underthings before stepping into her dress. He moved more slowly than she did, so like a gentleman—no sense of urgency because there were never any consequences for their actions.

"Charlotte…," before he could continue, Charlotte held a finger to her lips and peeked out from behind the curtain. They were still alone, and the clatter from below indicated that the rug beating was still underway. She must get him out of here, without a trace. Searching the floor of the fitting room, she gathered her shoes and pinafore, replacing all of the items to their proper place.

Dorset had seemed reluctant to dress and leave, but his sense had returned. He had abandoned his cravat and fastened only a selection of buttons at his collar, but his breeches and boots were respectable. Charlotte thrust the greatcoat he had tossed aside back into his arms and led him through the door to the staff stairs. She would never dream of taking a civilian through these narrow passageways, but at the tousled and flushed sight of them, there would be no doubt about how they had spent their time. Thankfully, they met no one and reached the door to the back alley without question.

"Charlotte, will you be all right? May I see you home?" Dorset asked. With his shirt unbuttoned at the neck and without his cravat, she could see his pulse rioting there, his muscles working as he swallowed.

"No, thank you. I must fetch my things from inside, and

my cloak. I shall hire a hack," she replied awkwardly, unsure how she should address him now. He called her Charlotte, but she knew she could not entertain such a friendly arrangement. "Thank you, my lord." His brow furrowed, like storm clouds rolling in without warning across a clear sky. He understood.

"You are very welcome. Goodnight, Miss Price."

*Goodbye.*

# CHAPTER 13

The next morning, Charlotte awoke to an empty room. She could hear Sarah through the thin wall, tending to the fire that just barely kept them warm. Charlotte pictured her friend, stooped low to avoid hitting her head on the slanted beams of the garret ceiling as she stoked the coals in the small grate.

She'd dreamt about Dorset that previous night, after she had returned safely home and trudged up the many stairs to her bed, exhausted. Almost as soon as she closed her eyes, he was there, running his hands through her hair and whispering beguiling nonsense into her ear.

*The skin below this point belongs to me...*

*I wish for you to be bare to me except for your stockings...*

*Peaches, you are the most beautiful woman I've ever seen...*

There's no way the last was true—Charlotte wasn't a swooning schoolgirl, easily led down the primrose path. She had marched down that path hand in strong hand with Dorset, once again unable to resist his pull toward her own emotional ruin.

The viscount was only one of two reasons Charlotte felt

unsettled that morning. The other, of course, was her potential impending ladyship. She rolled onto her side, pulled her threadbare quilt up around her chin to keep out the chill, and wondered what life would be like if she could install herself in a home like the Sutton Abbey. Sarah entered.

"You were so late returning last night, I didn't want to wake you," she said, slipping behind the screen in the corner to dress.

"I hope you didn't wait up for me," Charlotte replied, idly twisting a loose quilt thread and letting her gaze fall on the small, grimy window tucked so near the roofline that it provided them little light, even on a rare sunny day.

*When was the last time we spent a sunny day away from the shop?*

"I knew better than that, you were in one of your moods," said Sarah, doing up her buttons. "Did you manage to measure every yard in the store?"

"Not even close. I got distracted"

"Distracted? That's not like you, Lottie."

"True, although I had rather a lot to mull over," she replied, sitting up in bed. It wouldn't do to remain prone like some kind of invalid; decisions must be made, and an important one was just beginning to form, deep within the depths of her mind. "I'd barely started when Madame came and found me."

"Did you tell her about the duke?"

"Indeed, I did. She's thrilled for me," said Charlotte. She got up, crossed the room to the wash basin in the corner, and dipped her hands into the cool water. As she rinsed her face and then patted her skin dry with a thin cloth, Sarah emerged from behind the screen.

"We're all thrilled for you, Lottie. Or, we're prepared to be, that is." Charlotte could sense that her friend was being careful not to press her. What Sarah didn't realize was that Charlotte no longer needed convincing.

The stark contrast between their dark, decrepit home and the lofty opulence of Sutton Abbey had shocked Charlotte upon her return. Even as the illegitimate sister of a playboy duke, she could change the lives of those closest to her easily; Sarah would never again have to scrimp and save for new spectacles. They would always have coal for a fire, as long as Charlotte lived to ensure that Sarah's coffers were full. With a little strategy, she might even be able to help others like them in need. After all, money did solve problems, and due to pure luck, she could have more than she ever dreamed of—more than she would ever need.

"Well, I suppose congratulations are in order, Sarah," she said, replacing the damp towel on its hook near the shallow, chipped basin. "If the duke can find these supposed letters, I've decided to accept him." Sarah crossed the room and threw her arms around her, a gesture of friendship, and, Charlotte sensed, of relief.

The clatter of horse's hooves arose outside, followed soon by a swift knock on the street-facing door of their boarding house. Their landlady, who hated being disturbed, would not be pleased.

"Who could that be?" asked Sarah. Visitors weren't expressly forbidden, but they were not encouraged.

"Probably a peddler," Charlotte replied, dressing for the day. "One who doesn't yet know not to disturb Mrs. Jukes before she's had her third cuppa."

"The poor fool will soon learn."

The knock was answered, and a muffled conversation ensued. Before long, there were heavy footsteps on the stairs, and another knock—this time, upon their door. Charlotte finished with her final buttons just in time to rush to the door with Sarah. It was Mrs. Jukes; as expected, she was less than thrilled.

"Girls, there's a toff waitin', blockin' the street in 'is carriage! I told 'is man to shove off, I did, as my Simon won't be able to fit froo wif 'his pony cart, and I'm expectin' 'im back any second now, aren't I? Simon's been gone a week, I can't have 'im delayed, can I?"

"Certainly not, Mrs. Jukes. Did the gentleman say what he wanted?" asked Charlotte. Although her heart beat in her throat at the mention of "a toff" waiting for her in the street, she hadn't yet given Dorset her direction—the only possible gentlemen downstairs this morning would be Markby.

"Miz Price, I don't 'ave the time this morning to receive messages on your be'ahf, do I?" replied Mrs. Jukes, color rising in her formidable cheeks. "I'm waitin' for Simon to get back 'ome safe and I need that toff cleared out! There's no room for the pony cart, 'ees blockin' up the whole road!"

"Certainly, Mrs. Jukes. We'll get him on his way, won't we Lottie?" said Sarah, who thrust a cloak and bonnet into Charlotte's arms and moved them all out the door and into the small stairwell.

The three women marched down single file. Mrs. Jukes kept up her protestations and Sarah gamely soothed her as they descended, leaving Charlotte to realize that depending on what her brother the toff had to say, she and Sarah were potentially walking down these stairs and out the door for the final time.

Sure enough, it had been Markby's carriage blocking the road. He was his usual self that morning, all manners and impish charm as they rolled out of Cheapside, past Covent Garden, and then Hyde Park before slowing in front of a stately Kensington manse.

The interiors reminded Charlotte of Stapleton: gleaming, ornate, and pristine. It was a far cry from the garret they had just left, somehow worlds away but just across London. Markby offered Sarah his arm and led her through the halls, pausing occasionally to point out a painting here, or a clock there, never once letting his attention stray from the bespectacled seamstress at his side. Charlotte expected that this was more for her benefit than for Sarah's, and when he turned and gave her a small wink and smile, she sensed that he knew she would need a moment to take in the sumptuous surroundings without fanfare. She was grateful to him.

*Brother.*

Their stroll led them at last to Markby's study, a room clearly designed for the important work of duking. Charlotte assumed this meant issues of land usage, horseflesh, household budgets, perhaps hiding opera singers from duchesses? It seemed the ideal conditions for this important and regal work were dark wood panels and towering bookcases, jewel-toned wall papers with gilt peacock feather print, and a great oak desk where Markby, and his father, and his father's father and on and on had sat and managed all.

*Not just Markby's father's father...mine as well.*

"I do not wish to wait even a moment longer, ladies," said Markby, settling them in chairs facing the family desk, which he then took his place behind. "I've received the news we've been searching for: the proof that you, Charlotte, or shall I adopt Miss Ludlow's most charming appellation and call you Lottie as well? I think I shall try it! Lottie, we've contacted the legal people, and they've confirmed what I'd hoped. They've even sent me a letter from our late father to his man of business that seals it."

He opened a calfskin-bound journal and removed a delicate piece of parchment, and slid it over to Charlotte. She unfolded it and read the swooping, slanted script aloud:

*"Hawkins,*

*It is with the deepest sorrow that I write to inform you of the death of Miss Catherine Price. As you remember, she has been receiving £2,000 per annum at my request, for although she refused my proposal of marriage, I wanted to ensure her safety and comfort. Miss Price cut off contact with me before I could confirm my dearest hope; I have reason to believe that when we parted, she was with child. Her reason for ending our connection was that she wished to shield me from social scorn...as though I cared a damn.*

*I know that you will not regret her death, as you objected entirely to my support of dear Catherine, initially and many times over the years since. I will tell you now what I did not explain then, too heartbroken to admit the truth: I loved her. I loved her more than I thought possible. My years spent in her company were the happiest of my life following the death of the duchess, and I regret to this day that I could not make her my wife and stepmother to young Master Richard. And what of the child she feared we had conceived? If only I could have given my son a family...*

*I am beginning to feel keenly the ravages of age, Hawkins, and as I grow wiser, I know that this love was nothing to hide, nor to be ashamed of. I wish I could look into her eyes and tell her one last time, for the world to hear, "Catherine, I love you."*

*Alas, as I cannot cross into the River Styx until Death comes to collect me, I must make one final request regarding this matter: I request that you transfer a lump sum of £5,000 to one Madame Celeste Beaumont of London in complete anonymity. You shall see to this personally, with your usual discretion, explaining only to Madame Beaumont that she should accept it in memory of Catherine, and with eternal gratitude from someone who loved her friend.*

*As always, I remain,*
*Your Servant,*
*Gerald, Duke of Sutton*
*Sutton Abbey"*

So there it was—in her father's own hand. He had loved her mother, and would have raised her if her mother had allowed him. There was so much she wished she could ask her mother, so much she would say. Tears beaded in the corners of her eyes as she folded the paper carefully.

"I don't know what to say," she said feebly.

"Say, 'Thank you, brother, for finding this iron clad proof of our blood relation! I shall move in at once,'" said Markby, the scamp. Charlotte imagined that he had been just as impish and charming as a youngster—no doubt a headache for the nanny. Sarah giggled.

"Of course she's moving in, your grace," she said, "she told me just this morning before you arrived." Markby turned to Charlotte, aghast.

"You mean I don't need to beg? I was prepared to, you know."

"No, you don't need to beg. However, you must remember: I am my mother's daughter and must consider practical matters," Charlotte said, not wanting to deflate his rising tide of joy but knowing that she must.

"And what of those matters?" asked Markby, leaning back in his tufted chair now, looking not unlike a young man playing pretend at his father's desk.

"Much in the way that my mother sought to shield your father from scorn, will my existence not tarnish your name? We cannot print and distribute this private letter, and I know what the *ton* is like. Are you not worried that I will ruin you?" asked Charlotte.

"Sister, you might be intimately acquainted with the ladies of London, but you have much to learn regarding ducal privilege," he replied, not concerned in the least. He went on, "there aren't many of us—dukes, that is—and the even fewer of us who are unmarried enjoy a certain status amongst those same ladies you dress. Nothing can ruin an eligible duke, Charlotte."

"I only wish my mother had understood that," she replied, knowing that of course he was correct. No mother with a daughter out would dare question him, although they would have a field day behind closed doors.

"What a happy day for you both," said Sarah. She removed her spectacles and cleaned them with her handkerchief before replacing them and reaching for the letter to read it herself. "And this explains how Madame built a dress shop as grand as a palace."

"Indeed," said Markby, standing. "Now, to important matters," he said, beaming. Would you like a tour of your new home?"

"I'd love one."

"Wonderful. After you."

# Chapter 14

Dorset skipped breakfast and dressed as quickly as possible that morning, opting instead for a cup of his favorite Assam tea, enjoyed in one searing swallow as Stilton helped him into his jacket. He'd received a note from Markby, delivered by footman, that had him concerned.

*"Come at once—we need another man. Utmost importance, do not delay. - Markby"*

Not only had Markby signed with his surname rather than his usual dashed-off "Richard," there wasn't a nicety or ribald remark to be found. The footman who delivered it had no further insight, but it seemed serious, and Dorset feared the worst: a duel.

Thomas had the mare mounted and ready as Dorset flew down the path through the garden that led to the stables. He had to get to Markby's home quickly—negotiations would soon begin, and as Markby's second, it was down to Dorset to keep them from certain catastrophe in an open field at dawn. Was his friend the challenger, or the challenged? His mind raced with the possibilities as nervous sweat gathered on his brow and unshaven upper lip.

The horse may have been overkill—their townhomes were separated only by the expanse of the Kensington Gardens, but the bustle of mid-morning London prevented Dorset from driving the horse faster than a trot. He cursed those blocking his way, but it wouldn't do to panic, not when his dearest friend was less than a day away from facing down the barrel of a pistol.

*What will I tell Em? If he doesn't get himself killed, she'll finish the job.*

Markby's townhome came into view at last, with no outward signs of impending doom. With his horse safely in the hands of a groom, Dorset dashed up the steps and was greeted by the one and only Hanson, the only butler in all of England who seemed more disapproving than his own Mr. Barlow. Dorset steadied himself on the doorframe as he caught his breath.

"Hanson, what's happened? Is he inside?" Dorset asked, breathing heavily.

"Good morning, my lord. If you are referring to His Grace, yes, he is in residence. I believe he is in the ballroom." Dorset entered and Hanson took his hat.

"The ballroom? Whatever for?" asked Dorset. Hanson regarded him with suspicion, as usual.

"I expect he is there awaiting your arrival, my lord," said the butler, betraying nothing. Dorset set off in that direction and offered hurried thanks to Hanson. It was time to get to the bottom of this.

Making his way to the ballroom, Dorset's unease increased. Why could he hear the faint strains of music playing? Voices were chattering from within the great room, echoing as though it was mostly empty. He reached for the handle to the great double doors, but before he could grasp it, they opened. Sure enough, it was Markby. The duke didn't notice Dorset at first—his head was turned and he was speaking to someone inside.

"—yes, I know that, Em, fill in for me and I'll return at once—Oh! Nicky, what are you doing here?" With genuine puzzlement on his face, Markby angled himself so that Dorset could not see inside of the ballroom, nor any of its inhabitants. But why would he move to conceal Emmeline? Dorset swore under his breath and prayed that the conflict did not concern her.

"You mean to tell me you don't know?" asked Dorset, flummoxed. Emmeline appeared, prying the door open from Markby's side. They both looked ever so slightly disheveled, with flushed cheeks. Curious...

"Hello, brother. I see you received my summons," she said.

"Yours? No, I received a rather terse note from Markby asking for my aid at once," he replied.

"That's impossible Nicky, I didn't send a note," said Markby.

"You most certainly did. It was on your stationery, delivered by your footman, and signed with your name."

"No, no, no, *I* sent the note. It was from *me*," said Emmeline.

"Emmeline, if there is to be a duel, this is no time for frivolity—" said Dorset, cutting her off.

"A duel? Who said anything about a duel?" she replied.

"Dorset, have you been challenged? How much time do we have? I must fetch the pistols at once—"

"No, *I* haven't been challenged, have *you*?"

"What?!"

"Oh, for God's sake, neither of you has been challenged. There is no duel! I sent for you this morning, and I knew if I signed with Markby's name that you'd actually show. We need another man," replied Emmeline impatiently, as though her statement made perfect sense.

"And what, pray tell, do you need another man for? Could you not locate one on the premises?" asked Dorset, annoyed with his sister for worrying him but quietly relieved that neither he, nor Markby, would be up with the sun, guns loaded.

"Not just *any* man. We require a gentleman—for dance lessons of course," she said, suddenly fascinated by a bit of stitching on the cuff of her sleeve.

"Dance lessons? For whom?" he asked. There weren't any children in either the Markby or Dorset families at present, and even if there were, qualified teachers usually handled such business.

"This isn't how I wanted to tell you, Nicky," said Markby, looking for once in his life sincere. Dorset turned to Emmeline. Once again, in the masterful way of his family's women, she had managed them both with ease.

"Don't look so upset, brother. I think you'll be quite pleased," she said. Moving aside, she gave Markby room to open the door and lead him into the ballroom, where a curious but beautiful sight greeted him: Charlotte, conversing in a corner with some string players who were no doubt the source of the music Dorset had heard in the halls just minutes earlier. At the sound of their approach, she turned, and her eyes grew wide. As that familiar shade of peach rose on her cheeks, Dorset felt sunlight fill his chest. They must have found their proof; she had accepted her brother.

"Nicky, may I present to you my sister, Miss Charlotte Price."

"You most certainly may," he replied under his breath. As she rose from a prim and reserved curtsy, he stepped forward, took her hand, and raised it to his lips. Lips she had kissed dozens of times.

"It's a pleasure to meet you, Lord Dorset," she replied, gazing up at him through her thick lashes, as lush as mink. Dorset held tight to her hand, fearing that if he released it, she would vanish once again. But why had she felt the need to greet him as though they had never met, and with a curtsy no less? Just as he thought it, she answered his question, although indirectly.

"Was that alright? It still feels so unnatural," she said to Emmeline and Markby, who stood apart from them with discerning eyes. It was becoming clear now; Charlotte had begun her training.

*Lady lessons.*

"You're doing splendidly, Charlotte," replied Emmeline.

"Are you sure? It feels so forced," she said, dropping from Dorset's grip and smoothing her skirts, ignoring the slack-mouthed viscount completely. Markby, clearly the assistant to Em's head teacher, chimed in.

"Well, you know this one already, don't you, Lottie? It will feel less awkward on the day, I'm sure of it," he said.

"On the day?" asked Dorset, realizing that he had joined today's lesson many hours into its progress. He must make a note to have Stilton wake him earlier.

"Our parents' ball, of course. It's to be Charlotte's official introduction," said Emmeline, raising her chin in Dorset's direction. Ah, yes, the Stapleton Ball, where no doubt, his parents expected him to escort Tabitha Crampton, and where he was sure that the unattached lords and the gossips and all of their nosy mothers would be drooling for a chance to get their hands on the Duke of Sutton's newly discovered half-sister.

*Fresh meat.*

"Yes, I think you're right, I won't truly know until I meet a new one," said Charlotte, pulling Dorset from his rioting imagination and back to the nearly empty ballroom. She had once scoffed at him for offering her his protection—he knew now that he must provide it to her at any cost, for they would stop at nothing to tear her apart.

Just as he opened his mouth to make his intentions known, the violinist present gently cleared their throat.

"Excuse me, Your Grace, Lady Emmeline—shall we pick up where we left off with the waltz now that Lord Dorset has joined us?"

"A splendid idea, thank you. We mustn't waste any more time," replied Emmeline. "Markby, I'm afraid you must settle for me this time. Let us give Charlotte and my brother a chance to dazzle us all." She took her place near the center of the room. His friend did not object, and joined her there, leaving Dorset and Charlotte to follow.

He turned to her, the woman he had been so transfixed by, soon to be made a member of "polite" society that would ravage her if they weren't careful. He would do his best to prepare her, and would annihilate any man, woman, or Crampton who threatened the happiness of this remarkable person. Assuming the visage of a respectable gentleman attending a ball, he turned to her.

"Miss Price, may I have this dance?" he asked, with a slight and very proper bow in her direction. Gamely, she replied.

"You most certainly may, my lord," Charlotte said, offering him her hand. He led her to the dance floor where they joined Emmeline and Markby, who had already taken their places in each other's arms, looking rather comfortable at that. Dorset thought nothing of it—they three had attended scores of balls between them. Dancing a Viennese waltz would be as simple as walking for them by now.

The opening strains of music rang out in the cavernous room, not dampened by the usual crush of people. It would be easy for them to speak without being overheard, but he only had a few minutes until the piece ended—he must make himself plain, and quickly. Luckily, Charlotte danced well, if stiffly.

"Forgive me, I must fight the urge to look down at my own feet only to find them obscured by my skirts," she said, her gaze level with his throat. He let out a warm, low chuckle at her confession.

"When paired with a competent partner, you won't have to worry yourself. Your skirts will hide any imprecise foot-work, although I think you'll find 'on the day' that the free-flowing champagne will prevent any critics from looking too closely," he said, tightening his grip on her back. Dorset liked the feeling of her warmth through the fabric of her dress. He flexed his hand there as if to memorize it.

"I'm afraid those critics will need something stronger than champagne if they're to look the other way. I'm a walking scandal," she replied.

"You seem to be a waltzing one. You're doing quite well, Peaches," he replied, his voice a husky whisper so that only she could hear.

They stepped and twirled across the empty floor, performing a perfectly passable waltz with Dorset there to lead her. He suspected that she had been a good student, and as he felt her relax and grow more confident with each pass, he decided to make his intentions known.

"These balls, they can be quite difficult if one is not prepared," he said.

"Don't bother. Your sister and my brother have given me the same talk, both separately and together," she said with a small smile. "I don't think anything about this ball will be more difficult than poverty, do you?" A direct hit, for what did he know of poverty? Only that he didn't truly know what she had endured before his mother had practically stolen her from Beaumont's.

"Forgive me, of course you're correct. I only wish to offer my help as well," he said.

"And what exactly would you aim to help me with? What is it that I'm lacking?" she asked, her tone good-natured though forward.

"Not lacking, Charlotte," he said, his tone lower, and private. "That's just the problem. You possess everything and more: a scandalous and much-rumoured history, the *ton's* most notorious duke for a brother—"

"Oh, is that all? And here I was, assuming it would be a lovely evening," she said with a small laugh. "I'm quite aware of my position as an object of fascination."

"Then you must let me be your escort, as I am easily the most fascinated of all," Dorset said, keenly aware that their waltz would soon end, as would their private audience. At his suggestion, the peach deepened, but her placid demeanor did not falter. She was learning well.

"Are you not promised to escort Miss Crampton? I don't wish to invite scandal to your family home, and on my first night out, at that," she said, meeting his eyes with a playful smile.

"Haven't you learned by now? The best balls are the ones with something improper to talk about. Let it be us, dancing only together, to the chagrin of the lords and Cramptons alike."

Before she could give him an answer, the music waned. They parted politely, as one would in such a setting. He bowed, and she dipped, looking completely respectable.

"Well done, Charlotte, you dance beautifully," said Emmeline.

"You flatter me, thank you. I'm grateful to you all for your help," Charlotte replied. "You've taught me enough that your brother believes me a competent dancing partner."

"Indeed, I do," Dorset said. He couldn't leave it to chance

any longer. "My compliments to her teachers, for I intend to fill her dance card and enjoy the fruits of your labors as Miss Price's escort."

He was met with silence. From Markby, a puzzled, furrowed brow, no doubt weighing his closest friend's intentions with the reputation of his new sister, a responsibility he had gained whether he cared for it or not. Emmeline, unreadable as ever but pleased, like a cat who had just trapped her mouse before unleashing the final, lethal pounce. He was sure that she had hoped for this outcome all along.

And finally, Charlotte. She met his gaze with quiet determination. Something worked just below the surface as she calculated. What he would give to know her innermost thoughts...

*Everything.*

"Thank you, Lord Dorset. I shall be delighted."

# CHAPTER 15

With waltzing mastered, her tutors decided that it was time now for Charlotte to learn, from the privacy of the garden, how to properly promenade. Why one must learn how to take a walk, Charlotte did not know; clearly, the tutelage was necessary.

"The most important thing to remember is that you are constantly on display. Carry yourself as though all eyes are upon you, and never exert yourself," said Emmeline, walking with queenly posture and a pleasant, perfectly respectable expression. "Never let them find a flaw. Any betrayal of discomfort is like throwing meat to a tiger."

"Em, if you keep talking like that, you'll terrify her," replied Markby, who was walking next to Dorset, behind the two ladies. Emmeline did not turn around when she replied.

"Nonsense, she must know what to expect, Markby."

"You're quite right—I should like to be prepared for the worst," said Charlotte, doing her best to imitate Emmeline's signature tranquility.

They continued on down a winding path, at a pace just slower than glacial. This was fashionable, apparently. It seemed that the purpose of these strolls was not to arrive to a destination in a timely manner, but to be seen by as many posh onlookers as possible. The fresh air was a mere bonus.

"You will, of course, be sure to always be accompanied by your brother, who I do not doubt will be glad to act as chaperone whenever you wish."

"Emmeline is correct. You mustn't be seen in Hyde Park without me. I've never been anyone's chaperone before, and I won't miss my chance." Markby had to shout; he and Dorset were falling behind the ladies, who continued walking along the garden path.

"I never would have expected such a large garden, right in the middle of Kensington," said Charlotte, idly looking out over the perfectly kept lawns.

"Excellent, Charlotte," replied Emmeline, ever the consummate teacher. "Conversations must be mundane and innocuous. You will doubtless have eavesdroppers. And you're quite right, your ancestors secured quite a bit of land in their time."

"It's beautiful," said Charlotte. "But all this space, for so few people."

"Don't you worry, dear. Once you've been introduced, your brother will hold a celebration so large that you won't be able to see a single blade of grass. It shall put Vauxhall to shame," replied Emmeline, missing Charlotte's point entirely. Surely, this space could house hundreds comfortably. A school, a hospital? No. Instead, rolling lawns, a hedge maze, and rose gardens, all for the private enjoyment of the Markby family, which currently consisted of just two people.

"One could even imagine a wedding party," Emmeline said. "You'll be married in the church, no doubt, but there's something romantic about being married from home, isn't there? Especially a home like this. Were you christened, or should we make the arrangements?"

"Forgive me, Emmeline, but I wouldn't call this conversation 'innocuous,'" said Charlotte. She felt herself flush at the thought of a wedding.

*You mustn't appear upset; the tiger is circling.*

"My apologies, Charlotte, of course it isn't. But when I see you waltz with my brother, and accept his escort to the ball, the mind does wander."

Charlotte couldn't pretend that the thought had not occurred to her. She was a lady now, whatever that meant. She still felt like the same person, even if her brother had ordered her new dresses and given her a new home to live in. They'd decided it was best to not tell the duke that she and Sarah had made those dresses—Charlotte's final order as a Beaumont seamstress.

Sarah had elected to keep her position at the shop, which did not surprise Charlotte in the least. Dressmaking was her passion, and she was a true artist, taught at Madame Beaumont's right hand. Charlotte had learned the craft out of necessity, but for Sarah, it was so much more. Her work kept her from days like these, wandering gardens and dancing in empty ballrooms, but these were the sad practicalities of Charlotte's new life. It would take them time to adjust to seeing each other so much less.

*I wonder if Sarah will make my wedding dress as well.*

"You mustn't forget that your brother and I agreed to never marry on the day of our unfortunate first meeting," said Charlotte, remembering the topic at hand.

"Yes, and as far as I've heard, he swore the same to my parents. I blame the hangover."

Turning a corner, the ladies came to a small pavilion. The table within was laid with a tea service, no doubt brought by the footman dutifully standing off to the side. Without a word, the young man helped them into the two available chairs, which gave them an unobstructed view of the garden beyond—a beautifully trimmed lawn, like the richest green velvet. Hedgerows lined either side of the expanse, with a Grecian statue that Charlotte could not name in the distance. Charlotte thought she heard the faint sound of children's laughter, carried on the light breeze.

"How strange, I thought I just heard a child," she said, reaching for the teapot to pour for them both. As the lady of the house, it was her responsibility, even if it felt unnatural to have tea out of doors in the middle of what would have been her usual workday.

"I'm sure you did, Markby's cook has a brood. Curly heads and rosy cheeks, little cherubs."

"I still need to meet them. I haven't been down to the kitchens yet," said Charlotte, teapot safely settled again on the small table. "Markby told me that the three of you would sneak down for biscuits."

"I would never admit to such behavior, although I expect that may be where our companions wandered off to," Emmeline replied, smiling. She had settled back in her chair, with saucer in her left hand and raised teacup in her right, eyes focused on the middle distance. "When we return later, I'll show you where Mrs. Appleby keeps them."

"My most important lesson yet, I shan't forget it," Charlotte replied.

"Indeed, they're delicious," said Emmeline. The sounds of laughter met them once again, closer this time. "I suspect that the gentlemen are about to rejoin us," she said, and sure enough, Markby sprung into view.

Somewhere between the time they had last seen him and this moment, he had lost his jacket. A small child, the age of five at Charlotte's estimate, chased after him with a worn leather cricket ball in hand, which he tossed out onto the grass before them. The man and the youngster had matching flushed cheeks, as though they'd been playing for some time.

"They're always so good with the young ones," said Emmeline, her eyes softening. From around the corner of the path, more laughter—Dorset, sans jacket like his friend, emerged with a young girl sitting atop his shoulders. Her small, puffy fists held tightly to his temples, a beatific smile on her face.

While the older boy played with Markby, tossing the ball back and forth, back and forth, neither of them tiring, Dorset lifted his charge from his shoulders and settled her in his arms so that she could watch her brother play. Charlotte guessed that the girl was between the ages of two and three. Too young for the raucous game being played before them, but old enough to want to join in on the fun.

"Mrs. Appleby's cherubs, I presume?" asked Charlotte, transfixed by the scene before her. The little girl looked so small in Dorset's arms, perched in the crook of his elbow. He pointed to the game before them, speaking in her ear. Whatever he said made her laugh with infectious delight.

Charlotte had never seen a man holding a child; surely this was not common behavior for a gentleman. Dorset held the girl with the ease of a nursemaid; when the child leaned into his shoulder, he patted her back and gently stroked the fawn colored curls on the back of her small head. Charlotte knew it went against Emmeline's teachings, but she could not help but stare.

"There's something about seeing him play with them," said Emmeline, breaking Charlotte's reverie. She was just as transfixed, with her attentions on Markby, of course. Both women came dangerously near to open gawking.

"Is it usual for gentlemen to play with the staff's children?" asked Charlotte, her pulse quickening as Dorset continued to elate the little girl in his arms.

"Not at all, no. It is unusual for gentlemen to play with children at all, including their own. But Markby tends to do things differently than most dukes, and I daresay that those two revert to their school days when they're together. Overgrown boys, the pair of the them."

"It is rather charming, isn't it?"

"It is, and we must never tell them—we can't have them using these powers against us, can we?" replied Emmeline with a knowing smile. Charlotte blushed.

"It must have been great fun for the three of you, to play in such a grand place as children?"

"Markby and my brother were kind enough to let me follow along. I adored them both, and bless them—they were patient, even as rowdy boys. I think Dorset felt a certain responsibility," said Emmeline.

"Of course he felt responsible, you are his sister," Charlotte replied.

"Oh no, not for me...for Markby. He seemed determined, even when we were very young, to make Markby feel like he belonged with us, and that he wasn't all alone."

Charlotte felt the familiar ache in her chest as Emmeline went on, regaling her with tales of their childhood. Grand games of hide and seek that seemed to last for days, late night trips to the kitchens to beg the cook at the time for cocoa, an unfortunate incident involving a daring rescue from a murky pond—it all sounded like a monied dream. While Charlotte had been sent away to the boarding school, they were climbing trees and skipping stones on their school holidays. What could have been if her father had found her?

The little girl began to fuss, so Dorset set her down and watched her toddle away toward her brother and his two-man game of catch. Markby deftly tossed Dorset the ball in one graceful movement, which Dorset caught easily with one hand.

"Come, let us all play together," he said, close enough now for the ladies to hear. "Caleb, we must include your sister."

"But Annie's too little, sir. I don't want her to play," said the boy.

"Caleb, someday she will be grown, and take my word for it. It's a much better life having your sister as your friend, isn't that right, Markby?"

"That's right! And I have one of my own now, so I can confirm this is true," replied Markby. The two men sat on the ground and began rolling the ball back and forth between them, as the two children ran about, trying to catch it. Caleb even let his sister succeed, with a cheer for her when she did.

Two gentlemen, without jackets or hats, sitting on grass without so much as a cushion beneath them, playing with children in the middle of the day; Emmeline was not lying when she said that Markby did things differently than most dukes. For the first time, Charlotte felt well and truly lucky. These were good people who cared for each other.

"I must admit, I have not seen this side of him," she said.

"Dorset would never admit it, but he cares a great deal. But it isn't fashionable, so he must keep up the façade," replied Emmeline. She refilled their teacups and stirred a spoonful of sugar into her own.

"Façade?" asked Charlotte.

"Yes, 'Lord Corset,'" Emmeline replied, taking a sip. "It's nonsense, of course. He's the same little boy who taught me how to climb trees and sneak biscuits, and who stayed with Markby for days when your father died." Charlotte elected not to share the origin of the name, or the circumstances under which she heard the story: wrapped in Dorset's dressing gown and moments away from kissing him for the first time.

"If I were a suspicious person, I would begin to think you were trying to influence me," said Charlotte, smiling. Emmeline had made no secret that he wished to see them wed, and watching Dorset dote on young children stirred primal feelings deep within Charlotte, feelings that she could not help.

She imagined him at her bedside, with a baby in his arms—
their baby. Would the child have his blue eyes? She hoped so,
with all her heart.

Before long, it was time to return the children to the
house, where young Caleb was due for his afternoon lessons,
given by a tutor that Markby provided to all the children of
the staff of his home—another new detail that softened Charlotte further. Emmeline walked beside Markby with Caleb
between them, holding each of their hands as they went.
Dorset fell in with Charlotte, once again carrying little Annie,
who had dozed off against his chest, exhausted from the
excitement.

"I rather feel as tired as Annie," said Charlotte, stealing a
glance at the little one. "My teachers have been very thorough
today."

"Waltzing in the morning before a turn in the garden and
afternoon tea...it can't be more tiring than a day at Beaumont's, can it?" he asked. Their pace slowed, allowing them to
speak without the party ahead hearing them.

"Not physically, no, but it is a lot to remember. No one
has ever cared so much about my deportment," replied Charlotte. "I rather feel that I'm being fattened and led to
slaughter."

"Ah, yes, the ball. You may feel like livestock being sent
through a country gate in the crush, but try not to worry. I'll
be there to protect you from the butcher's knife," he said, as
though her formal debut in a society that almost certainly
would not accept her was no cause for concern.

"When you phrase it that way, it only makes me feel worse,
I'm afraid," she replied, unable to look at him without smiling.
His skin was aglow, flushed from the activity and the sunlight.

She was close enough now to breathe him in, that intoxicating scent so unique to him. It began to cloud her thoughts;
she wanted to congratulate his perfumer for their talents, for

they had perfectly blended the notes of leather and cedar that were so familiar to her now. Charlotte felt sure that a bottle of this potion could conjure him from thin air, whenever she wished. When he spoke, he roused her from her reverie.

"When I returned to town from Sutton, I heard rumors," he said, hesitating before he went on. "Rumors I desperately hoped were true."

"I asked Markby not to tell you. I'd hoped I'd get the chance to tell you myself," she replied. "I suppose the good news traveled rather quickly."

"He did his best, don't be upset with him. It was known in London that an unnamed person had joined the family, but when he told me that he had a sister but would not name her... you must forgive me for demanding he confirm my hopes."

"Your hopes?" she asked, her pulse in her throat. Every rendezvous up to this point had been with the explicit understanding that they would not continue, nor see each other again. Each time, they had failed. Did he still want her now that she was a duke's sister, or did their former boundaries still apply?

Rather than reply with words, he seemed to grunt in assent, his jaw working and his eyes cast down at the sleeping girl he still held. Was Lord Corset, the great seducer, charmer of children, and devoted brother nervous? Charlotte's heart swelled once more.

"I wasn't sure if you would welcome the news," she said, avoiding his gaze. A thought formed, a mere possibility, and she was afraid that if she looked directly into his eyes, she would lose her nerve. "We have been so careful, and now I shall be present and unavoidable."

His next words were whispered, private between them as though they were back in the fitting room, entwined on the velvet chaise. "Peaches, I have never heard more welcome news. I rushed to find you as soon as he told me," he said, his voice a low scrape, not unlike the sound of the gravel under their feet on the path that led back to the kitchens, where they deposited the children with their mother. Markby and Emmeline stayed to speak with her, but Dorset and Charlotte carried on.

"You know better than I, I'm afraid. Is there any hope that we can meet privately? I seem to be chaperoned at every turn," she said. She was his best friend's younger sister, now living in a home Dorset knew as well as his own, with footmen in every room and the new lady's maid waiting for her each time she had returned to the bedroom she had chosen. "I'm still learning my way here. We mustn't be found," she said.

He did not respond right away, and her heart sank. What must he think of her, now a lady and already planning a clandestine meeting with a gentlemen. "I'm sorry, I shouldn't have—"

"No, we must," he said, stopping her. They only had a few moments before Markby and Emmeline rejoined them, so he spoke quickly. "What color is the wallpaper in your bedroom?" he asked. She wasn't expecting this question; their companions neared.

"I beg your pardon?"

"The color, quickly." A flush rose on his cheeks, his gaze locked on hers.

"It is a soft cream, with small flowers and vines," she replied.

"And the counterpane. Is it blue?"

"Like the flowers, yes, but how did you—"

"Good. When you retire tonight, unlatch the terrace door. I shall come to you."

# Chapter 16

The rest of the afternoon and evening passed in a blur. After Dorset and Emmeline departed, all Charlotte could think of was retiring to her room to wait for the man she now saw in an entirely new light. When was the earliest possible moment that she could take her leave of her brother without causing alarm? She needed time to think, and to collect herself.

In the drawing room Markby had shown her to after their meal, she downed the rest of the sherry in her glass. He was introducing new rooms slowly, one by one, taking time to name the people in the portraits and to point out the provenance of each special trinket. He seemed to enjoy presenting their family's history to her, but tonight, she could not give him her full attention.

"Forgive me, Richard," she began, "I'm rather tired from the day. Would you mind terribly if I retired and we discussed this room tomorrow?" He turned from the portrait of their seventh great aunt on their father's side with a look of concern.

"Certainly, Charlotte. Are you feeling unwell?"

"No, no. I feel perfectly fine, just tired," she replied, hoping to put her sweet brother at ease.

"Today was long, wasn't it? Emmeline will make you a lady in no time, but at what cost! I shall speak to her about the pace of these lessons. And yes, of course, go to your room at once, young lady," he said with a twinkle in his eye at the last.

She bade him good night and found her room as quickly as possible, where she dismissed the young girl assigned to be her maid, as she had every night that she'd stayed in her new home. Accepting constant help was still difficult for Charlotte, but she promised the girl that she would do her best to make use of her more, as she settled in.

Alone at last, Charlotte checked the ornate clock on her dressing table. It was half past nine; bright moonlight flooded her terrace. Should she change into her night clothes? No, that would be presumptuous. Would he expect to find her sleeping? If she were to stay in her dress, shouldn't she wait up for him, perhaps with a book in the chair by her fire, or maybe she should wait on the terrace?

Her mind would not rest. She tried to arrange herself casually on the end of her four-poster bed, but she looked ridiculous. If she sat fully on the top of the bed, her feet didn't reach the floor, but if she settled her feet on the floor, she was left leaning against the side of the great bed rather than sitting atop—not a comfortable position in which to wait for him. Either option made her feel silly.

*Don't be a fool, Charlotte.*

With a deep breath, she collected herself. She blew out the candle on her bedside table and allowed the fire to die down in the grate as she usually would before bed. As Dorset had requested, she unlatched the large French doors so that he could slip inside, hopefully without notice to anyone but her.

As the firelight waned, she decided to rest her eyes, for just a moment. It really had been quite a long day, and the comfort of the bed beckoned.

*I shall simply rest atop the blanket, for just a moment…*

As soon as she laid her heavy head down upon the pillow, sleep overtook her. She dreamt of a beautiful, sunlit pasture, full of flowers. Dorset was there, how lovely; their children were laughing, and playing somewhere in the distance. They rested together on a blanket in the warm sunlight.

"Peaches," he whispered, smiling down upon her. He brushed an errant strand of hair from her face—nothing had ever felt more comforting. Warmth radiated from his palm to her cheek where it rested and spread through her whole body. She was perfectly content.

"Darling," she sighed, reaching her hand up to hold his against her face. She never wanted to leave. So warm, and so safe. Their blanket shifted; he was behind her now, arms around her, his face in her hair.

*"I love you, Charlotte," he said, the faintest whisper.*

*"And I love you," she replied.*

What a lovely dream, and so vivid considering she had just closed her eyes. It wouldn't do to be asleep when he arrived. What if he left without a word? She opened her eyes and found the room illuminated with silvery moonlight. The fire must have gone out quickly. But how strange; she still felt his arms around her waist, and the warmth of his body, just like in their dreamy meadow.

Her mind cleared as she blinked the sleep from her eyes and tried to raise her head. How did she come to be beneath a blanket? And how did that blanket, which smelled of leather and cedar, have her completely enfolded and secure?

"Charlotte," he whispered. "Are you awake?"

*Dorset.*

He had come to her, just like he promised. She looked at the clock—just after midnight. "I'm sorry, I meant to rest for just a moment. But I had the most marvelous dream," she said. The details returned to her; Dorset had told her he loved her, and she loved him, as well.

*Only in your mind.*

Dorset sat up with her, in just his trousers and shirt. He had discarded his boots by the door and draped his coat over her chair. "Don't apologize, Peaches. You needed to rest," he said in that low, husky whisper that enchanted her so. He turned her where she sat, so her back was to his chest. Pulling her close, he wrapped his arms around her waist and buried his face in that tender, sensitive space where her neck met her shoulder. Dorset took a deep breath and held it. She melted into his warmth.

The grit of his stubble against her skin sent tremors through her whole body. She'd never been happier to wake from a dream. "What did you dream about?" he asked.

"You, of course." He loosened his grip on her waist, and ran his hands over her back, up to the nape of her neck. Her hair was still pinned, but she could feel its structure failing. Before she could remedy the problem, he began to remove her pins.

"Me?" He continued unpinning and unwrapping, letting her hair fall. It felt like heaven.

"It was the most beautiful day," she said. Her hair undone, he threaded his fingers in her tresses at the base of her head, where it had been fastened since that morning. As she went on, he began to massage her tender scalp.

*Heaven.*

"We were in a beautiful meadow, full of flowers and sunlight," she said, her eyes closing as he continued massaging her head with one large, seductively warm hand.

"That sounds picturesque," he said, dipping his head to kiss her neck. "but I wouldn't trade being in this bed with you for anywhere else in the world."

Overwhelmed with sensation, she couldn't form words to reply; her pulse thrummed deep within her core. She rather felt as though she were purring like a housecat.

*Our first rendezvous in an actual bed.*

"I've wanted you in a bed since the moment I laid eyes on you, Peaches," he said, reading her mind. "A real bed, behind a locked door, with no interruptions."

"It is more comfortable than our fitting room, isn't it?" Charlotte sighed. Sweeping her hair to one side, he continued kissing her neck, slowly, and gently. She felt his lips curl into a smile against her sensitive skin.

"Infinitely more comfortable. But I do cherish the memory," he said, continuing his lips' lazy path up the side of her neck. "And if you'll allow me to, I'll endeavor to make you as comfortable as possible tonight."

"Certainly, my lord," Charlotte replied, in her most aristocratic tone; she was improving. "You may begin by loosening my bodice." Reluctantly, she left his warmth, slid off the side of the bed, and stood with her back to him, giving him full access to the buttons that ran down her spine to her waist.

"As my lady wishes." Once again, with care and his full attention, Dorset undressed her. She felt precious in his hands, as though he were unwrapping a priceless diamond from the layers of her mauve silk chiffon gown. This was the feeling Charlotte had longed for the most when they'd been separated and sworn to remain apart—the feeling that she was safe with him, and that he cherished every part of her.

If he lowered a strap, his sizeable hand would be there to warm the skin revealed beneath. As he untied her corset with one hand, he held the item to her in the front, just below her breasts with the other, never making her feel vulnerable, or bared to the cool night air too quickly. If he was not sure, he always asked permission, and he had never once coerced.

Only with her assent, Dorset dispensed of her corset.

Somehow, he knew exactly where the boning had marked her skin, and he soothed that tender flesh with his touch. With only the thin fabric of her chemise between those wicked hands and her skin, he turned her to face him. He was cast half in moonlight, half in shadow. His beard had grown just slightly since they had parted earlier that day, and somehow his skin still looked aglow from the afternoon sun.

Charlotte couldn't keep herself from touching him any longer—she felt the planes of his firm stomach beneath his shirt, which he quickly removed to grant her greater access. She felt his chest rise and fall, felt the measured beat of his heart. They would take their time tonight; of all her newly afforded comforts, this felt the most like luxury.

Dorset helped her into bed, and they settled facing each other, hands wandering, their noses nearly touching. She could feel his breath.

"This afternoon, in the garden. I watched you," she said. She took one of his hands in hers and brought it to her lips, just to rest there.

"And did the lady appreciate what she saw?" Dorset pulled her into his embrace. She could just feel his pulse against her cheek.

"She did, indeed." Here she was, in a bedroom in Kensington, *her* bedroom in Kensington, in the strong arms of a viscount. The very same viscount she couldn't seem to keep herself from, no matter how hard she tried...and now it didn't matter as much that they even pretend that they wanted to stay apart...

Dorset rolled, settling her on her back with her hair spread over the pillow below them. He gazed down at her, the sapphire in his eyes darkening to deep ocean water in the moonlight. He smiled, so confident and handsome. She was done with trying to resist him, done trying to convince herself that she didn't want this man for her own, for life.

"How did I get so lucky?" he asked.

"Am I not the lucky one? Transformed into lady within mere weeks by complete chance?"

"I won't deny that, Peaches. Call us both lucky, then." Dorset sealed his lips to hers, gently at first, before parting hers with the lightest sweep of his tongue. He did not gather speed nor urgency as they continued kissing; they were searching each other, taking the time that they'd never had before this perfect night. Learning.

Shifting himself, Dorset held himself above her with one leg between her two, his thigh so close to her center. Charlotte tugged at his bottom lip with her teeth, just a light, playful nip. He groaned in response, and the sound flooded her senses.

Rising above her, Dorset unfastened his buttons, never breaking eye contact with her as she watched. She couldn't help but writhe against the counterpane beneath her as she watched him lower his trousers and kick them away before returning to her, just as before, with that corded thigh against her. He raised his knee, giving her the friction she had grown desperate for.

"Here?" he asked her, through more slow, sensual kisses.

"There," she replied, shuddering against him. She could feel herself softening and could not ignore the length of him, resting against her stomach, growing harder for her. She reached for it, wrapping her hand around his shaft, delighted when he moaned against her mouth in reaction to her touch.

"Peaches," he whispered.

"Darling."

With their foreheads together and eyes locked, they teased each other. It was growing harder and harder to maintain their steady, sensual pace.

Charlotte was slick and desperate, ready to feel him inside of her once and for all—she had longed for this moment. She looked into his eyes as he continued to work against her; there was no question in his hungry gaze. He had longed for this too.

"Please, I need to feel you."

"Not yet, Peaches," he growled. He kissed her deeply, stilling her as she tried to arch herself against him. He fell to her side and helped her remove her chemise before lowering her back down to the warmth of their bed. "I want to touch you," he whispered. The way he looked at her, as she lay completely bare, set her skin to gooseflesh.

Slowly, Dorset trailed one languid hand from its gentle perch upon her chin to explore her. As light as a feather, he skimmed her well-kissed neck, then lower to her aching breasts. He held one and then the other, reverently cupping them before leaning down to taste her peaked and aching nipples. The pleasure of it made her shiver and sigh.

"Perfect," he whispered. "So beautiful." Charlotte smiled as he settled back beside her, with his face near hers. That roving hand continued its journey, brushing over her soft stomach and down into her curls, where it found her impossibly wet. She was so sensitive and needy that she couldn't stifle her moans and gasps as he circled her swollen clitoris. His touch was gentle but steady—the whirlpool within her grew and grew as he went on.

"Please," she begged, her voice little more than a gasp.

"Of course, Peaches," he whispered, his forehead against hers. "How does it feel?"

"Perfect," she breathed, her cheeks flushed as the string within her wound tighter and tighter. Bless this man, for he did not change speed, nor direction. Keeping the pressure steady and constant, he brought her to the edge, then leaned down and kissed her again.

The feeling of his lips on hers sent her swirling over. Her pleasure pulsed and radiated through her entire body, like crashing waves against a shore during a storm. The sensation seemed to go on and on, urged on by his steadfast touch.

He was with her as she returned to herself, there to kiss and soothe and hold her as she rode out the final tremors of her climax. She took deep, steadying breaths before she opened her eyes to see him gazing upon her, hungrily. Charlotte was dizzy with pleasure.

"I need you, darling," she breathed. She had never been so sure. He was still as hard as granite beside her. They had controlled themselves for weeks—no longer.

"As my lady wishes," he said, smiling like the devil as he moved between her legs and lowered himself above her, supporting himself as he kissed her with tender strokes. They watched each other as he guided the head of his cock through her folds, not yet pressing in, but covering himself in her essence.

Dorset notched his tip at Charlotte's ready entrance and waited here as he brought both hands to her face. Somewhere between whispered assurances and more kisses, he began to rock his hips, slowly, inching inside of her bit by bit, so that she could feel him fill the void within her with even, delicious strokes.

Charlotte watched his face as he continued, those waves of pleasure beginning to stir within her anew. His eyelids were heavy, and his cheeks grew red as he continued. She loved to hear him groan from deep within his chest as he took his own pleasure.

"More," she said, hands clasped against his back, legs hooked around his waist.

"More."

Rising onto his knees without withdrawing from her, he pulled at her hips and held her steady before continuing his masterful thrusts. He was glistening with sweat, and she watched a bead slowly trail down from his neck and over his heaving chest, so perfect and muscled. He was beautiful, and for now, hers.

"How did I get so lucky?" she asked, her voice a hoarse whisper from all of he gasped moaning he had coaxed from her. He exhaled a laugh at her use of his words, and tightened his grip. She could feel his pace quicken—he was nearing his peak.

He reached down and again found her clitoris as he continued thrusting deeply. A few sweeps of that wicked thumb and she felt herself building, once again, toward release.

"Don't stop, darling."

"Never, Peaches."

"I'm close," she breathed.

"I know."

With a few more strokes, she was over the edge once again, tumbling through waves of pleasure. As she cried out, she felt his grip tightening. He began to moan, chanting her name like a prayer.

"Charlotte," he said, neck strained and pulse rioting. "Mine."

*Yours.*

Dorset could no longer control himself. Releasing his grip on her flesh, he withdrew, his length soaked with her wetness. With a few strokes of his hand, she watched as he climaxed, spilling himself on her stomach as his great chest heaved, his face turned toward heaven.

*So lucky...*

Moments passed in silence, their shallow breaths the only sound in the room. Dorset rose, poured them each a glass of water from the jug on her dressing table, and dampened a cloth. He cleaned her, carefully and gently, making her feel once again like the most sacred thing in the world to him.

They drank their water, Charlotte in small sips and he,

large gulps. Now clean and both exhausted, they got under the bed linens without a word exchanged between them. It was understood—this was their night to spend together, in blissful afterglow.

With her head on his chest, Charlotte let her eyes grow heavier. Everything had changed now. Too drained to speak the words aloud, she made a silent demand of him as she drifted to her rest.

*Don't leave me.*

# Chapter 17

Dorset awoke just before sunrise, as the sky outside Charlotte's window had just begun to lighten with the dawn. She was tucked up against him, warm and asleep, his little peach. There was only one thing to be done now, but to do the thing properly, he must leave her.

It pained him to leave her there, peaceful and content in her bed. Still, there was much to be done, and as he arrived back at his home and rang the bell for a bath and his breakfast, he began to realize the importance of the next few hours.

He had made up his mind somewhere between his moonlit climb up the lattice below her terrace and her second climax. The idea had occurred to him already, of course, but he could not see his way around various obstacles—luckily, so many of those obstacles seemed to have taken care of themselves for him.

And now—now she was his. He had hoped with all his heart it was true when she accepted his escort to the ball without protest, but he knew not to assume. Surely, one could not stake the lifetime happiness of two people on the success of one ball, but he was willing to start there. After last night, he was left with little doubt that he would succeed.

He had found her last night, still dressed but in a deep sleep at the edge of her bed, facing the terrace. He had knelt at her bedside and watched her for a moment, so peaceful, her face so serene as she rested. In that moment, as he gently placed his hand against her cheek, he knew.

"I love you, Charlotte," he had whispered, practice for the day he would say it to her seriously, in the light of day and without fear of contempt or judgment for either of them. He had never expected her to reply.

"And I love you." Dorset knew she was sleeping when she said it, but still he hoped, with all he had, that she was addressing him, even from her dream state.

Would she remember that she said it? He did not know, and she had not repeated it once awake. But still, he hoped.

It had all led him to this day, and the task he must undertake that would lead him down a path to a life that he had sworn to his own father he would never take: marriage.

Charlotte was a Markby now, but even if she hadn't been, he would have taken the necessary and proper steps in their right and correct order. All eyes of the *ton* would be upon them—he, a degenerate rake, and she, a seamstress pretending to be a lady in their scornful eyes. This meant, without question, that Dorset must call upon Markby later that day; not as his friend, but as a suitor. He must ask for her hand.

*Let there be no doubt that our marriage is for love.*

Dorset replayed the memory of the previous night again and again as he dressed and prepared himself. He could still feel her softness, hear her sighs, even now as he dressed, alone in his room. The vision of her, resplendent in bed below him, her auburn hair fanned out around the pillows. He could conjure it so clearly, as though she was seared into his memory.

If everything went his way, this room would, of course,

become theirs. Would Charlotte like it here? He looked to the bed, with its grand mahogany frame and brocade canopy, and imagined her there. This is where he would bring her, carried over the threshold in his arms, as soon as they were wed. Here, he would show her with his mind, body, and soul that he had chosen her, and would continue to choose her for the rest of their lives.

First, he must go to Markby; and so, he did exactly that. Hanson announced him in the doorway of his friend's study.

"Viscount Dorset, Your Grace."

"Nicky, is that you? Come, I've something to show you," said Markby, who was seated behind his desk in his shirtsleeves and waistcoat, wire-rimmed spectacles perched on the end of his nose, reading a document closely. Dorset took a seat in an armchair and crossed his feet at the ankles, legs outstretched. Although his pose was his usual casual one, his heart rate betrayed his inner anxiety.

*Would he possibly say no?*

It was one thing to tell your closest friend about the woman you intended to marry, and that you had already spent a glorious night with that woman, a night and woman so divine that you were left with no choice: Marry her or die. It was completely another to tell that woman's *brother* such tales, and Dorset had never dreamed that he'd be asking for anyone's hand, much less asking Markby, his compatriot on so many ribald adventures.

"More family secrets?"

"The same, actually. We've found a bill of sale from a jeweler—a Messrs. Vane & Hobney Incorporated, who sold my father, according to this document, a 'perfectly matched set of amethyst cabochon and diamond cluster earrings' in 1819. Quite valuable—mother had passed by that time. I wonder if they were a gift for Charlotte's mother."

"Indeed, it seems rather likely," said Dorset. "That is why I came to see you today, come to think of it." He needed to raise the subject soon lest he lose his nerve.

"This is why?" Markby asked, peering at him suspiciously from above his ridiculous spectacles. "You came to discuss the earrings my father purchased for a small fortune even though it was not his custom to wear women's jewelry?"

"No, no, *that's* not why, *she* is why—Charlotte."

"Well, she's not at home, I'm afraid. She's out with Miss Ludlow."

"I don't mean to speak with Charlotte, I am here to speak with you—about Charlotte."

"Has something happened?" Markby asked, removing his spectacles and leaning back in his chair, bill of sale back in its envelope on the desk.

Indeed, something *had* happened. Physically, of course, but within him. Dorset found it difficult to reply, but if he couldn't voice his feelings in front of his closest friend, how could he expect Charlotte to accept his eventual proposal? "Yes, something has happened."

"Is she alright? If she's been compromised—" Dorset stopped him before he could go on, as by the most basic definition of the word, she had, in fact, been compromised.

*I shall give him the chaste version.*

"No, no...well? No. She's quite alright. I believe that she and I have a certain fondness for one another," he said.

"Fondness? Care to elaborate?" he asked, arms crossed over his chest. This was not going well.

"Indeed, I have had the pleasure of her confidence, on a handful of occasions, and I believe that she feels as I do. So, I have come to you today, not as your friend, but—"

"Confidence? What do you mean, 'confidence?' Have you been sneaking around? With MY sister?" Markby rose from his chair, fists clenched. Of all the outcomes Dorset had feared, this was one of the worst, and he hadn't even asked the question.

"Sneaking? No, of course not, no one has been sneaking," he fumbled, knowing full well that was exactly what they had been doing. Dorset had never been a well-behaved gentleman, but he imagined that some sneaking here and there was *de rigueur*, even for the most respectable matches. How did one effectively express their feelings with a chaperone present? Especially when those feelings were often expressed best via physical demonstration…

At that moment, while Dorset felt his brain turn to porridge as he tried and failed to come up with the right words to both be truthful with his friend but also to set his mind at ease, Markby did what he did so often: He laughed.

*The nerve of this menace.*

"Why are you laughing, you idiot? Can't you see that I'm trying to be serious?" asked Dorset, unable to keep himself from smiling as Markby collapsed back in his chair, grin wide.

"Forgive me, Nicky. Don't you see? I never dreamed I'd have the chance to play the concerned brother. What fun," he replied, setting his feet up on his desktop.

"I'm glad you find this so enjoyable," said Dorset, remembering why he was there to begin with. If all went to plan, the grinning fool behind the desk, who he had always loved like his brother, would actually become his family by law. But first, he needed that fool to cooperate.

"I *am* enjoying it. Now, out with it. I promise you that I shall not interrupt you this time," Markby replied, sitting up now so that he appeared somewhat respectable.

"Markby, you are my closest friend. I do not take what I am about to ask you lightly, and I want you to know that I have come to this decision after much thought. You may be surprised, as I have previously held that I should never consider what I'm about to suggest."

"I wish you would skip to the part of this conversation where you actually make the suggestion, as I feel like I am being led by a carrot that I shall never catch. Out with it at once or I shall have Hanson throw you to out."

*At least one of us is taking this seriously.*

"Fine, fine, I had hoped to be more eloquent, but here it is: I am here to ask for your blessing. I wish to marry Charlotte."

Markby leaned forward on his elbows, fingertips touching like the church steeple beneath which Dorset hoped to join the family. For the first time that day, and perhaps Markby's entire life, he fell silent and seemed to consider Dorset's request in earnest. Finally, he spoke.

"I cannot say that I'm surprised, Nicky. If you'll recall, I believe I'm the one who convinced you to court her in the first place. But before I weigh in, I'm afraid I must ask you, not as your friend but as Charlotte's brother, of course. And this is rather delicate, so forgive me—"

"What?" Dorset had not prepared to give detailed explanations of their private moments.

"Have you, or, rather, is she...no, that's not...damnit Nicky, is she with child?" Oh.

Dorset had been careful, but he supposed there was the faintest possibility. The longer they waited, the more likely a baby would become, for their brief history had proven that they could not keep their hands off of one another. And now that he knew what he'd suspected—that she felt like heaven on Earth and all he wanted was to worship her, every night until he died—he knew they'd best marry as soon as propriety would allow.

"She is not," Dorset replied, choosing his next words carefully. "I say that with as much certainty as possible, but I will admit, as your friend, that it is not outside of the realm of possibility."

"The realm of possibility? I see," said Markby, who also seemed to be choosing words carefully at this moment. "Then I will tell you, not as your friend, but as Charlotte's brother, what must happen next." Dorset braced for a scolding. "Stand up."

"What? Stand up?"

"Yes, you must stand up and face me. You have engaged in *activities*, we shall say, with my sister, who is not yet your wife. What kind of brother would I be if I learned of this and let you go unpunished." Markby circled the end of his desk and walked to the center of the room, where he bounced on his toes and rolled his shoulders, shaking out his fists. "Come, be brave, and do not deny me yet another brotherly duty. If you marry her and take her away, I shan't get to do these things anymore," he said, a hint of sadness behind his affable veneer.

Dorset had not considered this, that Markby had only just learned that he was not alone in the world, and here he came, asking for his blessing to marry Charlotte and remove her from the family home she had only just inhabited.

"Nicky, you know I will not challenge you to force you to marry her, and I don't believe I shall need to. But get up, and let's get this over with. One punch," he said, fists already raised. "I shall do my best to avoid breaking your nose."

If this was what it took to earn his blessing, Dorset would take the punch. He would not say aloud that he would happily endure much worse if it meant that he had succeeded.

"All right," he said, resigned. "Just the one. I suppose I deserve it." He faced his friend, and fought the instinct to raise his fists and protect himself, if not to fight back. Markby was not as tall as he was, but he was broader in the chest, and had always had a knack for boxing. This would hurt.

*Nothing compared to losing her.*

Dorset took a deep breath and held it, then closed his eyes. He regretted this almost immediately, as holding the breath seemed to increase his tension, and now he would not know when the blow would come. But, in an instant and before he could recover, Markby landed the punch with surgical precision—he was not a novice, and years later, Dorset would thank him for the speed with which Markby clobbered him. It was a kindness.

Dorset stumbled back with his hands to his face, vision swimming. Markby leapt forward and caught him, with the same grace with which he had directed the fateful blow.

"I'm sorry, Nicky. It had to be done, didn't it? And your nose isn't even bleeding," he said, helping Dorset into his chair. Maybe his head was spinning, but Dorset could have sworn that he saw the man smile. Markby rang for some ice, or a steak, or both, before pouring them both generous glasses of a fine imported bourbon.

"I deserved that," Dorset said, sipping his drink and wincing. He could feel the black eye blooming already. "But I hope you know now that I'm serious, about asking you for Charlotte's hand. And I'm not asking because of any *compromising* that may or may not have occurred. I'm asking because I love her."

"I know you're serious. And know that I'm serious when I tell you that, of course, you have my blessing. But I do not believe that her hand is mine to give you," said Markby, settling back behind his desk. "Charlotte is independent, and resourceful. I think that even if she had been raised here alongside me, she would feel the same. Her hand is hers to give, and hers alone."

Hanson entered with the appropriate remedies on a tray and left the men to their discussion, as it was not the first time one of the two of them had tussled and returned home in need of something to reduce swelling. Dorset set down his glass and opted for the ice cubes wrapped in cloth rather than the steak, noting that it was good to be the friend of a duke, for who else would have both of these luxuries on hand at all times?

"I mean to ask her directly, of course," he said, addressing Markby's correct assertion that Charlotte would not accept a marriage negotiated behind closed doors without her knowledge. "But I want to do it all properly."

"Of course, and we will," Markby said, refilling their glasses. "I raise my glass to you, Nicholas. To your health and happiness, and that of my sister. May you rot in hell if you ever hurt her," he said, clinking his crystal tumbler to Dorset's. "Oh, and do make sure you give me plenty of nieces and nephews, I should like to spoil them from the time of their birth. Another toast to those children, may they take after their mother."

After another clink and another drink for them both, the two men were beginning to grow tipsy—not nearly drunk, but loose and giggling.

"Markby, don't get ahead of yourself, she has not yet agreed," said Dorset, replacing the damp cloth and remaining ice cubes, quickly melting, back into the dish on the tray. "But once she does and we are wed, I swear to you that I will do all I can to make you a niece or nephew as quickly as nature allows."

"Dear God, spare me the details. Just deliver me a child that I shall happily corrupt and adore, in equal measure."

"Corrupt?"

"Yes, for example, I'll tell them all of the time their father came to me like a nervous twit and begged me for permission to marry their mother, and instead of saying yes right away, I blackened his eye." Both men dissolved once again into a fit of laughter. It was all rather absurd.

"It's quite painful, you know. Make it up to me by hosting the stag do."

"We'll go to Sutton, of course. A hunt, perhaps."

"If this swelling goes down and I can once again see from both eyes to aim, it shall be a miracle."

"You'll be fine, I barely tapped you," said Markby. If Dorset hadn't known him for decades, the utter cheek would have surprised him. "I'm getting rather peckish, what do you say we go on a hunt of our own this instant." It was barely the afternoon and they had had three glasses of bourbon, each. Food was needed, quickly, so the two men elected to stroll down to the kitchens where they would beg Mrs. Appleby to interrupt her usual work and make them sandwiches. She would put up a fuss, they would prostrate themselves before her, and she would relent—a time-honored practice since their boyhood.

With a ham sandwich to fortify him, and aside from the bodily injury, Dorset felt better than he had in some time. So much of his time spent with Charlotte had been uncertain and rushed; even the previous night had ended with him slipping away from her bed without waiting for her to wake.

But now, they had Markby in their corner, his blessing like armor. A duke could move mountains using only his whims, and his vocal support would outmatch any gossips or doubters who saw Charlotte as a social climbing seamstress.

"You're looking better already, Nicky," said Markby between bites of his own sandwich.

"Thank you, I shall hope that this bruise fades quickly," he replied, administering fresh ice, also provided by Mrs. Appleby.

"I didn't hit you that hard, and even if I had, you certainly deserved it. Now, tell me, when do you plan to make your offer to my sister?"

"I don't know; I'm much less nervous to speak with her than I was to speak with you, to be honest." Markby let out a low whistle.

"Don't be silly, Nicky. I'm the one who dealt you a blow,

but she's the one who's got to say yes. It is her decision." A correct assertion, but after what they had shared the previous night, Dorset had never felt more confident.

"You say that as though I'd forgotten," he said. "Do not fear, Richard. You'll be organizing the hunt before you know it."

It was time for Dorset to return home; they continued their conversation as Markby walked with him to the great front doors where Hanson was dispatched to have Dorset's carriage brought around.

"And to think, it was just weeks ago that you'd sworn off marriage entirely." Another correct statement. Did this man remember everything?

"True, although in my defense, I had made that vow against any marriage arranged by my parents. This one is for love," Dorset replied, smiling. The carriage arrived, and Dorset stepped in before remembering one final thing he had forgotten to mention. He would need to make a hasty retreat after this final confession.

"Oh! Markby," he called, head out of the window.

"What?"

"The ivy lattice on the west-facing lawn, below Charlotte's terrace—"

"What about it?"

"There may or may not be a broken slat, about halfway up. Awfully dangerous for anyone who fancies a climb. Just thought you might like to know." With that, he tapped his cane twice on the ceiling, and sped off toward home.

## CHAPTER 18

*Chez Beaumont* was bustling with activity, full of women preening and posing, being pinned, trussed, padded, and hemmed in the latest creations. A rainbow of silks, velvets, satins, and crystals covered every surface, every customer, and every seamstress in sight. It was mayhem, and all present were preparing themselves for the Stapleton Ball. It was sure to be the event of the season, especially if the rumor that the Duke of Markby had found a long-lost half-sister who would be making her debut proved to be true.

Half of the clientele, the romantics and naifs, believed the story at face value; how lovely that the handsome and orphaned duke had found his family at last! The other, more skeptical half, believed that the duke was in the clutches of a lady swindler, and an ambitious one at that (the very worst kind of either lady *or* swindler). Luckily for Charlotte, not a single customer there that day recognized her on her first outing as Lady Charlotte Price-Markby, Beaumont client, and the very "swindler" they were all discussing.

And yet, as she made her way into a fitting room with

Sarah for her final alterations before the ball, Charlotte felt that she was the one who had been tricked. She had awoken that morning expecting to find Dorset there beside her, still in bed after the night they had shared. The only traces left of him were the tender spot on her neck where he'd nipped her, and the scent of him on her sheets.

*Gone before the sun rose.*

She tried to tell herself that his disappearance did not void the experience they had shared, that it still had meaning. He certainly could not have stayed with her all morning, for no matter how they felt about one another, they were not married, and not even betrothed. But still, she could not help but feel disappointed. Doubt had begun to creep into the corners of her mind, lingering on the periphery of the memories of their blissful rendezvous.

It wouldn't do to sulk around her room, and Charlotte wished that she had not felt so disappointed by his departure. So, she was alone, and unable to turn to him for reassurance, but what did it matter? She had been alone for almost as long as she could remember. All she could think to do was to distract herself, and where better than Beaumont's?

As Sarah tended to her with practiced hand, Charlotte filled her friend in on the events of the previous night, from the moment she had fallen asleep by mistake until the time she rose, alone and unsure, that morning. The last bit seemed to startle Sarah, who pricked Charlotte with a needle as she adjusted the side seam of her bodice.

"Ouch! Sarah, do you stick all of your clients in the ribs?"

"You mean to tell me he just left?!" Sarah asked, not answering the question nor looking away from her work.

"Yes, he left. But he couldn't exactly stay for a lie in, could he?" Charlotte was in no small part trying to convince herself that this was true.

"That's true, but he could have left a note behind," said

Sarah, moving to inspect the length of the fateful lavender gown originally created for Tabitha Crampton and now purchased by and embellished for Charlotte to wear at her debut. She didn't say it aloud, but Charlotte agreed. A note would have been preferable to imagining the worst and not knowing. Although, what would he have said?

*"Thanks for the shag, Peaches. Don't send for me, I'll send for you.*

*xx,*

*Corset"*

Polly, still an apprentice but looking much more grown than Charlotte remembered, entered with a pair of lustrous lilac satin gloves and some jewels in a case on a tray. Not just any jewels; they were Charlotte's mother's amethyst earrings, kept for her all these years in Madame Beaumont's underground safe.

"Miss Ludlow, Madame asked me to bring you these, and said to send them home with the lady," said Polly, who set the tray down on a side table and dipped into a quick and serviceable curtsy before turning to leave. She did all this without turning her eyes to Charlotte even once, ever the proper apprentice. They were all very well trained to treat each lady with respect, never to linger, and most of all, never to stare. Polly had clearly learned well, so well that it seemed she did not notice nor remember the seamstress who had taught her how to finish buttonholes.

"Polly, how lovely to see you," said Charlotte. The girl turned back around, eyes down at her feet.

"Indeed, my lady," she said. Did she really not remember? Charlotte searched for a way to reach her, to make her recognize that she was standing right in front of her, still the same Charlotte who had taught her the difference between chiffon, organza, and tulle.

"Polly, don't you remember Charlotte? She's not dead,

just a touch fancier than before, that's all," said Sarah. Polly finally looked at Charlotte but didn't seem convinced.

"Yes, I can assure you I am still very much myself," Charlotte added, smiling at the girl.

"Certainly, my lady. How nice to see you again," she said, before turning to Sarah. "Do you require anything else, Miss Ludlow, or may I be excused?"

*Miss Ludlow?*

"Yes, Polly, you may be excused," said Sarah, as Charlotte remembered from both her Beaumont training and her lady lessons that staring with mouth agape was not proper. Polly turned and fled, off to tend to the scores of other ladies who still filled the shop.

"I haven't been gone that long, have I?" she asked, eyes trained on the curtain fluttering closed. "And why was she so formal with you?"

"You're not a seamstress any longer. I'm sure she fears the wrath of Madame if she's too familiar," said Sarah, helping Charlotte into the elbow-length gloves and doing up the tiny buttons with a hook. "Speaking of, Madame has promoted me."

"Promoted! How wonderful, Sarah. Why didn't you stop me and tell me first thing?" Charlotte had spoken only of Dorset since she arrived—so like aristocrats to think only of themselves.

"It's not as important as all this," Sarah said, gesturing vaguely at Charlotte in her finery. In her gown and with her hair pinned just so, she really did look like a proper toff.

*What have I become?*

Fighting a stinging tear that threatened to fall, Charlotte put her hands upon Sarah's slight shoulders before pulling her friend into a hug. "Of course it's important. You're important to me," she whispered, overcome by the feeling of loss she could no longer ignore. Their lives had been turned upside down, not just hers—Sarah's as well, and Charlotte had not even thought to ask if she was all right. "Tell me about this promotion immediately or I shall march into her office and ask Madame about it myself."

"Well, the season so far has been busier than last year, and Madame needs more time to do her sketches," she began, moving behind Charlotte to continue her inspection of the perfectly matched covered buttons that went down her back. "She's mostly just put into writing what I already do, and adjusted my pay to match. But I've a new title—I'm the head seamstress now, and she's going to let me try some designs soon," Sarah said, unable to hide her excitement.

"That's wonderful, Sarah. I'm so happy for you," Charlotte said, leaving out the sadness she felt at having missed such an important development. "I'm sure you will be a great success."

"I certainly hope so, but if she sacks me I shall come knocking on your door at once," Sarah replied with her trademark giggle.

"You must, if only to keep me company. The house is so large that I feel as though I'm living alone sometimes, and I find I don't care for it a bit." Charitably, Sarah did not roll her eyes at this confession.

"Nonsense, that house is full of people and you know it. Besides, Dorset may have slipped off like a scoundrel, Lottie, but something tells me he'll get one look at you in this creation and never let you out of his sight again."

Charlotte regarded herself in the mirror. The gown had been completely remade after an excellent suggestion from Sarah—namely, the careful addition of minuscule pearl and crystal beads, sewn onto a gossamer-thin tulle overlay and trimmed along the neckline of the bodice. The beads were so small and the overlay so sheer that one almost couldn't see them with the naked eye—but beneath candlelight, each tiny speck glistened. It was as though she had been gently dusted with starlight, and it was completely magical.

"Well, unless he has decided to renege, he is still my escort. He'll be stuck with me."

"He should be so lucky. I've got to go and check on Marchbank's girls, they're all being rather fussy. Here, put on the earrings, I want to see it all together when I return." Sarah handed Charlotte the dark green velvet case that housed her entire inheritance and was gone in an instant, the heavy curtain swinging shut behind her.

The case looked exactly the same as she'd remembered, protected from the ravages of time by the cool darkness of Madame's safe, where they had been safely tucked away for her for all these years. She wondered if Markby had a safe for such things. Surely, there was somewhere valuables were kept, although she supposed that everything at their home was valuable, kept in plain sight or not. And did he have any jewelry? Would he have kept his mother's?

As Charlotte leaned forward toward the mirror to fasten the first heavy earring, she caught a bit of conversation, drifting over from the next fitting room. Did her ears deceive her, or were the women next door discussing her?

"*...the Cramptons are not happy, as one can imagine...*"

"*...poor Tabitha, her good name sullied...*"

"*...well, I heard downstairs that Lady Harrington said that the girl is a beauty but nothing more...*"

A beauty, but nothing more.

Charlotte had tried so hard throughout this ordeal to keep her spine straight and her ears closed to the gossips. Emmeline had counseled her to ignore them at all costs; these were bored, wealthy women whose children were growing or grown, whose husbands paid them no attention, and whose idle minds led them without fail to the lowest form of social discourse. Still, this particular blow struck true. She could not stop herself from leaning into the partition and holding her breath to listen more intently.

"Well, we all know what the viscount is like, he's a perfect rake. Not a good match for any respectable young lady, if you ask me, although he is quite rich. I should think poor Miss Crampton can win herself a much more suitable husband," said one woman, who Charlotte imagined as toad-like, with a hairy chin.

*At least I'm not the only topic of conversation.*

"I just do not see how the duke has accepted the girl so readily. I would not allow a seamstress of *any* kind into *my* home for this exact reason—one can *never* know the motives of the working poor. And now, they shall be emboldened! Mind your social invites ladies, for soon we may all have supposed *half-sisters* arriving on our doorsteps, and *poor* Madame Beaumont will have no staff left to sew our dresses."

Charlotte knew this was what they thought of her, but it surprised her how painful it was to hear the women say it aloud when they thought no one could overhear their croaking. Emmeline and Markby had agreed that making her debut at the Stapleton Ball, a grand setting befitting their stature, was the correct and proper course of action. But as she seethed noiselessly against the partition, Charlotte wanted nothing more than to tear into their fitting room and debut herself to them immediately, to shame these smug old biddies who should have known better than to speak plainly when they could so easily be overheard.

*Imagine what they would say if they knew what Dorset and I had done on the very chaise they're seated upon...*

Sarah returned to find Charlotte with her ear to the wall, but she could hear no more. The women had moved on, off to squawk with disapproval elsewhere.

"Charlotte, why are you only wearing one earring?" She

didn't realize it, but she had the second unfastened gem balled in her fist.

"I—oh, it's nothing. I'm not sure why I'm surprised," Charlotte replied, loosening her fist.

"Care to elaborate?"

"I just got an earful, from next door," she said, modulating her tone in case anyone lingered and could overhear. "It seems that Lady Harrington thinks I'm beautiful, a compliment indeed, but nothing more and of no consequence. Dorset himself is unfit for matrimony, and poor Miss Crampton has had her good name sullied."

"What utter nonsense, Lottie. If any of those women have even met Lady Harrington, I shall eat your entire gown with a knife and fork for my supper. Now, put on your earring so I can see you all put together." Charlotte did as she was told, feeling slightly more at ease, though still ruffled. She needed to thicken her skin if she was to survive the ball, for there would be nowhere to hide from their comments in a crowded ballroom.

Straightening her spine and doing her best impression of Emmeline, for that is what she did when she felt unsure of how to act, Charlotte approached Sarah and dipped into a low curtsy, practicing what she'd learned in the empty ballroom at home just one day earlier.

"Lady Sarah, it is a pleasure to make your acquaintance," she purred, manners oozing from every pore. "You have a beautiful home, thank you kindly for the invitation." Gamely, Sarah played along.

"You are most welcome, Lady Charlotte," she said, in her best and most queenly voice. "I should like to see you dance with my son Reginald before the night is through. He has a member the size of a cricket bat and *never* leaves a lady after coitus without first bidding her *adieu*." They erupted into stifled giggles, unable to contain themselves.

"*Pardonnez-moi.*"

The tittering friends turned, mortified, to find Madame Beaumont, resplendent in cream-colored feathers, holding the curtain of their cubicle aside. She had most certainly overheard; Sarah clapped a hand over her mouth and blushed. Charlotte stammered.

"Oh, Madame, hello, we were just—" Madame held up one hand, with more rings visible than fingers, to stop her.

"Do not worry my pet, I was temporarily deaf. For *certainemant*, I did not just overhear my senior manager make reference to the sport of cricket." Now all three of them were giggling. Madame wrapped Charlotte into a gentle hug, air kissing each cheek and being careful to not disturb her carefully sewn and extremely delicate embellishments.

"Sarah, you were quite right about *les etoiles*. She is sparkling, just enough," she said, admiring the subtle but expert handiwork.

"Thank you, Madame, I'm quite happy with it," Sarah replied. Charlotte's heart swelled as she waited while the two women circled her and assessed the gown, two experts at the top of their craft.

"You will take over for me one day, Sarah, I am sure of it," Madame said with a wink. "Have a lovely time at the ball, *mon chérie*. Enjoy yourself," she added to Charlotte before blowing her a kiss and floating from the room, off to greet her other clients.

"I shall do my very best," Charlotte said after her, and she tried to mean it. Any time she felt unsure of her decision to live with Markby, she reminded herself that these things, the gowns, the balls, and the excess of it all, were a grand privilege —one she should be grateful for with her whole heart. For if she could not be thankful for her newfound comfort and safety, she should not have accepted them to begin with.

"I hope you will, Lottie," Sarah said. "I want every woman

at that ball to see you in this dress, and all of them marching back here to order the starlight tulle embellishment for their next event," she added, ever the businesswoman.

"Sarah, you had best take over for Madame one day, for only you have found a way to make her designs even more expensive. You shall carry the name well," Charlotte said, smiling but meaning every single word.

"Your mouth to God's ears, Lottie. You shall be my best advertisement," she said, moving to help unbutton the bodice now that their fitting was complete. "Now, off with those earrings—Madame is sending you home with an armed guard who shall see them safely locked away for you, and this gown will be packed and delivered later this afternoon."

"An armed guard? Is that really necessary?"

"I'm told that it is, Lottie, and I think your brother would agree if he knew how much your father paid for them." Charlotte stepped out of the gown and sat down to remove her satin slippers.

"I'm sure I would rather not know, for I would certainly not wear them if I knew the figure myself. I don't imagine that I'll ever get used to it," Charlotte said, "it" meaning the practical heaps of money that seemed to prop up every facet of her new lifestyle.

"Well, you must try your best, for I predict that you shall be betrothed to your roguish viscount before the end of the ball," said Sarah, helping Charlotte into the dress she had arrived wearing.

"I am not sure that I agree with you on that point." As she stared blankly at nothing in particular, Sarah handed Charlotte her bonnet, gloves, and shawl.

"No, he shall have to grovel first. And make sure that he does," said Sarah, correct as always. They bade each other goodbye at the top of the grand staircase, as Sarah needed to hurry off to her work. Charlotte regarded the showroom floor below her, more familiar to her than her new home.

She recognized every single girl working, knew them all personally, but not a single one would look her way. Charlotte knew she would always be welcome here, but still...it broke her heart. Despite her constant lessons and the new wardrobe, she did not yet feel like a lady. But it seemed that she did not have a choice in the matter, as she was clearly no longer part of the staff here, and now that she was a client with enough money to afford things like gowns that sparkled beneath chandeliers in ballrooms, they would not let her forget it.

Charlotte exited the showroom floor, the front doors opened for her so that she need not exert herself. There, beside her carriage, she was met with the largest man she had ever seen, who introduced himself as an associate of the bank where Madame Beaumont did her business. The man was not visibly armed, but Charlotte sensed that if his arms the size of mature oak trees were not sufficient, he had deadlier accessories on his person, just beneath the largest great coat she had ever seen. Never in her life did she imagine needing such protection, and never in her life had she felt so out of place in her own skin.

*It seems I cannot go home again, after all.*

CHAPTER 19

Dorset had never looked forward to balls. He found them tiresome, and far too full of people on their best behavior. The very same men he would see gambling, drunk, and cavorting at his club would doubtless be there, doing their best impression of gentlemen for all assembled. He had never put on a show for the sake of finding a wife, and he knew it had cost him his reputation, but at least he had never had to playact at a party to secure a dowry.

But tonight, everything was different—the outcome of a ball had never been so important. Dorset had dressed with more care than ever before, carefully selecting a black velvet evening coat lined with emerald silk. As he straightened his cravat in the mirror before departing for Stapleton House, he hoped that Charlotte would approve.

Opting to avoid the crush, he entered his parents' home through a side door, making his way to the already crowded ballroom from a servant's hallway. He heard the din of the guests and the music before he even entered—had they invited all of London?

The majordomo was still announcing guests, even though

the ballroom was dangerously near capacity. Quite the setting for Charlotte's debut, but she would not have to bear it alone. Dorset was her escort, and he would make sure that everyone around them knew it, and knew it well.

*She shall be off limits, and perfectly safe.*

"Hello, Nicholas, so kind of you to join us, and very nearly on time," Emmeline said, joining him where he stood near the edge of the room. "Did you not wish to be announced?"

"I did not," he said, scanning the room and on high alert. He wanted the lay of the land, and to assess all threats. He had already spotted two separate young lords he knew to have both crippling gambling debts and nosey mothers—they would doubtless be intrigued by a duke's new and hopefully naïve sister.

"You seem rather on edge. Here, take this, for your health." Emmeline took two glasses of champagne from a passing tray and handed him one. They clinked their glasses and sipped.

"I suppose I should go say hello to our parents," said Dorset, knowing it was true but still wishing to avoid them. He had not yet spotted them, nor had he told them about his intentions with Charlotte; did they still consider this the night he was to promise himself to Miss Crampton?

"In due time, yes, although if I were you, I wouldn't linger too long. The Crampton family has arrived and they are circling." Of course they were.

Guest after guest were announced at the top of the entrance stairway, which led down from a balcony that circled the entire ballroom, to the dancefloor. Guests who lingered in the dim light above the chandeliers enjoyed a bird's eye view of the activity below, from the dancing, to the orchestra, to the refreshments. Everyone who descended the stairs was on full display.

Dorset spotted his parents across the room, with nary a

Crampton in sight. Knowing this could be his only chance to speak with them alone, he decided to act. "Our parents have misled the Cramptons long enough—I shall speak to them," he said, leaving Emmeline wondering if he meant that he would speak to their parents, to the Crampton's, or both.

He crossed the floor to them on a mission. He did not wish for their approval, only for them to release him from the arrangement they had made without his consent, all those weeks ago when this ordeal began.

*Let there be no doubt.*

"Nicholas, darling, you look so smart in evening dress. Doesn't he always look so dashing when dressed for the evening, husband?" His mother was holding court, a perfect society maven. Her endless capacity for conversation and natural ability to see the best in everyone around her was perfectly suited to the setting. Dorset kissed her cheek.

"Thank you, Mother. You look lovely," he said. "Hello Father."

"Good evening, Nicholas. You are looking well, far better than when we last spoke," he said, referring, no doubt, to the worst hangover of Dorset's life. The earl went on, bringing up the subject at hand so that Dorset did not have to. "That reminds me, Nicholas. This ball has a very specific purpose, if you recall our conversation that day."

"I remember as though it were yesterday," he said, truthfully. That was the first day he had laid eyes upon Charlotte. How far they had come since then.

"Nicholas, dear, you must know that we simply wish for you to be happily settled," said his mother, her hand in the crook of his arm, which she squeezed to reassure him.

"I know that, Mother. Do not worry—I shall endeavor to settle myself happily," he replied.

"I am glad to hear it, son. The baron will be even happier,

I would imagine," his father said, referring to Miss Crampton's father. Dorset spotted Emmeline over his petite mother's head, some distance away and entertaining the entire Crampton brood, absent their daughter who Dorset assumed would be clad in yellow satin and easily spotted. Emmeline was buying him time.

The announcements of new arrivals had slowed, indicating that the crush had thinned and it was time now for the opening dance; people swirled around them in all directions, but Dorset did not yet know if Markby and Charlotte had arrived. He would have felt more confident with his friend there beside him, with Charlotte's hand in his own as he made his intentions clear to his parents.

"You misunderstand me, Father. I have not yet made an offer to the lady, but I shall do so in due time, and she is not Miss Crampton. I have her family's blessing, and I shall introduce you, although in some sense, you have already met—"

He was about to go on, to tell them of his stubborn, independent, smart, and entirely lovely future wife. He wanted them to know that he admired her strength, and that even though she was not raised in an aristocratic family, she was the most poised and fine woman he had ever known. Charlotte would be a credit to their family.

Just as he opened his mouth to tell them, someone nearby gasped. All conversation halted and the orchestra faltered and ceased their playing, as though some collective shock had rippled through the room. From above them, the majordomo hastily returned to his post and cleared his throat; all heads turned to the top of the stairs.

*She is here.*

The majordomo's voice practically bellowed through the silent room as every guest stood rapt. "His Grace, the Duke of Markby, and Lady Charlotte Price-Markby."

The room held its breath at the sight of them, and it was no wonder—she was *sparkling*. Was it some kind of trick? She glistened, as though her perfect violet gown was shot through with jewels, reflecting the light from the candles all around them. Dorset could not help but stare as they slowly descended the stairs. She was flawless.

Soon, the whispers began; many were craning their necks for a better view of the woman they had been hearing about for weeks, now real and here before them, outshining every other person in the room.

"...is *that* the sister?"

"Pretty, but I do not see any resemblance..."

"...Markby looks pained, surely he is not serious..."

As though surfacing from beneath water, the sound of the party came crashing back to him. Dorset needed to be by her side, as he had promised, immediately.

He was across the room in seconds. Charlotte caught sight of him as he neared, and he held her gaze with intention. Dorset knew they would elicit stares and yet more whispers, but he did not care—she was here, at last.

He was so utterly transfixed that Dorset did not even acknowledge Markby, standing beside them now and watching along with the rest of the crowd.

"Lady Charlotte," he began, his voice all propriety as his hungry gaze was anything but. "You look magnificent." He eyed the dance card dangling from her wrist, given to her as she entered, no doubt. She dipped into a curtsy before she replied.

"Thank you, my lord. How kind of you," she said, her voice a mere whisper. All eyes remained upon them, and Dorset did not care. He looked into her eyes, that familiar soft green shade looking back into his own.

Dorset took her hand and raised it to his lips. He kissed her delicate knuckles with a light brush of his lips wishing that they were anywhere but here, alone, where he could strip off this blasted glove and feel her skin against his, as he had the last time he had seen her. As the crowd watched, mouths agape, he reached for her dance card with his other hand and slid it off of her wrist, before placing it inside the interior pocket of his evening coat. No man would dare write down his name for her tonight; every dance was his.

The whispers intensified. In his periphery, Dorset saw Emmeline signal to the violinist—the same man who had been present at Charlotte's dance lessons. The music began again, and the spell that the Markby siblings had cast with their arrival loosened its grip on the assemblage. They could breathe, once again.

"Dreadfully sorry we're late, Nicky," said Markby, mopping his brow. "Emmeline thought it best if we come in last, to avoid getting trampled on our way in," he said, replacing his handkerchief. Emmeline joined them.

"Yes, we couldn't have a riot break out in the hall, could we? Charlotte, you look divine. Violet is your color." Indeed, it was. Dorset could not pull his gaze away from her. Charlotte's cheeks flushed with peach in the warm room. His eyes trailed over her exposed collarbone and further still to the edge of her bodice, trimmed in those magical twinkling jewels.

"Thank you, Lady Emmeline," she said, the sound of her voice shaking him from his trance. Dorset needed to pull himself together and be respectable if he was to give her the society debut she deserved. The music swelled—it was time to waltz.

"Lady Charlotte," Dorset began, meaning to ask her to dance the way he had during her lessons. She cut him off before he could go on.

"Yes, yes, let's dance, everyone is staring at us anyway," she said, smile plastered across her face, but quietly enough so that only they could hear.

They fell into the dance easily, his hand at her back and hers on his shoulder. This felt right to him—the two of them, hand in hand. Dorset could feel her relaxing as they turned across the ornate parquet floor, as though they had a thousand times before, but something was amiss. She would not meet his eyes.

"Are you quite all right, Peaches?" he whispered. She may belong to the *ton* as of a few moments ago, but his private name for her did not.

"Indeed, I am," she said, her voice betraying an emotion that her face did not. "Although—"

"Has something happened?" he asked. Dorset would crush anyone who had made her feel unwelcome.

"Well, yes, but—"

"Who, what have they done?" he growled, growing hot around his collar. His grasp upon her tightened, but he took care not to draw her too close as they danced.

"Dorset, please. Not here, I beg you," she said, still maintaining an insouciant appearance, as composed and calm as Emmeline had taught her to be. "This is a private matter, concerning only me, and you," she said.

*Oh.*

What could she possibly mean? The night they had spent together had been perfect, and he had done nothing since then but prepare to make her his wife. What had he missed?

"Tell me," he said, turning them away from the center of the room, toward the edge of the other dancers, where they were less likely to be overheard.

She stared straight ahead, directly at his chest. "You left," she said, her voice small. "You weren't there when I awoke."

"I did not want to leave, believe me," he said.

"I did not know if you still meant to escort me," she said. "I found it rather confusing."

Spinning them to a stop at the very edge of the ballroom,

he lifted her chin with his thumb, without a care for anyone who may be watching.

"Charlotte, darling. I'm sorry that I left you. I had a matter to attend to right away, I could not delay it another moment," he said, hoping she felt his sincerity.

"If we—I don't mean to be presumptuous," she began, choosing her words carefully. "but if we are to meet in such a way again, and you exit without a word…" She hesitated.

"Yes?"

"I will never speak with you again," she said, speaking calmly with her shoulders squared. How she managed to look perfectly composed while delivering this blow, he did not know, but she did it masterfully. Dorset had hurt her, and he knew that she meant every word of her threat.

*Not a threat—a promise.*

He opened his mouth to respond but was interrupted before he could speak.

"Dorset, old boy, introduce me at once or I shall think you're keeping this creature all to yourself!" It was Lord Chumbly, a sputtering, degenerate louse in debt to his own uncle after a poor speculation, face reddened by alcohol. He slapped Dorset on the back, too hard to be friendly. Just the kind of man he had vowed to keep away from Charlotte. Dorset ground his teeth and played his part, keeping alert for an immediate escape.

"Lady Charlotte, allow me to introduce Lord Chumbly, who is a complete ass," he said, sneering. Chumbly was an idiot; sure enough, he took Dorset's insult as a joke and laughed heartily, leaning too close to Charlotte for anyone's comfort.

"Pleasure to meet you, love," the drunk said, swaying where he stood as he reached for her hand. She did not offer it —smart.

"Now, now, Chumbly, I think you'd best visit the men's

salon and refresh yourself," said Dorset. The man reeked of booze.

"Nonsense, Dorset! I saw you snatch her dance card away, as though that would stop me. Save the next waltz for me, miss," he said, ignoring propriety and insulting her by not using her proper name, for the second time. Dorset could not allow this but did not wish to make a scene.

He twisted Chumbly's arm behind his own back with ease, as the scotch coursing through the man's veins had loosened him significantly. With all his considerable strength, Dorset dug his thumb into the drunkard's elbow and held him by the joint with his forearm pointed upward, between his shoulder blades. Dorset was one upward thrust shy of dislocating the man's shoulder. Exceedingly painful, though Chumbly was not yet permanently injured, and to anyone else watching, it simply looked like the two men were leaning in close for a private word.

"Chumbly, if you do not remove yourself immediately, I shall rip off your arm. Do you understand?" Dorset deepened his grip, and Chumbly cried out.

"Fine, fine, message received. Unhand me, Dorset."

"Not until you understand that *Lady Charlotte* is off limits. You will not speak to her, do you understand? Do not so much as look at her. If you disobey me, I shall find you," he said, fuming. Eyes were turning to them now; it had become clear that their conversation was not a friendly one.

Chumbly nodded, and Dorset shook him off. He stumbled away awkwardly, hopefully toward the exit; he was far too drunk to remain on his feet much longer.

The bastard had interrupted them—Dorset had been moments from begging Charlotte's forgiveness.

"Are you all right," he asked, scanning her person for any signs of the man's errant spittle. She remained radiant, and unblemished.

"I'm fine," she said, allowing him to examine her. "Thank you." Charlotte blushed. At the sight of that shade that always set him aflame, he began to feel hope. He needed to get her somewhere private, and quickly, so that he could explain himself.

Dorset did not care a bit if anyone noticed that the belle of the ball had slipped away with the host family's rakish son after just one dance, but he imagined that the belle might. Thankfully, he found Emmeline in the crowd and waved her over. Before his sister could arrive, he leaned in close and whispered to Charlotte.

"Peaches, please, I need to explain myself. Go with Emmeline, take a turn about the room, let everyone see that *wicked* dress that is driving me mad. Have a glass of champagne, let Emmeline show you off to her friends, and then make an excuse—any excuse to get some fresh air. I shall be waiting for you in the garden, near the pink rose bushes behind the fountain, in ten minutes," he said, finishing just as Emmeline arrived.

Charlotte nodded her assent, imperceptible to anyone who did not know her intimately, as Dorset did. He knew her sighs, knew the softness of her, knew the strength of her grip on his bare skin—he was sick knowing that he had disappointed her, and he intended to rectify the situation as soon as was humanly possible.

Emmeline whisked her away into the crowd, and Dorset slipped out through a side door into the crisp night air, so much cooler than the ballroom. No one had yet taken a respite from the heat on the great stone porch just outside of the room; hopefully they would both be unnoticed.

He disappeared into darkness down the steps, finding the granite path as his eyes adjusted to the night. The marble fountain, burbling happily as it always did, was in sight, the pink roses just beyond.

There, as he enjoyed the stillness of the evening compared with the raucous atmosphere inside, he took a deep breath, and waited. He did not yet know what he could possibly say to atone for his stupidity.

*You have ten minutes to figure it out, you blasted fool.*

# CHAPTER 20

Charlotte had dressed for the Stapleton Ball like a soldier arming for battle. Her gown was utter perfection; thanks to Sarah's abilities, Charlotte's appearance would be unimpeachable. The rest of her, the internal parts, the bits that were *important* were another story entirely. But as she stood at the top of the stairs, arm in arm with Markby, she realized that absolutely none of it mattered.

No one knows better than a seamstress that one cannot possibly please everyone. One can sew the most beautiful and intricate lace with the finest detail, and yet, there will always be a customer who detests lace. When the whispers broke out as they descended into what she now considered an environment akin to the pits of Hell, it became clear that if Charlotte were lace, no one present was buying.

That was, until she saw him. Dorset came for her with a gaze like steel, cutting through the crowd with decisive ease. When he greeted her as "Lady Charlotte," in a voice loud enough to reach the rafters, and then had the utter cheek to remove and pocket her dance card, the doubts she had held since he had left her alone in her bed evaporated.

*Mine.*

Still, she was determined to tell him how he had made her feel—like she was easily left and easily forgotten. And she would, in approximately ten minutes time when she was to excuse herself and find him in the garden.

*How do I slip away without notice when wearing a dress designed to grab attention?*

After their first waltz, an attempted drunken assault, and his whispered instructions to find him amongst some roses, Dorset had fled and Emmeline took her in hand. They walked —no, *floated*—gracefully about the room, as though there were no slippered feet beneath their rustling skirts. Two proper ladies. There were so many people all around them. Some turned to stare. Some made a show of turning away and ignoring them as they neared, suddenly fascinated by their canapés and flutes of champagne. The rest, and the ones that Charlotte liked the best, continued to enjoy themselves as normal, unbothered by her presence among them.

"Charlotte, have you eaten?" Emmeline asked, directing them toward the refreshments. "The figs are divine, you must try one." Charlotte accepted and agreed that the figs were, in fact, divine. They were just one of a spread of more fruits and cheeses with breads and sliced meats than she had ever seen outside of a market—enough to feed an army, but the army present was doing little more than nibbling as they passed by.

Discarded berries, smeared on an abandoned plate caught her eye at first, then, a half-eaten and forgotten square of cheese, absently placed right next to a platter of melting ice, meant to keep the salmon mousse cold. By all appearances, as the mousse sweated and congealed, it was no longer cold and no longer fit to eat as its serving dish floated on the shallow pool of tepid water. A fly circled.

Charlotte could not abide such waste. The food sitting there melting, wilting, and rotting was enough to feed hundreds, and the hundreds assembled did not seem to care a whit. As servants arrived and began clearing away the detritus and refreshing each dish, presenting freshly shaved ice for chilling an entirely new salmon mousse to replace the one that sat untouched and decaying, she wondered if she had not fallen into a nightmare.

*A very expensive nightmare.*

It would not do to embarrass Markby, who had been nothing but kind to her, nor Emmeline, for that matter—she had gone to great lengths to prepare Charlotte for this night. They had all hoped for her success. But here she was, unable to find any respect within her for this foul display of wealth and excess. Charlotte did not know if it had yet been ten minutes, but she needed to get out of this room, immediately—if a sharp-eyed gossip happened to notice that she exited the room too closely behind the gentleman in possession of her dance card, she did not care at all.

And so, with her eyes locked on the open doors that led to Dorset, she thanked Emmeline and excused herself. Head held high, she floated into the night. The crisp night air was a balm compared with the stifling, perfumed heat of the ballroom. Perfumed, no doubt, to mask the odor of turned salmon and evening wear sodden with perspiration.

Charlotte heard the fountain before she saw it, and let the sound guide her as her eyes adjusted to the night. There was no moon—all the better to meet in secret, she supposed. Just beyond the fountain, she saw roses. But were they pink? It was hard to tell in this darkness. What was not difficult, however, was finding Dorset. All she had to do was follow her nose.

*Leather and cedar.*

"Has it been ten minutes?" she asked, finding him on a low stone bench near the garden wall, just wide enough for two. He stood to greet her.

"It has been too long," he said, taking her hands and

pulling her to him. "I find that I do not much care for letting you out of my sight."

"And I do not care much for balls, I think," she replied, letting him wrap his arms around her. "I mean no offense to your mother and father."

"Believe me, I offend them enough for the both of us," he said, and she exhaled a small laugh into the lapel of his jacket. The velvet felt soft and warm against her cheek. They stilled, the sound of the water playing in the fountain such a comfort after the din inside.

After a moment, he spoke. "I'm sorry," he said, a whisper into her hair.

"I know," she replied, not wanting to leave his arms, but needing to—she could not think when he held her like this. "But you must understand. That night, you made me feel precious, and desired," she said.

*You made me feel loved...*

"But when I awoke and you had left—" She dipped her head and worried a button on her glove, finding it difficult to say aloud her most private thoughts. What if she told him that he'd hurt her, and he decided that she wasn't worth the trouble?

As he always did, he placed the pad of his thumb under her chin, as light as a feather, and lifted her face to his. He was beautiful.

"What, Peaches? You must tell me."

"I felt alone," she admitted, a tear threatening to fall. It had been a common theme in her life before she had returned to London from school, and taken her post at Beaumont's, and found Sarah. Left motherless far too young, and knowing that her father was somewhere out in the wide world, and that he did not want her...she detested the feeling, and still found it difficult not to detest the man himself.

Dorset took her face between his hands and held her still.

He looked into her eyes with such sadness in his own, so much sadness that he seemed unable to speak. He brushed one cheek with gentle sweeps of his thumb, holding her there with him.

"Charlotte," he said, his voice low and private. "I was a fool. Words cannot express how sorry I am. You must let me show you." He gazed down at her through those lashes, impossibly long and lush. There was promise in the words, but what did he mean? Was he implying that he could simply take her to bed once again and make her forget? That would not be enough.

"We are both foolish," she said, nestling her face back in the solid warmth of his chest. "You for disappearing, and me for knowing I would do it all again without a second thought." She should not have said it, should not have told him that she was so smitten with him, he could get away with treating her poorly. Why did she always reveal too much to him, and so often in gardens where they were not meant to be left unattended?

"Peaches, I need you to understand," he said, brushing one of those thick, wicked thumbs over the exposed skin at the nape of her neck. "I left that morning to make everything right, to do everything properly."

"Properly? Do what properly?" Her tone was suspicious —she must have been mistaken, for it sounded like he was referring to a state of being she knew him to have sworn off entirely: matrimony.

"I did not want to tell you like this. I had planned to ask you tonight, I'll admit, but I did not realize—" Charlotte could not believe what she was hearing. It must have shown on her face, as he did not finish his thought.

"I should imagine, and I suppose I have never made such an offer so I do not know, but it seems that one can only propose to another when they are in the same room. Or simply within earshot, at the very least," she said.

"It is not my custom, as you know, but I wanted to play by the rules, I suppose," he said, leading her now to sit on the small bench, and then taking both of her hands in his. "I left to collect myself and then to go to Markby." She knew the men were close, but could Dorset not complete a task without speaking to his friend first?

"Markby?" He looked into her eyes, saying nothing, his gaze full of meaning. Finally, she realized—he had gone to her only relation and asked for her hand.

She now understood what he had meant by "properly," but something about it rang hollow. There was nothing proper about either of them, and never had been. From the moment she spotted him, hungover and swaying on his feet at tea, to when he took her in the moonlight after climbing up her terrace like a thief in the night. No, Charlotte did not believe she could accept propriety. It did not suit them at all.

"Forgive me," she began, loving the way the shadows darkened his face and doing her best to contain her thoughts as she went on, "but I do not see how we can possibly do anything properly. Haven't you heard that the *ton* thinks me a swindler?"

"Then let them think my bride is a swindler," he said, his eyes turning wolfish, hungry. "You shall be *my* swindler, and I will live the rest of my days in happiness as your easiest mark."

*His bride...if only.*

He went on, leaning in closer to her as he spoke, his lips so near to hers now that all she needed to do was inch forward to claim a kiss. "I knew the day we met that it was you—or no one. And then, it seemed impossible." He was referring, no doubt, to learning her true identity. Viscounts did not marry seamstresses. Unfortunately for Dorset, Charlotte was still that same seamstress, playing dress-up in expensive clothes, unable to acclimate to aristocratic life.

"But now," he said, brushing his lips over hers as he spoke, softer than the velvet of his jacket. "Now, anything is possible. You do not have to pretend to be someone you are not, and we have your brother's blessing. No one questions a duke."

Charlotte imagined that a prince might question a duke, or even England's young queen—but surely, notice of a viscount's marriage to a mistress's child brought up in genteel poverty would not prove worthy of Her Royal Highness's notice.

"But that is the problem," she said, returning his gentle, teasing kisses before pulling away. She needed him to hear her, and to know what she said next was the barest truth. "In these clothes, these houses, away from my work—I am still pretending to be someone I am not. I have tried with all I have, and all I know for sure is that I am not 'Lady Charlotte,'" she said, sadly.

His brows knitted together, somehow making this devil even more handsome than ever before.

"I shall never truly be accepted here, in your world. And I do not think I can go back, either. No one at Beaumont's will look me in the eye, save for Sarah and Madame herself. I do not know where I fit, but it is not here, and it cannot be in even the most respectable union. The rumors would follow us forever." She trembled under the weight of this confession.

"Charlotte, I do not know how I shall convince you," he said, more seriously than he had ever been with her to date. "But I shall make it my life's work to make you feel welcome, like you belong, and most importantly, that you are mine."

"I want to believe it, with all my heart," she said, tears once again threatening. "But please, I cannot bear another moment in that ballroom. All it does is remind me that while I grew up without my mother, my father could have been at a ball just like this one, perhaps in this very house, drinking champagne and waltzing instead of looking for me. He knew how to reach Madame Beaumont, it would not have been difficult for him to find me if he had wished to. Maybe then, we could have had a real chance. But he did not even try, and here we are."

Dorset took her hands in both of his and held them to his mouth, his eyes closed, as though he were bowed in prayer, meditating over her words. Minutes passed before he spoke.

"Here we are, indeed," he said, in that low, private tone she liked so much. "Your father was an ass, Charlotte. He is lucky that he passed away of natural causes, for I should like to wring the neck of any person who ever made you feel that you are not worthy. If it is what you wish, let us get you out of here and safely home before I must resort to throttling every last guest inside."

Rising, he offered his hand, and she took it. Without a care for who may see them, they walked back toward the glowing party within, slowly, and somberly, garnering stares from those who had fled to the garden to escape the heat within. Charlotte did not know where she and Dorset now stood with each other. If only she could have played her part more convincingly, been the darling of the *ton* with impeccable manners and taste, and without a checkered history that had ruined their chances before she and Dorset had even been born. Then, everything would have been perfect.

*So much for my flawless debut.*

"We shall find Markby and get you home," he said quietly, stopping as they neared the heat of the room, radiating out into the night. With his free hand, he took hers and tucked it into the crook of his elbow.

They spotted Markby with Emmeline dancing a waltz, the pair of them an absolute vision, the platonic ideal of a peer and a lady. He, in impeccable evening dress, and she, in a soft gold satin gown that glowed against her skin, flushed from their dancing but without a drop of perspiration on her person, not a hair out of place. They were perfect—Charlotte and Dorset would never come close.

The music waned and the dancers came to a stop, thanking their partners and going their separate ways, but not Markby and Emmeline, who seemed entranced, unable to release contact with each other. Charlotte felt a twinge of shame as she and Dorset approached them, still arm in arm, to interrupt their private moment. Before she could signal to Dorset that they should leave the two be, Markby caught sight of them above Emmeline's twisted coif, and the spell was broken.

"Oh, there you are, we thought you'd run off," he said. "Em, they've returned."

"Ah, they've returned," she said, sounding, for the first time that Charlotte had ever noticed, flustered. Quickly, she recovered. "Are you quite alright? Why do you both look as though someone has died?"

It did feel as though something had died—their expectations for this night had been so high, and Dorset was even planning to propose. They should have been so happy, rushing to share their joyous news.

But before either of them could respond to account for their absence, an unfamiliar voice interjected from behind them. Unfamiliar to Charlotte, at least. From the pained look on her face, Emmeline recognized it instantly. Dorset closed his eyes in anguish as realization dawned for him as well.

"Well, well, well, if it isn't the chit who had to steal my name to get herself out of the gutter." It was Tabitha Crampton, with a gaggle of smirking friends flanking her, holding a brimming glass of red wine.

Dorset spoke first, furious. "Miss Crampton. Apologize, or I shall see you escorted out."

"Me? Escorted out? I believe I am the one owed the apology, Dorset. Or do you not remember that she tricked *you* by pretending to be *me*?" He opened his mouth to respond, but Charlotte squeezed his arm, stilling him instantly. She did not require his help, nor his defense. If Miss Crampton wanted to cause a scene, she would have it.

"Miss Crampton, I believe you were speaking to me, were you not? I will admit that I'm surprised to see you here, as I understood you to be a lady unable to keep her own appointments."

"Appointments! As though I care a bit for *dress fittings*," she sneered, eyes dropping from Charlotte's eyes to her feet and then back up to her face. "Is this the gown they made for me? You will take anything you can get your dirty hands on, won't you?" The girls around her snickered.

Charlotte did not flinch. It was not the first time she had been insulted by an entitled and cruel lady. It would certainly not be the last. "Oh, this gown? No, of course not. This one is much more expensive, and the design is not yet available to customers. You would know that if you had shown your face that day." Tabitha's cheeks reddened, and her eyes narrowed. Clearly, she was used to her targets backing down, and tonight, she had chosen the wrong one.

Tabitha began to sputter, the *Bordeaux* in her glass sloshing dangerously close to the brim. "You snide little *crook*, how dare you speak to me in that tone. Dorset, how can you stand by and allow this, this, *imposter* to speak to me like this?" Dorset opened his mouth to speak, but again, Charlotte stilled him with another gentle squeeze. She was in complete control.

"Miss Crampton, surely, when you start a fight, you must not expect someone else to finish it for you. Since you are so clearly out of your depth, I would advise that you take your friends and your cloudy diamonds and leave this home immediately before you bring further embarrassment to our kind hosts. Oh, how silly of me. Are the jewels paste? I'll admit that I cannot tell the difference in this lighting, but regardless, they are as dull as your skin tone against that buttercup satin. Do not worry, I shall speak with Madame Beaumont about finding you more suitable shades for next season. It's the least I can do."

Miss Crampton gasped; her friends looked truly alarmed now. The ballroom was silent, with all eyes on the entertainment before them when she cried out.

"You COW!" she yelled, furious. Her friends began to back away from her; Miss Crampton looked around, frantically, and realized that she had been bested at her own game. Like an unholy combination of a spoiled child and a trapped animal, she snarled, and unleashed the final weapon she had at her disposal: her full glass of wine.

With a flick of her wrist, the liquid went flying, and time stood still. Charlotte held her breath and closed her eyes, prepared for the wine to hit her square in the face, for there was no time to move out of the way. She heard Dorset yelling, and felt Markby rushing forward—but the impact never came. Chaos broke out, and Charlotte opened her eyes just as Dorset grabbed her and spun her away from the madness.

Had the wine vanished in mid-air? She was completely dry and her gown spotless. No...as the crowd parted, she saw that Emmeline had taken the bullet for her. Her perfect, golden gown was stained from the top of her bodice and down across her skirt with a massive, inky splotch. Emmeline must have leapt to shield her, and it seemed that Markby, who now had her in his arms on the floor, had caught Emmeline and broken her fall.

Bodies were rushing everywhere, no doubt to separate Miss Crampton from the rest of them, and hopefully to see her tossed out for causing such havoc. Charlotte wanted to tell Emmeline that she should treat the stain as soon as possible, with a white wine if no vinegar was available, but she could not get to her in the chaos.

"I think this is our cue to exit, Peaches," Dorset said, ushering her out of the ballroom at a clip.

"Is Emmeline all right? What happened?" Charlotte asked, nearly dumbstruck. She had expected many things for that night, but a confrontation complete with wine-laced assault had not made the list.

"She is quite all right, if a little soggy. Markby will take care of her," Dorset said, leading her outside to the grand portico where carriages stood waiting. He found his own and put her inside, closing the door without entering himself. Standing on the runner and leaning through the window, he gave her rushed instructions.

"Go straight home, and speak to no one. I shall call upon you tomorrow, with your shawl and reticule," he said. He leaned forward and grasped the back of her head, mussing her pinned hair, and then claimed her mouth with a searing kiss. They were electric with adrenaline, their kiss full of promise.

"And Peaches?"

"Yes?" They were so close that they shared panting breaths.

"I love you," he said, jumping down to the ground in a flash and sending the carriage away with a startling lurch.

*And I love you.*

## CHAPTER 21

Charlotte had to admit, as she arrived back home without her reticule, nor a key to any of the numerous doors, that it was convenient to live in a house with staff members there to let her in. If those staff members were confused as to why she arrived back home in a carriage belonging to someone else and without her brother who had escorted her, they said nothing.

She would not have cared a bit if they'd questioned her, for she felt as she climbed the stairs to her rooms that she was floating on air. Dorset had told her he loved her, and hearing him say it had elated her. The practicalities of their earlier conversation could wait until tomorrow. Tonight, she would go to bed at peace, knowing that even if she still could not see their way to a happy future, right now, he felt as she did. And that was enough.

Sleep did not come easily, for her heart had pounded long after she got into bed, her sparkling gown draped over her settee. When she awoke, the sun blazed, high in the sky; it seemed she had slept away the morning. Charlotte had never done such a thing, and as she dressed quickly after splashing some cool water on her face, she wondered when Dorset would come for her, as he said he would before he stole her breath with a kiss and said the words she had longed to hear.

Charlotte left her room in search of food, for she estimated that it was nearly mid-day, and she had not had much aside from the lone fig given to her by Emmeline the night before. Thankfully, Mrs. Appleby took pity on her, and made her eggs and toast in a great cast iron skillet on the massive stove. Still unused to being waited upon, Charlotte made them a pot of tea to share.

"Did you have a nice time at the ball, my lady?" Mrs. Appleby asked, kindly. The staff here had observed and facilitated her preparations for days; they must be curious about the outcome of the grand reveal.

Charlotte paused over her teacup before answering. It had not been fun at all—the event had been disastrous from beginning to end. But Dorset's declaration at the last possible moment was all she could think of now, in the light of day.

"I am not sure that I would call it fun," she replied, choosing her next words carefully.

"No?"

"No; but it was a great success."

The food restored her, so after many thanks to Mrs. Appleby, she set out in search of Markby. He was not in his study, nor was he in the library, nor the garden. Could he still be asleep? Or, perhaps, had he not come home the night before? Charlotte had long suspected there was something between her brother and Emmeline, but Dorset had maintained that the two were friends akin to siblings and nothing more. So like a man to be clueless about these things, she thought.

With no brother at home with which to discuss the previous nights' events and their repercussions, Charlotte paced the halls. She had never felt at such a loss for activity; the workload at Beaumont's had been never ending, leaving no time to idle.

*Surely, there must be something to do in this enormous house.*

To end her spell of aimless dithering, Charlotte decided to settle in with a book. She did not know when Dorset would call upon her, but surely the thick, leather-bound volume she had selected could occupy her until then.

Ultimately, it did not. She found the story bland and uninspired, especially when compared with the drama of the night before. Were events like Miss Crampton's eruption common at balls? As Emmeline had not warned her of this violence in her lessons, Charlotte imagined it was not.

And what would the Harringtons think of it all? Charlotte had felt completely confident in her behavior the night before, not afraid for a moment to defend herself against such atrocious behavior. Now, as she turned the page of the book she was not reading, she wondered if she had embarrassed them, her hosts and the parents of the man she loved.

It would not do to dwell, and book reading had become quite as idle as dithering. She would write a letter to Sarah—yes, that would fill some time. Charlotte would tell her that the violet gown was effervescent perfection, so envied that it was very nearly drenched in wine, and oh, yes, she must also warn her that Emmeline's gown would need a thorough cleaning.

With her letter written and sealed with wax, she deposited it with a footman who would send it for her via post. She did not even need to leave the writing desk where she had composed the letter, and it was already off and on its way to her friend. This task had taken her five minutes, at most.

*Where is Dorset? I wish to tell him I love him, too.*

If only she had learned needlepoint by now, or how to play violin. She now understood why ladies were so often partaking of these hobbies, and she wished, not for the first time since moving away to her new life, that she could return to Beaumont's and get back to work.

As she considered her options, she remembered that Dorset had advised her to speak to no one. And, as she had no sense of what had gone on at Stapleton after she was whisked away, she realized this was still the most sensible plan. What she did not know as she tapped a nervous finger upon the inlaid marquetry desktop, is that she would receive the news from the most unexpected source, very shortly.

Hanson found her at her writing desk, still in agitated contemplation. He moved into the room silently, and startled her when he spoke.

"Lady Charlotte, I am sorry to disturb you. The Earl of Harrington and Lady Harrington have called, and wish to speak with you. I have escorted them to the solarium." He said all of this as though Charlotte would know exactly what to do. She looked at him, eyes wide and mouth open for longer than was polite, unsure of what to say.

"Is my bother at home?" she asked.

"His Grace is not, my lady. Might I suggest, if I may be so bold, that you simply offer them some refreshment, and ring for it if requested. One would imagine, after your greeting, they will state their purpose." This was helpful advice, so needed that Charlotte did not care a whit that it had been delivered as though to an imbecile.

"Yes, I think I shall do just that. Thank you, Hanson," she said, rising and crossing the halls to the solarium. She felt like a child being called to the schoolmaster's office.

*No, this is closer akin to a gallows walk.*

As promised, Dorset's mother and father awaited her in the sun-drenched solarium. He, looking like Dorset's future, still handsome but graying even more than when Charlotte had met him so briefly all those weeks ago, and she, dressed impeccably in a magenta creation that Charlotte remembered well from when it was purchased. Duchesse satin with pearls and feathers for day was awfully extravagant, but Lady Harrington wore it with aplomb.

Charlotte greeted them, and offered refreshment as Hanson had suggested; they refused. Whatever their purpose, this did not appear to be a social visit.

"You must know that I am terribly sorry for the *events* of last night," she began, hoping to head them off. Charlotte did not know if she could withstand a scolding from them. The embarrassment threatened to swallow her whole.

"Oh, *darling*, it was very clearly not at all your fault, was it," said Lady Harrington, her tone dripping with her usual effusive warmth. Still, Charlotte found it difficult to relax. "You must not worry yourself over it. The unfortunate Crampton girl was taken home swiftly by her parents, and they assure me that she will be dealt with privately."

*If I am not in trouble for causing a scene, why are you here?*

"Indeed, and, Lady Charlotte, that is not why we have come to speak with you today," said the earl.

"No?" Charlotte asked, trying to mask the surprise in her voice, and failing. Lady Dorset smiled at her as though nothing was amiss, and this was a completely normal and common social call; the earl's tone contradicted her demeanor entirely.

"It has come to our attention, that our son has shared a certain affection for you," he began, his gaze stern. Charlotte rather felt as though she were being questioned, even if he had not asked her—he had told her. Dorset's words from the night before echoed in her memory.

"*... speak to no one.*"

"I see," she replied, doing her best to stick to Dorset's advice. If they expected her to say more than that in response, they would be disappointed.

"Yes, and although you have secured a rather advantageous connection with the Duke of Markby—" At this, Charlotte could not stop herself from interrupting him, earl or not.

"Forgive me, my lord, but I would not call my questionable parentage, upbringing in poverty as an orphan even as my father lived, and eventual reunion with my half-brother with so many years between us lost, 'advantageous.'"

"Of course not, *dear girl*, he meant nothing of the sort, did you, husband?" said Lady Harrington. If he was the salt, she was the sugar—here to sweeten whatever blow they were preparing to deliver.

"Certainly not, certainly not. Allow me to make myself plain," he said.

"Please," she replied, her tone betraying the impatience she was trying so hard to hide.

"Our son has expressed his desire to marry you, which of course you must know by now. Naturally, this cannot come to be, and we are prepared to provide you with funds to that effect."

*Funds?*

"What?" she asked, her annoyance plain now. If ever she could make use of her privilege as the sister of a man who outranked the one speaking to her so rudely, and in her own home, now was the time. "And what, exactly, do you mean when you say you are prepared to provide me with funds? I am not sure if the setting or my presentation contradicts this, but as you can plainly see, I do not find myself short of them at the moment," she said, rising from her chair. "And furthermore, if I ever did find myself in need of money, I would earn it honestly, as I always have."

Her tone was full of anger, but she did not see why she should have to make these people comfortable, especially not if this man was suggesting the unthinkable: paying her off to end her connection with Dorset—to be rid of her.

*Do they really think so low of me?*

"Now, now, Lady Charlotte," began the earl. "You must understand our position. Our son has a duty to his family, to marry well and continue the Dorset line. While we understand that you are no doubt capable of entering into matrimony with him, as a member of society yourself, and surely capable of bearing a child, we have a much larger reputation to consider. We cannot approve of your marriage, but we have landed upon a figure that we feel would be appropriate. Should you accept this offer, it must be with the understanding that you shall have no further communication with our son."

"Appropriate? What is the 'appropriate' value of your precious bloodline, that you feel I have threatened?" Charlotte was furious, and they both knew it. The earl sputtered and broke her searing eye contact before he could respond.

"£2,000."

Somehow, hearing the number itself made the entire proposition even more degrading. Finally, by naming the price, he had expressed what they were all thinking and what Charlotte had long assumed was true. They did not consider her good enough for their son, for their *family*, regardless of her brother's title, and they would never accept her. Even worse, they would pay her a fortune to be rid of her. Truthfully, she did not give a damn for their approval, and she suspected that Dorset did not either. But he was not here, and she could only stand up for herself.

The earl gathered himself and returned his stern focus to Charlotte; the countess beamed as though nothing were amiss, and Charlotte wondered if the woman had a hearing problem. Nothing this strange and enraging had ever befallen her when she worked for a living, and returning to her former routine seemed more enticing then ever at this moment.

"In fact, I do not understand your position, Lord Harrington. For you see, your son has not made his intentions known to me, only that he loves me. No proposal of marriage has been made, and therefore, there is nothing yet for you to object to. Your offer, though generous, is both premature and completely preposterous," she said. The earl scoffed; she continued before the man could speak. "Sadly, I have not yet had the chance to make it clear to him that I love him as well, more than I ever dreamed was possible. And, it is precisely because I love him so much, that I will decline any offer of marriage that he makes, just as I shall now decline your offer of money."

"Good girl, wonderful. Do not be too sad, *dear* Charlotte, this is for the *best*," said Lady Dorset.

"No, it is not for the *best*, my lady. I love your son. So much so that I feel lost when he is out of my sight, and I cannot bear the thought of living the rest of my life without him. But as you said yourself, I came from a broken and scandalous home. I cannot wish the same upon him, knowing that it would doom us and our children to a lifetime of scorn, starting from the time of their birth from their closest relations.

"I knew that my past, which was far beyond my own control, mind you, would be questioned, and that it may reflect poorly upon your son. I will not allow this insulting conversation to continue, and I will not bring children into this world who would be forced to call the likes of *you* family. You hate them already and they aren't even born. You should both be ashamed."

"Now, miss—" the earl blustered. Charlotte silenced him. His impudence would not continue.

"Enough. You will not disrespect me in this manner any longer, nor ever again. Good day to you both." Charlotte swept from the room, furious. She had meant every word she'd told them. If her connection to him brought shame on his family, she would not doom Dorset to a life sentence as her husband.

She met Hanson in the halls, tears threatening. The dear man said nothing and awaited instructions. "Please see them out, Hanson," she said failing the battle to hold back her tears. "And have my trunks brought to my room, if you would be so kind."

"Certainly, my lady," he said, and went about his work.

As she reached her room, hot tears had streaked down her face and neck, dampening the neck of her day dress. She had known it from the start and could not bear to hear it said again: She did not belong in this world, and it was time for her to make her escape for good, and the sooner the better, for they would all be better off once rid of her. She had never once in her life been a burden to anyone, and so help her God, she would not start now.

Dorset saw his path forward so clearly now, after the chaos of the previous night, that he awoke the next morning determined to begin immediately. When the dust had settled and he finally left his parents' home in the wee hours, he was furious with them. They had needlessly raised Miss Crampton's hopes and then done nothing to correct her expectations before the ball. They easily could have intervened to prevent the scene that ended with him rushing Charlotte out of the fray and with Emmeline on the ballroom floor in Markby's arms, soaked through with their priceless French wine.

If the riot that ensued clarified anything for him, it was that he must shield Charlotte from this nonsense if they were to have any chance. People were not playthings, manipulated for entertainment, and he would not allow her to be the subject of scrutiny any longer.

As he went about his careful work, for it would take him some time, he thought back to the day that Markby revealed that Charlotte was his sister. It had seemed so easy then; she is a lady and I am a viscount, and we shall be wed and that will be the end of it. He had been so foolish; only now did he understand what Charlotte had struggled to explain to him in the garden the previous night. The very society he believed had paved the path to their future happiness was the only thing standing in their way.

From behind his desk, he drafted letter after letter, setting in motion the only possible remedy for the situation, irreversible once his orders were completed. When he finished his tasks, late in the afternoon, with the sun just beginning to set, he set out for the Markby home to call upon Charlotte, as he told her he would.

It was time for him to reveal his plans to her. Would she protest? He doubted it, for she was smarter than he was by a mile, and this would be their only possible way forward.

*The only way we can be together, and love each other without scorn.*

He walked to the Markby home that night, enjoying the evening breeze as he went. Where they were going, a carriage would not be a guarantee, nor would a stable full of ready horses with a groom to tend to them. Besides, it felt nice to stretch his legs after a long day spent behind his desk, signing papers and firing off correspondence as quickly as his footmen could carry it to the post.

He arrived and knocked upon the door. It was opened by Markby himself, looking frantic.

"Dorset, where is she?" he pleaded. Something had happened, something grave, and Dorset prayed that the "she" in question was not Charlotte, although something within him knew that of course it was.

"I've just come to see her. Is she not here?" he asked, growing concerned.

"Hanson said she asked for her trunks this afternoon, after you parents called."

"My parents? Markby, start from the beginning," said Dorset, trying to remain calm. Why had his parents called upon her without telling him, and dear God, what had they said to her?

Markby recounted what he knew, which unfortunately did not include topic of the conversation between his mother, father, and Charlotte, earlier that day. All that was known, as Charlotte had done a perfect job of obscuring her objective, was that she had packed her trunks and entered a hack with them, destination unknown. While she had left Markby a hurried note reassuring him that she was safe, it contained no further information, and no clues as to her objective.

It was after dark now. Dorset and Markby agreed that she was smart, and knew how to take care of herself. She would not walk willingly into danger, and Dorset rather thought that by leaving, she had walked straight out of it.

*She does not even know that we are in complete agreement, even now.*

"Markby, eat something, and go to bed. If she comes home, send for me at once. But I do not think she will, and you must not worry yourself," said Dorset, trying to calm his friend.

"Not worry myself? How is that possible? She left without a trace."

"As your future brother-in-law and your lifelong friend, I swear to you," he began, embracing Markby before he went on. "I will find her."

# Chapter 22

To Dorset, as he stood on a cramped stoop in drizzling rain, still clutching the violet shawl and reticule he had promised to return to Charlotte, the night was darker than it had ever been. The moon had only just risen. No starlight reached him where he stood, taking cover from the weather under the eaves of what had once been her home. The delicate beads attached to the handbag shone weakly under the dim light from the street lamp, a far cry from the dazzling sparkle that had stolen the breath from an entire ballroom.

Dorset had gone straight to Beaumont's, where he could not help but feel he was being purposefully dismissed. When asked, none of the women working that day had seen her, they said, but they would certainly send word to His Grace if the lady arrived for an appointment. No, Madame Beaumont was not in at present, they were afraid; Miss Ludlow was otherwise engaged.

His next stop was here, the boarding house where Charlotte and Miss Ludlow had lived. The landlady, a Mrs. Jukes, informed him in a raised and rather severe tone that Miss

Ludlow was no longer her tenant, the garret had already been let, and how dare he, a gentleman who should know better, interrupt her evening meal. Apologies were made and not accepted; the door, slammed.

His carriage arrived in the narrow lane to collect him, as it could not wait there for him without blocking the flow of traffic.

"Where to, my lord?" asked his driver. He could not reach Miss Ludlow, nor Madame Beaumont, the two people he imagined that Charlotte would turn to in a time of crisis. To whom else would she confide?

*Emmeline?*

It was possible, he supposed. He knew Charlotte and his sister were friendly, but would she run to Em, at Stapleton House of all places, if she had just been accosted by his parents? It did not seem likely, but Emmeline would certainly have a stronger grasp of where women went when they wished to hide. With this in mind, Dorset signaled to the driver to take him to Stapleton, as quickly as he could.

Dorset rode on in misery through the increasing rain, his carriage in nearly complete darkness, save from the dim flickering of the lantern. He could not in good conscience keep his driver out in these conditions, nor the horses, so he sent them home once he arrived at Stapleton. Wherever Charlotte had gone, he would walk through the downpours if he had to, for as long as it took him to find her.

Shaking off his rain-soaked jacket in the foyer, he asked after his sister. Carter informed Dorset that Lady Emmeline was not at home, because *of course* she was not. Charlotte had vanished without a trace, as had any person he knew her to confide in. It was as though she did not wish to be found—and she was doing a damned good job at hiding.

What could his parents possibly have said to her? She had vanished. Not only had he promised Markby he would find her, he could not marry a woman who had gone missing—although, he supposed he would make the attempt if it came to that. Nothing would stop him, but he must know what his mother and father had done.

Carter showed him to the music room, where he found his parents seated in silence, reading separately near a roaring fire. The pianoforte sat untouched, and the harp Emmeline had practiced upon as a child was now little more than decoration. If he had not been in such a foul mood and on such an important mission, he would have laughed at the irony; one could hear a pin drop at the present moment, as not a note of music has been played within this room for years. The warmth from the fire spread through him and strengthened his resolve. Before he could make himself known, his mother spotted him as he entered.

"Nicholas, *darling*, we did not expect you. Have you eaten? You look rather pale, doesn't he look pale, husband?" As he always did, Dorset approached his mother where she sat and kissed her on the cheek in greeting.

"I have not eaten, Mother, but I am not hungry. I am here to speak with you," he said, eyeing his father, who regarded him suspiciously from over the wire rim of his reading spectacles.

"Good evening, Nicholas."

"Is it? I find I do not agree, Father," Dorset replied. His tone was insolent, but he could not help himself. "What have you done?"

"Oh, Nicholas, *whatever* do you mean? We have scarcely left our home at all, we are *so* done in by the ball, as I am sure you know. Such fun but rather taxing on one's faculties, are they not?" Dorset found this feigned ignorance "rather taxing," and felt it was a mistake to have come here at all.

"Mother, I have been told that despite your exhaustion, you were able to call upon Charlotte at her home today. There is no use in denying it," he said, stopping his mother before she could speak further. "What I endeavor to find out is what you said to her, as she has since disappeared completely."

"Now, Nicholas, it was nothing so serious as all that. The girl must be somewhere," his father said, removing his spectacles, folding them, and placing them on the side table at his elbow, next to his evening whisky.

"Father, 'the girl,' as you so rudely called her, packed her things and fled the safety of her home after you spoke with her. If you do not tell me what was said, I shall find out anyway, and I fear I shall not ever forgive either of you for as long as you live," Dorset said, his tone rising.

"If you ask me," said Lady Harrington, marking her place in her novel and setting it aside, "she handled herself exactly as I had hoped she would. I was not sure last night, of course, but I think I shall be delighted to have her as a daughter-in-law." Dorset felt that if she spoke another word of nonsense, flames would erupt from within him. He had never been this angry with his parents, not even when they had promised him to a woman with a penchant for throwing glasses of *vin rouge* at her rivals.

"Mother, how am I to marry her when you have run her off?"

"Nicholas, we did not 'run her off.' We simply put her to a test," said his father, as though this was a completely normal thing to do with their son's beloved: toy with her.

"A test?"

"Yes, of course, darling. We do not know the girl, and as you seemed so set on her, we wanted to make sure that the rumors had no truth whatsoever," said his mother, rising to join Dorset on a settee. The look on his face must have betrayed his inner fury; his father endeavored explain further.

"You must understand, Nicholas. The proof of her background is not conclusive, and even you cannot deny that

Markby is somewhat excitable. We had to be sure," said the earl, as though it should all make perfect sense.

"And what did this test entail? Did a doctor examine her to find traces of nobility? Did you have her blood taken and checked against Markby's? Utterly absurd," he seethed, settling his head in his hands where he sat. He knew he had not been the best son to them, but was this what things had come to? Perhaps if Dorset had been less of a cad, better behaved, more like Emmeline, they would not have questioned his intentions to marry Charlotte—and to love her, for as long as they both lived.

"Do not be ridiculous, Nicholas, of course no one laid a hand upon her. We simply made her an offer that, if one were after only financial gain, one could not refuse."

"Do not tell me..." Dorset could not bring himself to say the words aloud. Had they offered her money? By the looks on their faces, that is exactly what they had done. "How much? How much did you offer her?"

"Now, I do not see how the figure itself is relevant," his father blustered.

"How much?" Dorset asked again, his face like stone.

"We offered her £2,000. And, much to her credit, she declined immediately," said his mother. It was a large sum, certainly more than she could ever have hoped to earn as a seamstress—but was that all they thought him worth?

"So, you put a price on me, then. I see," said Dorset. He rose to leave, exhausted. How could they be so cruel? He resolved to go back to Markby, to decide together how they should proceed. Maybe Emmeline would turn up and give them some direction, as she usually did. In any event, their callous behavior had made him more confident than ever before in his future path. A path that he would walk happily, even if the worst should happen, and he never saw Charlotte again because of this farcical and insulting ruse.

"Darling, do not be upset with us," said his mother. "We thought you would be happy to know that she loves you, and not because you are wealthy. She told us herself, just after she rejected the offer."

*She loves me.*

He had hoped that she did, and longed to hear her say the words. When he confessed his own love for Charlotte through his carriage window after the ball, he sent the driver away as quickly as he could, unable to bear the possibility that she might not say it back to him. He had not expected to hear it secondhand, from his mother, and because they had interfered.

Nothing between them had been neat, nor tidy. Their first meeting was preposterous, their first kiss abruptly halted by a scandalous confession and later resumed after fate intervened to lock them away together underground. Their first ball had ended in a melee, and now, if he did not act, their journey together, that he had hoped would last for their lifetimes, would simply end. Dorset would not allow it.

"Nicholas, darling, we would have told her immediately that we meant no such thing, and that *of course* we approve of her," said his mother, a pleading look on her face.

"Indeed, son. I was ready to explain on the spot, but your lady had us removed immediately. She had Mr. Hanson throw us out," said the earl.

*Good girl.*

"Indeed, it was somewhat exciting, was it not, husband? I have never been escorted out of anywhere before," said his mother, grinning. "She told us she loved you, and can you believe that in the end, it was *she* who objected to *us*—she made very clear that we should be ashamed of ourselves, and I should imagine we would be if we had made such an offer seriously, don't you agree, husband?"

Dorset was proud of Charlotte for tossing them out, but

could not hear another word of this absurd explanation. He spoke before his father could continue. "I have half a mind to follow her leave and reject you both as well. Now, before I disown you as you have threatened to disown me on so many occasions, let make myself clear," he said, training his serious gaze on his father.

Later, he would look back and realize that this was the first time he had used his father's own somber look of disapproval against him, but in this moment, he could find no joy in it. "Serious or no, you *should* be ashamed. People are not pawns for you to toy with for your own amusement. I intend to find Charlotte, and to marry her. But make no mistake—if I fail and she will not have me, know that you both, along with every other so-called 'noble' person in this God-forsaken town, ruined everything. This may sound dramatic, but I promise you it is the honest truth. Now, if you will excuse me, I must go."

"Nicholas, darling, I know we have upset you, but do you not see the good in it?" Lady Harrington asked, directly to Dorset's turned back. Without facing her, he responded.

"No, Mother, I am afraid I cannot see any good at the moment."

"But it is simple, is it not? She gave up everything, for you. *Dear* Charlotte told us as clear as day that she would give up her entire life, ladyship included, if it meant protecting you, and protecting our family. Surely, you must be glad to know it."

Still incensed, Dorset could not turn to face them. Was he glad to know that she had run from the opulent comforts of a ducal home to protect his honor? No, not in the least. But he knew without doubt that he would follow wherever she had run, and would gladly shed his own privilege if it meant getting her back.

"No, Mother. I am not glad to hear that the terror you

caused within her is so profound that she believes *me* to be the party in need of protection. If I cannot find her, I shall never forgive you."

If they called after him, he did not hear it. Replacing his coat, he stepped out into the rain, focused only on returning to Markby's to explain to his friend what he had learned. It was his fault that Charlotte had disappeared, for Dorset had failed to make his parents see how serious he was about her. And why should they have believed him? He had never been serious a day in his life.

The streets were deserted as he walked. As the rain continued to fall, he removed his hat, letting the drops soak him, the cold renewing his resolve. He walked on, and thought back to what Charlotte had told him in the garden during the ball. He had insisted that their standing in London society would be their salvation—they could marry now that she had debuted. How foolish he was. And Charlotte, always ahead of him, already knew that she would never be happy as a notorious viscountess with a murky past.

As he walked, the splashes of his footfalls the only sound apart from the pouring rain, he wished with all his heart that he could find her and explain that even before he knew of his parent's disgusting offer of payment, Dorset had resolved to reject all. He had spent all afternoon dispersing funds and reorganizing his investments—reducing his estate to something more akin to an average between their two disparate backgrounds. He wished to create a new standing for them both, where they could meet each other on neutral ground, somewhere between excess and ascetism—and without titles.

But would it matter? How much damage had his mother and father done? Dorset reached the steps of Markby's home and found the front door unlocked, no doubt left that way just in case Charlotte found her way back.

*She must find her way back.*

Dorset thanked Mrs. Browne, who took custody of his sodden outerwear. In his shirtsleeves and waistcoat, completely dejected, he found Markby in his study.

The duke was slumped in an overstuffed chair near the fire. He grunted when Dorset entered, the only sign that he knew his friend had joined him. Dorset poured himself a glass of the same bourbon he had drunk too much of just a few days before, and joined Markby in another chair by the fire.

"Nicky, your hair is soaking wet," he said.

"I walked," Dorset replied, sipping his drink. It warmed him.

"From where?"

"It does not matter. I have not found her," he said, unable to mask the hurt in his voice.

"I gathered," replied Markby, his eyes fixed on the dancing flames before them. "But it will not do to catch your death. Stay here tonight, I am a duke and you must do what I say." Like Dorset, he was utterly dejected.

"All right," Dorset replied, pulling off his dampened boots to warm his feet more quickly. He told Markby of the saga revealed to him by his parents, and expected to get punched once again, without the kind avoidance of his bones this time. But the punishment did not come—Markby did not seem angry in the least.

"That's Charlotte," he said, the corners of his mouth turning into what would slowly come to resemble a smile. "Do you not see, Nicky? This had to happen."

"I do not see, as a matter of fact," he replied. Was Markby drunk?

"She is just like my father," Markby began.

"Do not tell her that," said Dorset, meaning it seriously. Charlotte still felt a great deal of anger toward the man, and rightfully so.

"I would never, and I'll kill you if you ever reveal that I

think it…but they are the same. She cannot be persuaded. Charlotte acts on her own terms, always. Luckily for her and also the rest of us, she is generous and kind as well. She must have got that from her mother," said Markby, sipping his drink. "She got the best of both of them."

Dorset did not doubt that he was correct, and also that his friend had had too much drink. He could not see the silver lining that Markby had apparently found. "I do not doubt it," he said.

"And now, when she returns to you, which I know she will," continued Markby, sitting up in his chair and swaying slightly, drunk indeed, "she shall come back because it is what she wants—me, her family, and you. Her love." It was worse than Dorset had guessed; Markby listed in his chair, and Dorset caught him. It was time to put him in his bed.

"Do not fear," said the young duke, leaning on Dorset, who practically carried him up the stairs. "Charlotte is good, and you know it." Stumbling through the doors to Markby's chambers, Dorset laughed for the first time in what felt like ages.

"She *is* good," he replied, knowing it was true. Dorset helped Markby onto his bed, and left him on top of the covers, fully clothed save for his boots, which Dorset removed with great effort.

"We shall see her tomorrow, Nicky. I am sure of it," he said. Dorset was not sure how Markby had arrived at this assumption, and considered it for a moment before he opened his mouth to ask why he thought so. Before he could speak, the loudest snore he had ever heard filled the room; Markby was out like a snuffed candle.

Dorset crossed the halls to Charlotte's rooms, replaying Markby's words in his mind as he went, like an incantation.

*She shall come back because it is what she wants.*

He entered her chamber to find it just as he remembered,

but they had not lit her fire this evening. Clearly, no one expected her back that night. The armoire was empty, as was the water jug on her side table. He shucked off his shirt and pants, leaving them at the foot of the bed, and as he hoisted himself into her bed, he thought longingly of the last time he had been here. His chest ached as he recalled that night. What a fool he had been. And what a fool he was now, hoping with all his heart that Markby was correct.

*She shall come back because it is what she wants.*

He repeated the words to himself silently as he settled in her bed, the scent of her still lingering on her pillows. He was so tired—sleep was coming for him, and for the first time since he had loaded her into his carriage and told her he loved her, he gave himself up to rest.

*Do not leave me.*

# Chapter 23

Charlotte knew that Dorset would not find her here—the girls downstairs had agreed to shield her at Sarah's direction, and she was thankful to them all. Just as she had hoped, Madame Beaumont had accepted her back without a question when she turned up on the doorstep that day, just as she had when she arrived in London after leaving school as a girl.

Luckily for Charlotte, Sarah's new promotion had come with quite the new amenity—the lushly appointed penthouse apartment on the top floor of the building, until recently inhabited by Madame herself, who had decided to move to a quieter neighborhood nearby. If this wasn't the precursor to Sarah's complete takeover of the Beaumont legacy upon Madame's retirement, Charlotte would walk naked through Tottenham Court Road.

The penthouse had the same plush carpets as the store below, tall windows with exquisite views of the rooftops surrounding the shop, and thankfully for them both, two bedrooms with en suite bathrooms—a marked upgrade from the garret they had shared.

"Are you sure I'm not intruding?" asked Charlotte for the fifth time since arriving. It was a strange feeling indeed to not have a home of one's own, and she did not want to disturb Sarah who had only just moved into her new, luxurious flat.

"Of course not, Lottie," she said, helping to unpack her second and final trunk. "As far as I am concerned, you live here with me for as long as you like. Although, I expect that your man will grow suspicious of our repeated denials and will return sooner rather than later."

Sarah was likely correct, and Charlotte knew it. She would need to prepare herself, to find the words that could express to him the decision she had made.

*I love you so much that I will not ruin your life.*

With trunks unpacked, they moved to the sparkling and very French kitchen, where they opted for wine rather than tea, and cake rather than biscuits. This was an evening for the strong stuff.

"The girls are all aghast at the stories coming back from the Stapleton Ball," said Sarah, taking a forkful of rich tea cake into her mouth. "I'm shocked that you survived it."

"I very nearly did not survive it," said Charlotte, sipping her wine. Madame had left some bottles in a dark corner of the pantry she had outfitted to house her wine collection. It was delicious. "And poor Emmeline did not escape unscathed— you should have seen her gown."

"I did see it, a footman brought it in earlier. We thought it ruined, but it's not, of course."

"What do you mean?"

"Well, you know Emmeline, everything she wears sets off a frenzy. Now we have ladies in every day asking for a splash of this and an artful splatter of that. Madame had to contact the dye houses in Paris to see what they could do. They think she has gone mad."

"At least something positive has come of it," said Charlotte, raising her glass. Sarah clinked it and they both sipped.

"Now, I want you to start at the beginning," said Sarah, finally getting down to the business at hand. "The last I heard, you were planning to make Lord Corset grovel at your feet because he left in the night after pleasuring you relentlessly." She broke out into giggles, but Charlotte found it difficult to see the humor.

"Yes, very funny," she said, the corner of her mouth turning up just a touch—the first time she had come close to smiling since she was told that the Harringtons were awaiting her in the solarium, a preposterous and absurd room that no house nor person actually needed.

Charlotte recounted her feelings about the ball, and balls in general now that she had been subjected to one.

*Foul affairs, the lot of them.*

She then detailed their conversation in the garden, which she left with more questions than answers. There was no doubt that they cared for each other, but she could not see her way to it. Dorset felt that because she was now known to be of half-noble birth that they could be together happily, and Charlotte knew that for that exact same reason, the blasted half-noble birth, they could never be truly content. They had reached a stalemate, marched back to the ball downhearted, and straight into chaos.

"And then what happened?" asked Sarah, cutting them both more cake. The night was young.

"What do you mean?"

"You did not spend the night in the ballroom surrounded by spilled wine and drunk toffs, did you?"

"Well, no, of course not. Dorset put me in his carriage, and then—" Charlotte stilled. She could not hide her emotion as she remembered their final kiss.

"Tell me immediately or I shall pour my wine on you as Tabitha intended."

"He said 'I love you,' and sent me home." Sarah very nearly swooned out of her chair.

"Lottie, that's wonderful!"

"Is it? I am not sure that I agree, to be frank," she said, refilling their glasses.

"Of course it is. You have always been far too practical for your own good. Love always can and always will conquer *all*. Everyone knows this." She stated it as if it was simple fact, sipping her wine casually. Love was not that easy.

"Sarah, this is not one of your gothic romance novellas," said Charlotte. "And I am not sure that love conquers parents who are willing to pay any sum to keep you away from their son in order to prevent the horror of a tainted bloodline."

"Lottie, since when did Dorset ever listen to a word they said? They have meddled with you both from day one. If you ask me, they are bored and hurtling toward their own dotage with nothing else to do to occupy their time." Sarah had a point.

"Maybe, but you were not there. Their offer was base and insulting. It is as though they heard all the rumors that I'm a swindler and a cheat, and believed them without a second thought. You say they could not possibly believe that I would accept their money, and yet, they offered it."

"True, I cannot deny that. What does Dorset have to say about it all?"

"Dorset? I do not know," Charlotte said.

"You do not know? Haven't you talked to him?" asked Sarah, incredulous.

"Of course not. They asked me to leave, and I did. I won't have him or his children ruined because of me. I can't bear it," she said, eyes stinging once again.

"Lottie, don't you see what you've done? You have made

the choice not only for yourself, but for him as well. You've sealed your own fate. Don't you think you should hear what he has to say about it all?"

Charlotte pushed a crumb of cake around her plate, not wanting to receive this lecture but hearing the truth in it. Yes, she had decided for him, but what choice did she have?

"If you ask me, Dorset would be the luckiest man alive to father your children. Half of *you* is far better than half of some society darling like Tabitha, throwing wine at balls like a common drunkard. I would bet this entire flat that he agrees with me," she said, rising to clear their dishes. They fell into their familiar roles: Sarah washed and Charlotte dried, returning the plates, forks, and wine glasses to their proper places.

They moved to the drawing room, collapsing on comfortable, overstuffed chairs upholstered in the peacock feather colors that Madame favored so much. Charlotte was about to restate her position, to make herself clear and her word final, when there was a light knock on the door.

"Oh, lovely, she's here," said Lottie, rising to answer the knock.

"Who is here?" asked Charlotte, wary of any visitors. The door opened and their visitor replied before Sarah could.

"Why, it is me, Emmeline, of course," the lady said airily, entering and kissing Sarah on both cheeks, as she usually did with Madame. The transition had begun, whether Sarah knew it or not. "I wish you had sent for me earlier, Sarah. I believe I could have saved us all a rather dramatic evening, running about London in the pouring rain."

Charlotte let Emmeline's words sink in—it seemed that Sarah had gained considerable power as the new management of Beaumont's, able to summon ladies without setting foot outside of her rooms.

"Please, pull up a pouf and join us, I was just explaining to

Charlotte that she's made a terrible mistake," said Sarah. Charlotte rolled her eyes in silent response as Emmeline settled herself in a comfortable wing back chair.

"And what would you have done in my position? They offered me payment to disappear. What choice did I have?"

"It was dreadful of them, Charlotte. Really dreadful, and I am sorry. I was not informed until after the fact, and you must know that if I had known—"

"I know, you would never have allowed them to tell me to my face that I am unfit to carry and deliver their son's heir. But they did, and here I am," Charlotte said, feeling the anger she had felt that afternoon anew. Emmeline came forward, out of her chair, and knelt at Charlotte's feet. She took Charlotte's hands in her own before she replied.

"Charlotte. I cannot ever understand the pain you must have felt when hearing them say it. And I want you to understand that our family would be the luckiest in the world to have you join our ranks. My parents do not deserve it, but I hope you can forgive them."

"Yes, Lottie, you must endeavor to try," said Sarah, her feet up on an ottoman across the room. "I was just telling her, Emmeline, before you arrived, that Dorset will not give a damn what they think, and I am correct, aren't I?"

"As always, you are exactly right, Sarah. I do not have every detail, but I have some information that may convince you of that, Charlotte." Emmeline rose and joined her where she sat on a jewel-toned settee, opposite Sarah.

"Has he asked the Queen to revoke his peerage?" asked Charlotte, sure that anything less would be insufficient to change her mind.

"I do not know, although I would imagine he would inquire if you wished it," replied Emmeline, removing her bonnet and gloves to make herself more comfortable. "He sent me a note this afternoon, marked 'urgent,' and while I do not entirely understand its contents, I believe it gives shape to his intentions." The note was produced; after a moment's hesitation, Charlotte took it and read aloud.

"*Em—*

*You must speak with Carter straight away. See if he can find places for eight footmen, four maids, two kitchen maids, and two scullery maids at Stapleton. I shall pay their wages and any boarding costs, but they must be settled as soon as possible. Do not take no for an answer.*

*Your brother,*

*Nicholas*

Charlotte did not understand; was Stapleton in need of more staff? And why was it that Dorset had a list of people in need of urgent employment? Sarah, too, looked flummoxed. If he could afford their salaries and boarding, why not simply employ them himself?

"I will not pretend that this makes perfect sense, but I did some digging," said Emmeline, breaking the silence in the room.

"And what, pray tell, did you find?" asked Charlotte, growing impatient. If the purpose of this note was to set Charlotte at ease, she could not see how this information was relevant.

"It took some doing, but I managed to get my hands on the roster of Dorset's domestic employees. As luck would have it, in addition to a cook, a valet, a groom, and one young stable hand, whom I believe to be the groom's son, my brother happens to employ exactly eight footmen, four maids, two kitchen maids, and two scullery maids."

"Why should he wish to settle them at Stapleton? Is he moving back in?" asked Sarah with a humorless chuckle.

"On the contrary, Sarah. I have it on good authority that he sent an identical note to Markby, asking him directly to install the very same list of staff members in his homes, should I fail to secure them places at Stapleton House. From there, my investigation continued with the help of Fiona, who's uncle is a banker at Lloyd's. I paid this uncle a visit, and made some discreet inquiries that have confirmed my assumption."

"Brava, Emmeline. Someday you must teach us how you influence record keepers and bankers with such ease. Has anyone ever told you no?" asked Sarah with a yawn. It was growing late. Emmeline laughed weakly, no doubt as exhausted as them both after her afternoon and evening spent tracking leads in the rain.

"Indeed, your skills are quite impressive. But do you care to share your assumption with the rest of us?" asked Charlotte, still not clear on how this information pertained to her relationship with Dorset and its viability moving forward.

"You must forgive me for this, Charlotte, but I do not. I rather think this plan of his, if it is what I assume, is his to reveal," she said, as seriously as Charlotte had ever heard Emmeline speak. "You must see him."

Charlotte was not entirely sure that she *must* see him, but her curiosity began to grow. If Emmeline was correct, he had spent the better part of the day making efforts to relocate his staff, as urgently as possible. Dread pooled in her stomach, and her mind raced. Charlotte knew this feeling well, and recognized that her natural inclination was to assume the worst—the remnant of her tragic childhood.

*It is foolish to hope.*

"If you asked me to determine the aim of someone desperate to relocate their staff as quickly as possible, I would venture to guess that they were going abroad—permanently," she said, emphasizing the last. Sarah gasped.

"No, Lottie, do not say that—" Charlotte stopped her.

"When I left today, I did so with the intention to make a clean break. You might call me selfish, and you would be right, for I do not wish to relive the same heartbreak again and again. If Dorset goes abroad, it shall be a gift of mercy to us both."

Charlotte's words hung in the air like the rain clouds outside that continued to release downpours over all of London. Maybe he would travel to America. Surely, he would find a suitable wife in no time at all, perhaps a newly minted railroad heiress who would be dazzled and charmed by him, and his promise of a title—the very thing that sickened Charlotte to her core, even as she loved the man attached to the lordship. As she pondered this, neither Emmeline nor Sarah attempted to dispute her conclusion; it was as good as confirmation.

Sarah rose from her chair first. "I am afraid we are well past my bedtime, ladies. Emmeline, you are welcome to stay—I do not think the rain shall let up tonight."

"Thank you, Sarah, but I shall return home," she replied, before turning to Charlotte. "I do not doubt that you could be correct, Charlotte. Let us not lose hope just yet."

There was that word again—*hope*. Charlotte had lost it years ago.

She and Charlotte embraced, and Emmeline took her leave after promising to be in touch as soon as possible if any new information became available. Charlotte thanked her but did not want it, wishing with all her heart as she got in bed and failed to sleep that she had never read the note Dorset had sent Emmeline earlier that same day.

Charlotte knew what grief felt like all too well, and as she pulled her blankets closer around her face in the unfamiliar new bedroom that Sarah had so kindly given her, she let it wash over her. There was no avoiding the pain, and the loss of Dorset would surely leave its mark. God willing, it would ease with time.

She slept in fits, and when she awoke the next morning, Charlotte found the streets below her window damp and gleaming; the sun broke through the clouds and shone down upon the early commuters, hurrying to their destinations. She dressed and went down the ornate but private stair that led her down to the shop, full of anticipation and gratitude, ready to distract herself, and hoping for a day so busy she would have no choice but to collapse when it concluded.

If any of the seamstresses she worked with found it odd that she had returned to Beaumont's after her brief and spectacular failure, they said nothing. Thankfully, none of the customers did either; her work dress and apron created a sort of camouflage, rendering her once again below their notice. Charlotte relished the anonymity it afforded her and hoped it would last.

Alas, it was foolish to hope, and she cursed herself for forgetting this long-held truth. A week after her return to work, the post brought news along with the usual letters—Charlotte was found. Polly delivered her the note, written in that unmistakable, sloping and masculine hand, the paper imbued with leather and cedar. There was no salutation, no signature, and no indication of Dorset's plans. Aside from a return address that she did not recognize, it simply read:

*Meet me tomorrow, under the peach tree.*

# Chapter 24

Charlotte had taken some convincing, and if anyone was surprised by this fact by now, it was their own fault. Sarah had told her straight away that of course she must go—she would regret never knowing Dorset's intentions, and where on Earth had he found a peach tree in England?

Emmeline sent her arguments via post, and felt similarly. She urged Charlotte to do nothing more than to listen. "Hear what he has to say. If you still wish to be apart from him after he has explained himself, at least you have made the decision with all knowledge." It was signed, very dearly, from Em.

Fussing with a bit of embroidery, she pondered her options. Remain here and continue living in ignorance, working herself to the bone to forget her sadness, or take Markby's carriage to a quaint village called Pembroke where, depending on what awaited her there, her sadness may worsen a thousand-fold. Ultimately, it was Madame Beaumont who made her see the value of making the short journey.

"Without risk, what is life, *mon petite*? Your mother chose the safer path, and look what it got her. Do not live in fear like she did," she said, taking the needle from Charlotte's aching hands. It was a painful truth. Her mother had done her best, but time and illness had cut her life short. What would have been had she chosen to live openly, fearlessly in love with her father?

Before she could doubt herself, Charlotte bolted up the private stairs and changed from her work dress into one more suitable for travel, wrapping herself in a warm shawl. As quickly as she'd come, she was out the door and rushing to find Sarah, who, when found, revealed that the carriage was waiting for her outside. Best wishes were exchanged, as were hurried goodbyes with the other seamstresses; spirits were high.

It was not just a carriage that awaited Charlotte that day. Markby was there, a cautious smile on his face, hand outstretched to help her into their conveyance. Charlotte realized when she saw him that her escape must have hurt him a great deal. He had only ever been good to her, and he had been so happy to know that he had a sister, even if they could never prove their relation definitively. Here was a man who could teach her a thing or two about blind faith.

"I cannot imagine what you must think of me," she said, choosing her words carefully as the carriage set off. "I am sorry I ran." Markby smiled at her, his eyes sparkling.

"Apology accepted," he began. "I cannot think of much more terrifying than the Earl and Countess of Harrington calling upon you unannounced," he said. "I rather think I would have run myself. Come to think of it, it is a wonder they have not offered me the same deal." It felt nice to laugh with him.

"Do you know where we're going?" she asked, looking out the window as they passed through London.

"Vaguely, yes, although he has not told me much. I am not sure that anyone knows exactly what Nicky has planned."

"And that does not worry you?" Charlotte asked. Answers would soon come, but she wanted some reassurance that she was not being brought all this way to see Dorset off on a worldwide search for a more suitable wife.

"Not in the least, to be honest with you," he said, removing his hat and ruffling his sandy blond hair. "I trust him with my life. And, more importantly, with my sister," he said. Charlotte felt the sincerity in his words.

"You are a credit to him," she said.

"And you shall be, as well."

"I do not think I am prepared to agree with you," Charlotte replied, remembering the contemptuous look the earl gave her as she admonished him. "Not when my avoidance of him is worth so much to his parents."

"About that—" said Markby, stopping himself before he went on. "Apparently it was not a genuine offer."

"Not a genuine offer?"

"No, you see, it is rather my fault, I suppose. Nicky found out what they had done, and nearly shot through the roof, he was so angry. He went straight to Stapleton to get to the bottom of things, and it seems the earl explained that my word on the subject of our shared parent was not proof enough for them. They think me rather impulsive."

"A reputation you earned, no doubt," said Charlotte, exhaling a small laugh.

"Indeed. So much so that Lady Harrington suggested they perform a small test. Cruel, yes, but designed only to determine if you were simply after money, as the rumors would have them believe. If you had not had them removed, which I approve of completely, by the way, they assure me that they would have explained this with their sincere apologies on the spot."

So, they had put her to a test. It was callous, classist, and Charlotte did not know if she could forgive them, regardless of what Dorset had to tell her once they arrived and found the mysterious peach tree.

"Do you believe them?" she asked. Markby had known the family for most of his life; Charlotte trusted him to give her an honest answer. He considered her question for a moment before he replied.

"I believe that they are sorry, and also that they will never understand how deeply they have wounded you." This was a certainty. Charlotte could not imagine that either of them had ever worked for anything, nor had their worth and value questioned in such a manner.

The carriage trundled on, and soon the scenery changed from the London outskirts to gently rolling pastoral hills. Small, wooly sheep dotted the landscape; it was sun-dappled, and charming. If Markby knew what they would find when they arrived at the direction provided in Dorset's note, he did not reveal it. Charlotte pulled her shawl tighter around her shoulders, admired the green hills beyond the muddy road they continued down, and let herself believe that whatever lay waiting for her, she would rather know for sure than live another day wondering.

Soon, they came upon a small hamlet. It featured an ancient, moss-covered chapel and accompanying graveyard at the end of a lane with a decaying road sign indicating that they had finally reached their destination: Pembroke. There were few structures aside from the chapel and some scattered cottages; few people were about, and Charlotte wondered how Dorset had found this place, charming as it was. The driver pressed on a bit farther, which brought them to the edge of the small village, overlooking a field of wildflowers, with a charming home just beyond, surrounded by mature trees. Charlotte had never seen this many flowers in bloom at once; the recent rain had done wonders.

The carriage lurched to a halt where the road met graveled

path leading to the home. Markby took Charlotte's hands in his, and after a moment, revealed the little that he knew.

"This is where we must part, for the time being, at least. I shall wait for you in the village in case you decide that you'd like to leave," he said, seriously. Charlotte nodded; she understood. "Follow the path, and see what you think of it," he said, referring to the charming little house with the thatched roof that sat at the side of the pasture. He gave no indication that Dorset was present; would she know a peach tree by sight alone?

Nerves propelled her down the path. The crunch of her feet upon the gravel was the only sound, aside from the occasional and distant bird call, and the sound of the light breeze in the trees nearby. It was peaceful, but her anticipation kept her from enjoying the scenery.

Should she call out to him? There was no sign of another carriage, nor of a horse, but as she approached the home, she let the warmth of the sun, shining through the passing clouds, warm and comfort her.

*Of course he will be here.*

Charlotte hesitated at the great wooden door, her hand outstretched for the brass knocker, its color dulled by patina. But Dorset would not be inside—she must find the peach tree like he had told her to in his cryptic note. She entered the garden through a low wooden gate, and passed around the side of the cottage, the sound of her heartbeat so loud in her ears that she felt sure it would give her away.

The garden was modest but well-kept, with neat vegetable beds, a small and currently vacant chicken coop, and there— just beyond a row of bramble bushes—was Dorset. Charlotte stopped in her tracks, and took a moment to simply gaze at him, standing beneath what must be a peach tree. Here, surrounded by sunlight and greenery in this garden, he seemed so far from the brusque and sallow-skinned man she had met at tea all those weeks ago—for here he stood, handsome, healthy, and beaming at her with a smile that belied his more wolfish and secret desires.

*Lord Corset, brought from darkness into the light.*

Once she felt sure that she had memorized the image of him, she could no longer restrain herself. Charlotte ran to him, craving his embrace. If he was to give her bad news, he must do it with her safely installed in his arms.

"Charlotte—" he began, catching her and hauling her off of her feet as she reached him. He held her for just a moment before lowering her back to the ground, allowing her to look up at him properly. "You came."

"Of course I did," she replied, feeling a familiar swoon grow deep within her. This man was uncommonly beautiful, with lashes like fur and a smile that made her forget that she did not yet know why he had brought her here. "We did not get to finish our last conversation," she said, recalling the disastrous end to the ball and his carriage-side send off. If this was the end of their story, she would not let him leave without hearing her response. "I love you, too."

Drawing her close once more, he sighed, which felt to Charlotte like a low rumble from deep within him. His hand found her hair, as it always did, and held her fast to his firm chest. Would she be able to remember these sensations, so unique to their time together, if they were to part?

"Peaches, darling," he began, taking her face in both of his hands, gently grazing the delicate and sensitive skin along her jawline. "I want nothing more than to make you repeat that statement to me, in greater detail and for all eternity," he said, pausing as he continued to run his wicked thumbs upon her flushed cheeks.

"But?" she asked, sensing that he was holding something back. Her heart, afloat at the mere sight of him, sank once more. As much as she wanted to give herself up to him here, under this tree and in the glorious sunlight, she needed to hear him explain what he had been planning, in secret even to those closest to him.

Without answering her, he leaned down and kissed her. His kiss was gentle, his soft lips parting hers with exquisite promise, as though they had not already explored each other passionately. Was this his way of saying goodbye?

Charlotte could no longer bear the wait, the question of his intentions hanging over them like the branches of the peach tree above them. She broke the kiss and spoke before he could say what she feared he was preparing to.

"I shall miss you," she said, her voice a whisper. He had taken her breath with his kiss. And damn the man, he could keep it for all she cared. What use would it be to her now?

His brow furrowed, not with emotion, but rather, confusion. "Miss me? Where, pray tell, are you going?" he asked, not loosening the grip he now had on her waist.

"Do not make fun," Charlotte replied, sadly. "It is hard enough that you're going abroad, do not laugh at me as well." She settled her gaze on his cravat, and straightened the lapels of his jacket, unable to look at him. One look of confirmation from those eyes, so blue they should be illegal, would devastate her.

"Charlotte—"

"I am sure you will settle yourself nicely in New York."

"Darling, why—"

"The Marchbank girls visited once and said Rhode Island is quite pretty. Surely, you shall want to visit, perhaps they can make introductions for you."

"Peaches," he said, his tone resonant and firm. Charlotte started and nearly gasped; she could not help but meet his serious gaze. "I am not going abroad."

"Oh," she replied, quietly. "But where will you find a wife?" She was genuinely puzzled. He could have chosen any woman in London and heretofore had denied the lot. Before he could speak, Dorset responded in a manner that Charlotte would never had predicted, considering the sincerity of her question and its delicate nature. He barked out a laugh, continuing as though she had told the most clever and charming joke ever before heard.

"A wife? Charlotte, with all my heart and the entirety of my soul, I have already found her," he said, his laughter slowing. "I would like to tell you that I have known it since the day that we met. Alas, I was a fool that day, and did not yet realize what I had just discovered. I was not yet ready for you then," he said, his gaze turning serious. Charlotte held fast to him, rapt.

"I am sure you are wondering why I brought you here to this quaint and little-known place to tell you this, and I shall explain all to you, of course. But before I do, you must know, and know well: I love you, Charlotte, desperately. It is my solemn hope that you will do me the honor of becoming my wife."

It was everything Charlotte had hoped to hear, nearly identical to the words she would replay in her mind as she lay in bed each night, imagining him and their lives together as she drifted. Had they met as equals, without their pasts and families and societal expectations hanging around their necks like rope, she would have done him that matrimonial honor without a second thought.

"Dorset—" she began, using his title, the very thing that stood in the way of their happiness.

"No. Not Dorset. If we are to be married, you mustn't," he said, finding her chin with his bent forefinger and tilting her face to his as he had so many times before. "Call me by my name."

"Nicholas," she said, the name feeling as natural as breathing as she said it, even as it sounded unfamiliar and new to her ear. "If only we could. You know where I stand, that we cannot be together happily. I shall never be worthy."

"On the contrary, my darling. You are a beacon of goodness to me, and your presence in my life has been nothing short of a miracle, brought about by a lilac dress and my presumptuous mother. To call you unworthy is to misunderstand everything about you—my uncommonly brave, uncommonly beautiful, and perfectly proper Peach. After the ball, I took your words to heart. And I agree, we could never be truly happy as long as we tried to play by the rules, as it were."

So, he agreed with her. Charlotte opened her mouth to say so, but he stilled her with a gentle finger upon her lips. "What I mean, Charlotte Price-Markby, is that it is *I* who am unworthy. I have spent every waking moment since we parted at the ball attempting to make myself into something even close to a suitable match for you, something more like an equal—a partner. I shall not pretend that I have succeeded, but I swear to you that I shall continue to strive for worthiness, for as long as we both shall live." Realization dawned with his words.

"Your plans?" she asked, referring to the secretive dealings he had alluded to but kept even from Markby and Emmeline.

"Indeed," he replied, running the back of his knuckles across her jaw once more. Tingles spread from the spot as anticipation radiated through her body. What had he done?

*Maybe he has inquired with the Queen after all...*

"You told me, in the garden that night, that we would never truly be seen as equal."

"That is correct."

"And you continue to feel deep anger—justified, of course —toward your unfortunate father."

"I am afraid that remains true."

"The solution became so clear to me that night. I was furious with myself for not seeing it before. We should never have tried to force you to become something you were not.

And to make you truly happy, to love you as I intend to until the Lord takes me, I had to give it all up."

"What?"

"It is not yet complete, but I have alerted all the important people. I am walking away."

"Your staff—you had asked Emmeline," Charlotte began, stammering as the pieces began to fall into place. He was not going abroad, nor leaving her. He was divesting from the aristocracy.

"That is correct, I wanted to make sure that those in my employ were well taken care of. Markby has found positions for them all, and they shall be provided for via a trust that I have created with the funds I have accrued from some rather lucrative investments. It is more than I would ever need, than *we* will ever need. A much better use of it, I should think."

"But what about your home? And the cook? Emmeline said that the list of people you relocated did not include your entire household."

"Correct again, but that is because we shall keep the rest on," he began, the blue of his eyes darkening as he continued. "That is, if you will have us." She wanted to scream with delight, to answer yes without reservation, but still, she needed further answers.

"But where will you live?" Charlotte asked. At her question, his eyes rose from her face to the cottage behind them.

"I hope, with all my heart, that you meant to ask where *we* shall live—and all that depends," he began, taking her by the hand and leading her toward the home. "It is for us both to decide, of course. But I had rather thought that we should keep the townhouse, for our usual residence." They stopped at the front door, hand in hand, before he went on.

"But this cottage felt rather special. It met my requirement of complete seclusion, but I knew it was perfect when I learned that it had a peach tree in the garden—it seemed like a sign. And at present, only Markby, you, and I are aware of its existence. Call it an extravagant wedding gift—a quiet retreat where we can hide from gossiping, meddling mamas and anyone else whenever we like. No staff, no post, no ballroom."

"And how, my dear, are we to support the cost of two homes?" she asked, warming to the idea of them coming here, alone, and as often as possible.

"We shall work, of course. I have already begun, in fact," he said. "And Madame Beaumont has assured me that your position is quite safe." Charlotte was aghast—when, in the time since the Stapleton Ball, had he found even a moment to learn a trade?

"I shall ignore for the moment that you spoke with Madame Beaumont without my knowledge," she began.

"Just letters, but yes, please go on," he said.

"What exactly are you doing to earn a wage?" At this he smiled, not in jest—he was proud.

"Well, over the years, I have had rather a knack for investing," he said. If his so-called knack could provide a lifetime of wages to a number of staff members, Dorset was being modest.

"I have endeavored to use that talent to the benefit of those in need. I shall make investments, safe ones, using accounts in their names. Spread the wealth, if you will; use my ill-gotten powers of privilege for good, for a small but fair fee."

Nothing promised complete exile from the *ton* like taking on paid work—he really meant to change, to reshape himself into something Charlotte could understand. It was perfect. Unable to find words in that moment, she leaned forward and once more claimed a kiss from him, sighing against his soft lips.

After deepening the caress and making her feel, as he always did, like the only woman he had ever had the pleasure of kissing, he released her. Eyes still closed, Charlotte silently cursed the loss of his touch. However, any sadness she had felt at the interrupted kiss vanished when she opened her eyes to see that he had settled himself on one knee before her, at the threshold of their new and secret oasis.

"Charlotte Price-Markby, queen of my soul and owner of my heart...will you please, answering definitively now and for all time, do me the honor of becoming my wife?"

# CHAPTER 25

Pain shot through Dorset's knee as he knelt directly upon an unfortunately placed pebble and awaited Charlotte's response to his proposal at the door of their cottage—*her* cottage, for everything he would do for the rest of his life, if she would let him, would be for her. Blessedly, for his heart and for his aching knee, she did not make him wait long.

"Of course I will," she said, smiling down at him.

"Thank God," he replied, her hand still grasped in his. "Let your first act as my future wife be to help me to stand." With a laugh from his bride and great effort from Dorset to rise with one leg, she did just that.

Finally, after all they had been through, she was his. Dorset knew after their conversation in the garden at his parents' farce of a ball that it would take more than words, mere promises, to show her he loved her, and would not lose her. The only bit that surprised him was how staggeringly easy it had all been—aside from a few raised eyebrows and condescending letters from his bankers, presuming that he had lost his head over a woman and was behaving rashly, it was no trouble at all to rid himself of most of his money.

*And I do not miss it in the least.*

Now that Charlotte knew he was serious, the cottage before them standing sentry as proof that his promises were not empty words, he could not help but draw her into his arms.

"Peaches," he said, little more than a grunt in her ear as they stood at the doorstep. "Let me take you inside." He knew she caught his double meaning by the flush on her luscious cheeks.

"I wish you would," she replied, cheekily. Her consent inflamed him, and he felt himself grow heavier in anticipation as he opened the door and led her inside by the hand. The cottage featured just three rooms. The empty sitting room, which they now entered, a kitchen which featured a great stone hearth and washed wooden table, and beyond, the as-yet-unfurnished bedroom. Dorset watched her as she took in the humble surroundings.

"I have been in contact with a builder, in the village. We shall refurbish the kitchen," he said, leading her to the window that marked the future location of the basin. "And through there, in the bedroom, we shall add a washroom, of course." Once again, he drew her near, desperate to kiss her.

"It is perfect," she said, eyeing the large table behind him. "But, can we—"

"Yes, anything. Of course we can," he said, leaning down and stilling her mouth with his lips. She sighed and softened against him. He loved everything about her, and everything about pleasuring her, but this—the quiet, needy sounds he coaxed from her with his lips—they were his favorite. They continued searching, their lips opening to each other as their fervor grew. For as long as they lived, he would never tire of this, of her. To his chagrin, she broke the kiss.

"Can we have a bathtub?" she asked. At the sight of her, with lips reddened from their kisses and hair askew, peach-colored cheeks to match the fruit that would grow in their very own garden, he would have given her anything she asked.

*More.*

"Absolutely, Peaches." The thought of sharing a bath with her, in complete privacy where no one could find them, was enough to drive him wild. As he removed her shawl and kissed her neck, he felt so hungry for her—it was primal.

"Are you sure we're alone?" she breathed. He could feel her losing herself to the sensation.

"Yes, darling," he replied, turning her and then backing her up until her backside met the edge of the table in their kitchen. Dorset settled both hands on that curvaceous bottom and squeezed before lifting her from the floor and placing her on the tabletop.

"I require your shawl, my lady," he said, opening his hand while gazing down at her. She looked up at him through her lashes, a coy smile upon her lips, his naughty peach.

"Certainly, Nicholas," she replied, removing the soft knit garment and placing it in his open palm. The sound of his name on her lips—it was all he had ever dreamt of.

Carefully, he spread the shawl over the table top and settled her down upon it, before lowering himself to the floor before her. He took one ankle in hand, and then the other, running his thumbs over the silk of her stockings. She sighed, then rose up on her elbows so that she could gaze upon him.

"Will you not join me?" she asked, her tone polite and proper even ask he gathered her skirts and pushed them up above her shapely knees. Slowly, cradling her left leg in his hands, and taking all the time he pleased to, he brushed kisses up the inside of that leg, beginning at her ankle, and inching higher and higher as he went.

"At this moment, with heaven spread before me, I would

not trade this view for anything," he said, his lips brushing her skin at the inside of her knee. He continued with his gentle teasing kisses, pausing at the top of her stockings, where the delicately woven fabric gave way to her skin. Charlotte was trembling now, sighing above him. He looked up at her, met her hungry, hooded eyes, and nearly keeled over at the wanton sight of her.

*She is perfect, and she is mine.*

"Nicholas, please," she breathed, her chest rising and falling more quickly now.

"Peaches, I will spend my life working myself to the bone in order to give you everything you wish." He began moving to her right leg and repeating his leisurely ministrations from ankle to thigh. Between kisses, he continued. "But I will not be rushed."

Bundling her skirts higher, Dorset rose and stood before her where she sat at the edge of the table, one hand on each of her exposed thighs, which he stood directly between. With his fingers spread, and careful not to clench her too tightly, he sank all ten of his fingertips into her flesh, gently kneading her pleasing softness. Leaning forward, he met her lips, unable to resist them as she sighed and panted in response to his touch.

"I would not dream of it," she breathed, "but I find I am growing impatient." She reached for him and fisted the lapel of his jacket, pulling him nearer and deepening their kiss.

"So greedy," he said, his voice a near rasp. Dorset was struggling to keep himself together as his cock stiffened inside of his trousers. He tried to slow his shallow breathing, to keep his pace slow. This was for her.

With Charlotte's help, Dorset peeled off and discarded his jacket and waistcoat. He loved the feel of her hands as they trailed over his stomach and chest, and then up to his throat to untie his cravat.

"If I allow you to continue, you shall have me nude in

seconds," he said, dipping forward to take her flushed face in his hands.

"Then you must allow me," she said with a coquettish smile. Dorset kissed it away with one hand holding her face steady, and the other searching her hair for pins and plucking them out, one by one. As he did so, Charlotte found the waistband of his trousers and untucked his shirt before she slowed.

"Be my guest," he growled, loving the feel of her palms on his bare skin as she inched his shirt higher, a slow and teasing drag not unlike his treatment of her legs just moments earlier.

"Two can play at this game," she purred, raking her thumbs over his sensitive nipples as she pushed the garment up over his chest. He hissed at the sensation, which sent unexpected heat to his groin and sparks around the corners of his vision. His body was desperate for her, and for this. Once again sealing his mouth to hers, he silently thanked God and vowed that she may use him for her pleasure as she wished for as long as they lived.

Dorset fisted a hand in her loose auburn waves, and gently, reverently, stilled her movements. Her eyes had darkened with pleasure, and that secret smile he loved so much returned to that lush mouth. He had long considered himself a skilled lover, and had been told by many a partner that he possessed a considerable talent in the bedroom. But here, with Charlotte confidently matching him kiss for kiss, touch for touch, with a playful quality Dorset could not name—he had met his match at last.

"Charlotte," he breathed, looking down into those green eyes, lids heavy. "I know you do not care for titles."

"Indeed, I do not," she replied, her brows knitting just slightly. He kissed her at the faint crease between her brows and let his free hand trail from its seat upon her knee, up the inside of her thigh, closer to her warmth. She shivered as he went.

"There is one that rather suits you, I think. I should like to confer it upon you," he said, relishing a small moan as his hand grew nearer to the slit in her pantalettes, already askew from her impatient squirming. Her eyes closed as his fingers parted the fabric there and finally reached her center, stilling with the slightest possible touch. Charlotte's eyes fluttered shut with a gasp at the feather light contact.

"Is that so?"

Unable to resist, he parted her curls and folds, already wet with her desire.

"Indeed."

She moaned, and rocked forward from where she sat, desperate for more of this feeling.

"Name it."

He circled his thumb, coating it in her slickness and coaxing more of those gorgeous sounds from her as he rubbed it gently over her swollen clitoris.

"Lady Corset," he growled, capturing the next blissful sigh with his mouth.

"I accept," she replied, exhaling a laugh, cheeks flushed and beautiful. How had he done it? How had he been so lucky?

"You are the first and only, my love," he said, leaning over her and angling her back, her weight resting in the palm of one hand. Carefully, he slid two fingers inside of her with the other; she was impossibly warm and growing even more wet for him. His thumb once again found her engorged clitoris, where he continued his slow and steady circling, mirroring those small movements with his other fingers as well.

"More," she said.

"Here?" he asked

"There," she replied. "Just there, do not stop."

Even death could not have stopped Dorset then, so deter-mined he was to please his future wife, for what he hoped would be the first of many times that day alone. He felt her grip upon his waist tighten. Her breaths grew deeper. She was nearly there.

*Lord & Lady Corset, wanton and insatiable, and desperately in love.*

"Nicholas," she whispered as she began to shudder. She was over the edge now, coming apart in his hands, lost to her pleasure. "Nicholas, I'm—"

"I know, Peaches," he said, his face buried in her hair. "I know."

Charlotte did not know how Dorset, how *Nicholas*, could sense her climax so readily. And yet, just as she was about to tell him she was very nearly there, just about to beg him not to change his pace or his pressure, he simply held her, continued exactly as he had been, and said, "I know."

She had never felt such comfort in her life. As the shuddering pleasure took hold of her, he remained with her, whispering his encouragement in her ear, never leaving her side. Only then, as she returned to herself and he gently laid her down upon their tabletop, did she truly realize that he never would.

"That was marvelous," she breathed, still out of breath.

"Indeed," he replied as he leaned over her, pressing himself into her swollen and still pulsating flesh. This man, wicked as ever, trailed light kisses over her neck as he did so, stealing her thoughts along with the breath he had already taken.

She would, of course, continue her work at Beaumont's, and he seemed to have found an advantageous use for his financial acumen—but how, dear God, would either of them get anything done with unfettered access to each other? She would save critical thinking for after they had announced their engagement. For now, their fervent, chemical desire was all she could focus upon.

As Dorset kissed his way down her neck and chest to the edge of her bodice, she could not help but rock herself against his length, so solid and ready for her. Charlotte locked her ankles behind his back, lamenting that it had been too long since their first night together. If she had been impatient before, soon, she would go mad.

"Please, darling," she sighed, unable to keep herself from circling her hips. The sensations were too potent, and she only wanted more. Limp and trapped between the table and his solid body, she could not lift him to pry off his trousers. With all her effort, even limited as her strength was still dulled by pleasure, Charlotte reached for his waistband.

She felt Dorset's lips curl into a smile upon her cheek, where he stilled his kissing. "Allow me, my lady," he said, in that deep register that she heard every night in her dreams. Slowly, he rose above her but did not back away from the tight circle of her legs around his back.

A fortuitous beam of afternoon sunlight, breaking through a passing cloud and straight into the kitchen window, illuminated him. Charlotte could not help but take in the sight before her, and she did not attempt to hide her hungry stare, trailing over his sculpted chest, muscled and dusted with hair. He was strong, *vital*, and best of all: hers.

"You look awfully pleased," he said, unfastening the fall of his trousers without looking away from her.

"I am," she purred. He freed his fully erect shaft, letting it fall forward before stepping back from the table to kick off each pant leg.

"Not pleased enough, if you are still capable of speech," he replied, wickedly. With a devilish grin, her betrothed reached below her, gripped her bottom firmly, and pulled her toward himself, nearly off the edge of the table. She gasped.

"Do not worry, Peaches," he said. "I have you."

"Of course you do," she said. The sight of him, nude and engorged, was making her giddy. He tutted in response.

"Still able to speak, this will not do." Dorset sank down on his knees at the edge of the table, lost behind a pile of her bunched-up skirts.

"Where have you go—" Charlotte began, rising up on her elbows to see him just as he found her clitoris, still throbbing from his earlier attention, with his tongue. Her head fell back, mouth agape. The sensation stole her thoughts and rendered her dumb—this handsome rogue had reached his goal, and she could not finish her question aloud.

"Mmhmm," he moaned, directly into her flesh. How was he capable of keeping his pace steady and slow as her pleasure built? It coiled deep within her with each sweep of that luscious tongue, matched now with those perfect probing fingers. That she would have this devious man at her disposal, ripping only her corsets for the rest of their lives...the thought was enough to take her growing orgasm from wish to reality.

"Nicholas—"

"Mmmm—"

"Darling, I—"

"Mmhmm—"

Like a dam breaking, the orgasm surged through her. As before, Dorset stayed steady, present, and unwavering. It was as though he could pluck a string deep within her, each strum sending unrelenting vibrations through her body. Charlotte breathed deeply, losing herself to tumble in these waves of pleasure. And all the while, with a firm grip and disciplined dedication to the tempo and pressure that she liked best, he stayed with her to the very end.

He rose, chest heaving, and wiped the slick evidence of her from his mouth with the back of his hand. If he had been patient before, his focused and clouded gaze told her that patience had run out. The man was a lion stalking toward her, and God help her, she could not run.

*As though I would ever run from this man again.*

Dorset clasped one hand behind her head and kissed her. His tongue felt warm and languid against hers, his lips swollen and soft. He threaded his hand more deeply into her hair, holding her forehead against his, then tightened his grip and spoke.

"Peaches, darling," he said, nearly out of breath and straining to control himself. Before he went on, she felt him notch the warm head of his cock at her opening, his beaded and dripping moisture no doubt now mixed with hers. Still face to face, breathing the same air, they both held their breath at the sensation. Charlotte had never felt anticipation like this in her life. "I need you," he rasped, his eyes locked on hers.

All she could do was nod her head "yes," for he had rendered her speechless after all. At her assent, he pressed himself inside, inch by inch, going as slowly as his desire for her would allow. Only once he was fully seated within her did he exhale.

As slowly as he had entered, he then dragged himself away, again and again, allowing her to feel each glorious union anew. She loved the subtle curve of him, and how it seemed tailor made to fit within her depths. If she could have spoken aloud at that moment, she would have told him so; instead, all she could do was sigh and delight in the secure, intimate connection they had forged.

*Together.*

Although he remained standing at the edge of the table, Dorset was able to cradle Charlotte in his arms, rocking himself in and out, in and out, taking his pleasure as he lavished it upon her. His earlier words echoed back to her now as he continued, groaning with pleasure.

*Do not worry, Peaches. I have you.*

Charlotte had built a life for herself. It had taken hard work, careful planning, and cunning. The safety and comfort she enjoyed thanks to her career had been hard won, and she knew that she had been lucky to secure and keep the position she had held, at an uncommonly successful dressmaker's shop in the center of an unforgiving society.

But never, in all of her memory, had she ever felt as safe and as protected as she did now, in Dorset's arms, at her most vulnerable. Finally, she could give herself to him—first her mind, now her body, and as soon as they were wed, her eternal soul. This man was walking away from everything he had ever known to prove to her that she could trust him with it all, to her last breath. For the first time since her childhood, she felt free.

Dorset's pace quickened as sweat beaded at his temple. Charlotte kissed it away—it was his turn for release, and she knew it would not be long now. Once again, he groaned; his breaths grew shorter, quickened.

"Nicholas, my love," she whispered. His eyes screwed shut. "Yes—"

"You feel perfect," she said, encouraging him. He marched on, faster still, his hands an iron grip on her waist. The table began to shake.

"I need to—"

"Yes, darling," she said, as he was unable to finish the thought. "Stay inside of me, please."

As soon as she said it, his composure broke.

"*Fuck*," he swore, loud enough for Charlotte to thank him for selecting a cottage set apart from any neighbors who may overhear. Beyond the curse, Dorset could do little more than groan as he finished, still sealed deep within her, throbbing with such pleasure that she could feel every pulse with her own spent and quivering muscles.

Dorset drew her fully into his arms now, and Charlotte

did not mind one bit that he clutched her so hard she could scarcely draw breath. He joined her on the tabletop and drew her into his arms, again clutching her tightly. The table wobbled frightfully as he settled beside her.

"One day in our new home and already breaking things," she said, kissing his cheek as he tucked her under a thick but exhausted arm at his side. Dorset exhaled a laugh and mopped his brow with a corner of her shawl.

"I shall learn to repair it," he said, his eyelids heavy, mouth drawn in a satisfied smile. Of course he would. They would no longer be able to count on unlimited wealth to pay for unlimited tables. "And we must be sure to keep to the bed," he added, wrapping her in his arms and turning to face her.

"That, Lord Corset, is a promise I am unwilling to keep," she replied, enamored with the length of his lashes and the sharpness of his jawline. Again, he smiled. She could look at him forever.

*And I shall.*

# EPILOGUE

*London*
*Three Months Later*

Lady Harrington, in her estimation, had never been so sought after in all her life. Following the news that her son had liquidated a great many of his assets before getting married to that *notorious seamstress* everyone remembered from the Stapleton Ball, it was no wonder—all of London wanted to know if the story was true. Had he really given away the bulk of his fortune? Was it true that he had done so for love? And was it possible that his bride, herself somehow connected to none other than London's beloved Duke of Markby, was continuing to *work* for her living?

There had been too many social invitations to even count. One simply could not drink that much tea without upsetting one's humors, and although she fancied that she was aging rather well, Lady Harrington was not at all anxious to hasten the ill effects of any form of stress. Therefore, at her *dear* husband's *brilliant* suggestion, she elected to remain at home, and would receive guests as often as she felt up to the task. In the days following the wedding, to which none of the ladies flocking to her doorstep had been invited, she had to admit that she felt very much up to that task and would speak to any who cared to listen.

Lady Marchbank and her *lovely* daughters were the first to call. They were shown to the salon, where Mrs. Moore had laid out a most impressive buffet of delicacies, and on the *good* china, to boot. Her son may have rejected the comforts of his upbringing, but Lady Harrington thought it best, at this time, to embrace them.

"You must tell us what the wedding was like," said Lady Marchbank, sipping daintily from her hand-painted teacup as her daughters looked on. "We were terribly grieved to miss the happy occasion." Lady Harrington chose to ignore the acid in the lady's tone; the wedding had been a lovely affair and her son was happy—nothing, not a cutting remark, nor a reproachful look, could sink her spirits.

"I am sure that you were, *dear* Lady Marchbank. Of course, it was my son's and his bride's express wish that their wedding be a small occasion, as the Markby family chapel at Sutton Abbey is *terribly* small, you know."

"Is it? I have not had the pleasure of attending a service there."

"Oh, indeed," said Lady Harrington, selecting the reasoning her son had provided her when she asked what she should tell all of her friends who he had chosen to snub. That the Markby chapel rivaled the churches of London with its full chancel and nave nearly as long as St. Paul's Cathedral was information best concealed.

With each new guest, the questions continued. Who had attended on the bride's side, if the poor girl had no living family? Guests were reminded that the duke himself is her living family, as she was herself, now that Charlotte and *dear* Nicholas had married. Yes, but was her side of the chapel simply empty? Of course not. It was filled with the most wonderful assemblage of people. Madame Beaumont herself, of course, and all of the other seamstresses and their families as well, who very nearly filled the church, in fact.

The examinations continued into the second week after the wedding, with still more ladies of London desperate to confirm the tales they had been told. Was it true that the duke's cook's children, a boy and a girl, served as the attendants? Why, of course it was, replied Lady Harrington, still delighting in her role as official source of information regarding the blessed event. The children were simply *darling*, carrying the beautiful bride's train with such pride.

But what, the ladies begged, did the bride wear? Surely, a favorite of Madame Beaumont's would be outfitted in only the finest creation. And what a pity it was that so few people were able to see the gown. Indeed, it was quite beautiful—a powder blue silk gown with sleeves and high neck made of French lace, and yes, the lace pattern was designed for Catherine de Medici herself and seldom used since her time. It was dyed to match the silk, of course, and the bride wore it all with some carefully chosen Markby family baubles, and a wreath of white flowers pinned beautifully into her *chignon*. How did she get the lace? Well, one must assume that Madame Beaumont had these things at her disposal.

Could Lady Harrington see about getting yet more of the lace for a daughter's upcoming debut? It was unlikely, as it had been created especially for this occasion, the gown and trousseau being a gift from Madame Beaumont, of course; but certainly, Lady Harrington would be *delighted* to inquire. And yes, the rumors were true. Charlotte, now as close to Lady Harrington as her own natural-born daughter, had been an *absolute* vision in her wedding clothes.

Was there a ball to celebrate the occasion? No—it was not the formal affair one would expect of a London society wedding. But, this was by design—the bridal couple wanted a simple, country wedding, and that is exactly what they had. Never mind that the nuptial location, while it *was* in the countryside, was one of England's grandest estates—what Lady Harrington's guests did not know could not cause them further pain than the exclusion already had.

And where, pray tell, had the happy couple gone to after the wedding? Could two working people expect to take a honeymoon? Had they, perhaps, gone to the continent? That, Lady Harrington was afraid, was not entirely clear. While they had certainly gone *somewhere*, Lady Harrington had to admit that even *she* did not know exactly where, and no, she was not entirely sure when they would return. If anyone *did* know aside from the *darling* newlyweds, they were keeping mum.

Was it unconventional? Undoubtedly. But it was just what they had wanted, and Lady Harrington could not think of anything more romantic. No, there was not a dry eye among the assemblage as they shouted their best wishes to the bride and groom as they waved goodbye from the departing carriage. And yes, *of course*—everyone was terribly happy.


THE END

# Acknowledgments

Above all and forever, thank you, Reader. I hope you enjoyed spending time with Charlotte and Nicholas. As you may have guessed, Emmeline and Markby's story is up next and coming soon!

Lottie & Nicky would not exist without the early and constant support from my friend, original beta reader, and honorary manager, Gaby Pariente. Thank you, Gaby, for taking some time away from your favorite genres to champion this story and for all the bolstering when I needed it most.

To Bianca Ursillo, the universe blessed me when it cast Johnathan Bailey in Bridgerton. Forever grateful for your writing expertise, our shared love of Tessa Dare, and for your correct advice that we must never fear a bad draft.

Lynn Andreozzi, thank you for your brilliant cover design. Sydnee Thompson, editor extraordinaire, thank you for your guidance and polish.

Finally, sincere gratitude to Zoe York and Jane Friedman for their excellent and comprehensive self-publishing guides and advice. Without them, I might not have realized that my dream of publishing was well within reach.

# About the Author

Goldie Thomas lives in sunny Los Angeles with her cat Pepper. She loves long sits on the beach, reading romance, and daydreaming about new plot ideas when she should be writing. Visit www.goldiethomas.com for updates!

# Next From Goldie Thomas

*They've been in love since they were children, if only she can get him to remember...*

Lady Emmeline Felton is the very image of perfection and poise. Everyone in London looks to her for the latest fashions, but she has eyes only for the charming Duke of Markby, who has possessed her heart from the moment they met as children.

Markby, so quick to joke that few consider him serious, has finally found the courage to ask for Lady Emmeline's hand in marriage following a night of intense passion.

But before he can declare his intentions, Markby is found badly injured and with complete amnesia. Will Emmeline be able to restore his memories and their love along with them, or are her carefully laid plans over before they could begin?

A DUKE TO REMEMBER

COMING SOON IN EBOOK AND PAPERBACK